DEATH
AND THE
DREADNOUGHT

Published in 2019 by Elbow Publishing

© Robert Wilton 2019

A catalogue record for this book is available from the British
Library ISBN 978-0-9574090-8-8

Printed in the UK

Also published electronically in 2019 by Sharpe Books.

DEATH
AND THE
DREADNOUGHT

Robert Wilton

[signature]

with all good wishes,

Also by Robert Wilton

The Comptrollerate-General novels:
Traitor's Field
Treason's Spring
Treason's Tide
Treason's Flood *[projected]*
The Spider of Sarajevo

Sherlock Holmes and the
Adventure of the Distracted Thane

Extract from *Le Figaro*, 16th November 1968

DOSSIER DU AVENTURIER GENTILHOMME

A curiosity is reported in Biarritz

M. Tretiot recounts that a charming oriental trunk, sold at auction as 'the property of a lady', was found to have a false bottom. Concealed within this space was a dossier of papers. These proved to be the work of an English Gentleman, Sir Harry Delamere, who in the years before the First World War was a renowned traveller, adventurer and libertine. His later years remain a mystery, and indeed rumour and scandal attached to much of his life, so it is thought that this dossier may be enlightening. The Minister of Interior has directed that the papers shall be first reviewed by his Department before any further steps are taken with them.

1.

A Dreadnought battleship dwarfs a man. And the man slumped at my feet, with his head bent up against the monster's keel, certainly looked small enough.

A shipyard, at night, was a damned odd place for a rendezvous. But Sinclair had insisted, and he'd seemed pretty het up, and he did owe me thirty guineas, and so I'd trekked across to London docks from the West End and spent twenty minutes stumbling around in the darkness until I'd bumped into the biggest latest thing in British naval warfare.

Cathedrals of the new century, and all that. Most advanced specimen of man's vision and engineering brilliance. And damned eerie if one finds oneself skulking underneath it in the small hours.

H.M.S. *Thunderer* was nigh on 600 feet long, a bit shy of 100 across. If St Paul's Cathedral were made of iron, Sinclair had said; more than once. And if St Paul's Cathedral had ten guns capable of firing one-ton shells to a distance of ten miles or more, and were an instrument of colonial rivalry designed to overawe Germany.

Not a very helpful comparison, all in. Sinclair's, not mine.

This was just the hull. The superstructure – funnels, guns, bridge, portrait of the King and so on – was still to be installed; she wouldn't be ready to start overawing Germans until 1912. The crudeness made her immense bulk even more ominous in the gloom.

I'd not looked closely, but I was pretty sure it was Sinclair slumped at my feet. Against the keel of his beloved battleship.

He'd not given me exact directions, so at the gate I'd slipped the night-watchman a shilling, and he described where the offices were, and shortly afterwards I was properly lost in the vast metal jungle of the shipyard. They left a few lights on at night, but all those did was hint at the shapes around them, and make the whole effect more ghostly. I walked past corners of large buildings, under the metal feet of enormous machines, through seas of shadow. My dress shoes splashed through puddles of unknown liquids that shimmered faintly in the gloom. Cranes and gantries loomed over me.

Eventually, my wanderings through the wasteland of metal and oil and darkness brought me to the dry dock, and what I first took to be a wall: a blackness that closed out my vision and rose in front of me; but it rose and went on rising and back over my head and far up into the night, and instinctively my fingers reached for this mammoth and found the rough chill of iron, and I knew it was the *Thunderer*.

I seemed to have come at her from the river end, her stern. With a faint idea that the offices might be at the head of what was clearly the main area of the yard, I set off along those 600-odd feet of shadow towards her bow.

Tiny metallic echoes boomed in the ship, as the wind rolled a rivet off a plank, or a rat nudged a bolt and sent it plummeting into the abyss of the hull.

At the bow I'd found the body. There was a light strung quite near, and it caught the pale splashes of starched shirt and empty face.

Something was dark and glistening on the shirt front. Now I bent to the body.

It was Sinclair, alright.

Someone had stabbed him to death right under his battleship. The commission that he'd hoped would save his company had become his tomb.

Something gleamed faintly under his clenched left fist, and I picked it up: a cufflink, with a battleship design.

My fingers brushed at the knife still embedded in his chest.

At which moment the shipyard came alive with light, scorching

3

the metal and blinding me and from behind there were shouts, and whistles, and boots converging on me.

2.

'You are Henry Delamere?'

Now, many shrewd observers feel that this isn't something to be proud of, but it's true enough and I said so.

'It says here you're a baronet.' He looked up. It hadn't been a question, so I didn't answer it.

'Whatever that may mean. I have to call you sir, is that right?'

'I've never much cared either way.'

He watched me for a moment longer, then considered the papers in front of him again. I re-examined the room: small; damp; brick painted an appalling green.

'It also says here that you're more or less bankrupt. That you've no profession as such. "Traveller", it says. On the omnibuses, would that be sir?' I smiled encouragingly at this hilarity. '"Gambler", it says too. Not married, but known to have been associated with a number of different ladies. And more than once linked to scandal. Theft at a country house in '03. Gossip about a duel a couple of years later. Various bits of murky business abroad.' He stretched the "murky" like a connoisseur. 'French police wanted you for killing a man, it says. Until it was hushed up somehow. Some political trouble in Con-stan-tinople. Another death.' He tutted heavily. He looked up from the papers again. 'No stranger to hot water.'

Still not a question.

They'd worked fast in an hour or two.

'What were you doing in the Thames Ironworks Company Shipyard, Mr Delamere?'

'Sinclair asked me to meet him there.'

'Why?'

My vis-a-vis was a shortish solid object, a policeman – Inspector, he'd said – but in civilian clothes. A grey suit with an ill-advised check and an enormous thickness that looked like it could stop bullets and, given its general state of wear, might have done so.

'He didn't say. We'd played cards in St James's, and afterwards he grabbed me and said he needed to talk to me about something.'

'But he didn't say what?'

'No. He didn't. Seemed pretty emotional about it, though.'

'Why didn't you talk in St James's?'

'Damned if I know. He insisted. I was a bit reluctant, as you'll imagine; no chance of a cab back to civilization at that hour. He insisted some more. Emotional, as I say.'

'Did you kill him, Mr Delamere?'

The face was as solid as the rest of him. A heavy, yeoman-of-olde-England affair topped with red hair.

He didn't seem to blink.

'No, Inspector. I did not.'

Still he didn't blink. He just watched me.

'The assertion is offensive and fantastical.'

'Mm. Thing is, sir, business like this, we like to go step-by-step. If you follow me. I'm trying to establish who killed this gentleman. I find another gentleman, bent over the body, with the knife in his hand. Perhaps you'll think me unimaginative, sir, but it seems only logical that I explore that second gentleman's fit as a murderer, before I conceive of any more... fantastical hypotheses.'

I nodded.

'Sort of a journey, sir.'

'Well, bon voyage, Inspector, and don't dawdle; you're well

short of journey's end at the moment.'

'Mm. You played cards, you said?'

'Yes.'

'Who won?'

'Tonight, I did. A matter of thirty guineas.'

The Inspector's eyes widened a fraction.

'Any… trouble about that, sir?'

'No.'

He made a charmless noise through his lips, like a cow sneering at a thistle. 'Sum like that, sir: might easily cause a bit of unhappiness.'

'But not on this occasion. I was happy to take his I.O.U.'

He was just gazing at me again; implacable, suspicious. I didn't like it.

'Listen, old lad, I know you're not a regular at White's, but does it really strike you as likely that a chap wanting to clear a debt, welsh on a debt, or smoke a cheroot and chat about a debt, would invite his creditor to a shipyard at the arse end of London in the middle of the night to do so?'

'Not much, your worship. But it's the ideal place for you to invite him, if you wanted to do murder.' It was rather a good point. 'Another five minutes and you'd have found somewhere to put him he'd never have been seen again.'

'Or I'd have found somewhere less elaborate in the first place. Or perhaps I didn't do it at all.'

'You'd quarrelled over a lady.'

'I beg your pardon?'

'We've done our digging, Mr Delamere. Story's well known. You'd quarrelled over a lady.'

'I deny that utterly. We were briefly – Gods, to have to discuss it in these sordid circumstances – what someone with your intimate knowledge of the Sunday papers would refer to as rivals for a lady. He lost. He took it in good heart. I subsequently learned there had been an… understanding, and I stepped back for him.'

'May I know the lady's name?'

'You may not.'

'I could find it easy enough.'

'No doubt. You're clearly a connoisseur of fatuous errands.'

'A journey, sir. As I say. And lookee here, I've found two healthy motives for murder already.'

3.

Like Polyphemus the Cyclops stowing Odysseus and crew in his cave for future consumption, the desk sergeant had put me in cold storage in a sort of holding cell. My companions were a couple of drunks, a pimp who'd caught a truncheon across the phiz during his arrest and was having trouble breathing through a grotesquely swollen purple nose, an old boxer I was pretty sure I'd seen once in an unofficial bout south of the river, and an evil-looking little personage who'd bagged the driest corner and everyone was avoiding.

I slept fitfully. It's a habit of travel in out-of-the-way places that I sleep as and when I can. But it's also a habit not to settle until I'm sure of the company, and the holding cell of Wapping Police Station was a dashed sight more dubious than many places I've dossed in the Balkans and the Levant. And having to prop oneself up against a damp wall with a grille above you open to the night don't make for cosy slumber.

In the dawn – the cold light coming in from the grille made us look like the tombs in St Paul's crypt, frozen on our benches – I was chatting with the pug when I heard voices from along the corridor. I knew they didn't allow visitors along, but for some reason they were making an exception: a door was opening and now heavy feet were approaching the cell.

After a night of unpleasant surprises, a moment of good news.

'Good morning, sir,' he said to me. 'Did you sleep well?'

He was carrying a loose parcel. 'Tolerable under the circumstances, Quinn. Sorry to have dragged you out like this.'

'Not at all, sir. I regret that the person at the desk insisted on examining the contents. I hope you'll find them in good order.'

He pushed the parcel through the bars, watched by the sergeant. Again, I had no idea whether this was normal, but my valet had bribed, bullied or charmed them into acquiescence.

'I think you will have to appear before the magistrate this morning, sir.' Quinn gets more formal in company; in his habitual Cornish drawl, the average sentence drags on for hours. 'Some improvements to your appearance and hygiene may help.'

'No need to get personal, Quinn. What news from Fawnsley?'

'I regret that Mr Fawnsley has said he is unwilling to act for you, sir.'

'Ah. The quality of mercy has taken one look at my predicament and buggered off, eh?'

'His excuse was a matter of an unpaid bill, sir. From his other comments… he does not care to associate, sir.'

The parcel contained a change of linen, a razor and soap, a small volume of FitzGerald and a packet of sandwiches. A nod of courtesy, and Quinn was gone.

I'd begged a cup of water and used it to shave, and was sharing the sandwiches with the pug when the sergeant came back to confirm that the magistrate would indeed be casting his eye over me during the morning. He said it as if they'd be skipping a committal and trial and reaching for the black cap right off. He then confiscated my razor.

I returned to my sandwich. The pug was halfway through his as I sat, but then he stopped mid-mouthful, looked confused, and – having checked that the policemen weren't watching – cautiously pushed something out through his lips. He wiped it on his trousers and handed it to me.

'Looks like your bloke ain't confident,' he said.

It was a tiny pen-knife.

I pocketed the knife quickly. 'He gets snooty if I don't keep my nails in good order.'

4.

My valet mightn't have been confident, but the magistrate was in a good mood. I was politely asked to remain available to support the police in their enquiries, and bailed.

I was enjoying the sweet air of freedom in the lavatory-like corridor outside the courtroom, until I saw someone watching me hungrily. Red hair, mighty suit. And not happy.

'Ah, Inspector. Sorry to disappoint you.'

'Nice to be able to buy yourself out of justice. I'm still after you. Every step.'

'Better luck next time, eh?'

'Sure of it, sir. Two healthy motives already, as I say.'

'Give me enough rope and I'll hang myself, eh?'

'That's the spirit, sir.'

And he managed to smile. Sort of wolfish; implacable. I didn't like it; I was starting to feel as though I might have stabbed the chap after all. Then he was gone.

Then Quinn, coming from the public gallery. 'Congratulations, sir.' It didn't sound much in the Cornish grumble, and neither of us was feeling it.

'I have a question, Quinn. You're moaning at me more than usual about our finances. My lawyer has passed by on the other side of the road because I owe him, and he's in pretty distinguished company among the local tradesmen. You're restricting me to second-rate wine and hiding the racing pages. How have I just met bail?' The lumpy face shifted uncomfortably. 'And anyway, what possible power induced the magistrate to give bail on a capital charge?'

'Perhaps your distinction, sir, or a friend–'

'Rubbish. I couldn't get a stray dog to piss on me, even before the police sized me up for murder. There's no-one who'd… Quinn, why are you looking so damned shifty?' He tried to compose himself, and failed. 'Who, you blighter? Wait. No… No, Quinn. If you've gone to her, you'll be on the street in the hour.' That put him on his dignity again. 'A woman? You went to a woman?'

'Naturally I went to no-one, sir. Her butler and I happened to be in communication on – on a private matter, and when he asked after you it would have been odd not to mention your present inconvenience.'

He was looking solid again. 'Very clever, Quinn. Quite the politician, aren't we?' I turned away. 'Of all people…' I was off down the corridor. I needed air. 'Her!'

5.

Eaton Square always has me on edge. Some queasy combination of the Eden from which I have been cast out, and so many generations of ill-gotten and ill-inherited wealth staring down so smug from the elegant windows. It's a couple of generations since Delameres stopped being acceptable in Belgravia; I've had better welcomes from Turkish bandits.

I took a deep breath on the doorstep of Number 22. She had

to be faced; although some yellow corner of my gut was hoping she wasn't there.

She was there.

There as she always appears in my mind, standing by the mantelpiece when I'm shown in, long and elegant and the handsomest face in London.

The handsomest face was considering me with something like fondness, which made me uncomfortable enough, and what might even have been a touch of pity, which was intolerable.

'Why Henry, I'm disappointed. I'd hoped for prison rags, and perhaps a manacle or two.'

'I spruced up to impress the Law.' She nodded. 'You shouldn't have done it, Victoria. You had no—'

'I thought champagne, to celebrate your liberty.'

'I'm not stopping.'

'It's the '98' She was pouring it already.

'You'll have the money by nightfall.'

'Don't be an idiot, Henry.' She'd stopped in the middle of handing me the wine. She was glaring at me. 'In the extremely unlikely eventuality that you can find it, it's much better spent elsewhere.' The wine finished its journey. She raised her glass near mine. 'To liberty.'

Another deep breath. I drank, and grunted ungraciously at her.

She knows I'm a sucker for the '98.

'Victoria, you know my attitude to debt.'

'And to gainful employment and marriage, and similarly impractical. If you've a penny you'll want to spend it on finding out who killed poor David.'

I was about to protest again, and stopped at her face. So damn' certain. So damn' wise about me.

'You don't think I killed him, then? The intelligent money's agin you.'

She looked rather austere. Inappropriate levity, I suspect. Victoria Carteret is in her way the most ruthless woman I've ever known – ruthless in her rationalities, her certainties – but the most truly sympathetic to creatures weaker than herself; which is most of us. She'd known David Sinclair; known him for a decent man.

'You're certainly capable of killing, Harry. Had it been a sword, I'd have thought it quite possibly you. Had he suffered some inexplicable accident I'd have known it for a certainty.' She sipped at the champagne, tasted it, looked at me straight. 'But a knife, as the newspaper said?' She shook her head and tutted.

The door opened behind me and a voice said 'Victoria – oh. Didn't realize–'

'Daddy, look who's here!' There was just the hint of mischief in her voice.

'Delamere!' The old man spoke hoarse; appalled. One of the many comforting principles of Magnus, Lord Aysgarth – along with the British Constitution, the Gold Standard and the eternal timetable of the shooting season – is that I should not be in his drawing room. 'Del– But wait: I thought you in prison. You're arrested for murder!'

'And guilty as all hell, sir. Victoria caught me hiding the knife in your box hedge.' I didn't make it sound like a joke, and he didn't laugh. His face turned a funny colour, though.

'Daddy, would you kindly excuse us? Henry is innocent, of course. He's only here because I summoned him.' She had too, in her way. 'I wished to learn certain points about the matter, before Henry continues to assist the police in finding the real murderer.'

Lord Aysgarth shook his head, and left. His late wife – a woman I'd truly respected and liked – had bequeathed to her eldest daughter the unique ability to deflate him, and he swallowed this latest atrocity and the door slammed enough to shake the lamps. Come the 1st of October, the pheasants would be suffering for this incident in their thousands.

Victoria was gazing up at me. Inspecting. Considering. Eventually, she said:

'I know you'll refuse, but couldn't you get to the Continent for a spell? Hide out until this blows over?'

'No.'

'I know you'll refuse, but I repeat that if you need—'

'No.'

'More wine?'

'No. Thank you.'

'You're hunted. But – for David; and for your pride – you're going to take on the police, and whoever is responsible. You're going to find out who did this.'

It hadn't, I realized, been a question.

I raised my glass to her, and then emptied it. 'Yes.

6.

The city roared around me, and I didn't notice a thing. She's a glorious old girl, London, and in the right mood I get a kick out of rambling through her streets. The buildings – the immensity of all that history, of all that it's built on and all it has been and all it represents now. The grandest men in the world, mingling with some of the most wretched. And sometimes, just for a moment, the lives touch. And the energy of it all, the power: horses, carriages, omnibuses, motor cars, and a million pairs of boots. The high windows of Mayfair sneered down at me. Hyde Park Corner was a merry-go-round of the city: news-sheet hawkers and fruit-sellers and clerks having a gasper and nurses pushing perambulators and street gypsies careering between them. There was some sort of public meeting in the park, a fellow on a box roaring out his message to a silent watchful mob.

It all became nothing: a hum and a blur around me.

Could it have been mere thuggery, Sinclair's death? A robbery gone wrong, a disgruntled worker scorned? Somehow it didn't seem so. Sinclair's concern, his insistence that we meet. Found in his yard, by his battleship. It was... consequent, somehow.

And that explained the police, too. In the normal run of things they'd think twice before pinching someone of my relative status. The world's not that far gone yet. But this, clearly, wasn't the normal run of things. The police had decided immediately that this was something stranger, something that wore his collar stiff not soft. And they had pulled together my dossier in record time. What in hell was going on?

Had the walk from Eaton Square to Piccadilly been a dozen times longer, perhaps I'd have reached some brilliant conclusion with my thinking. Probably not. As it was, in those twenty minutes I covered the mile and a half to my rooms briskly enough, but got nowhere mentally.

I'd given Quinn a list of errands – things I'd need and things I wanted found out – so I had to let myself in. The dark familiar hall – sticks, coats, a few prints of places I'd been and places I'd rather be, the hatstand made from a buffalothorn branch I'd once spent the night on – seemed inadequate. I made for the sitting room, and brandy.

There was no valet in the place, but there was a man with a brown Homburg hat, a loose-fitting suit, and a pistol pointing at my stomach.

So, more than enough company.

He was sitting in the armchair near the window. 'One of us seems to be in the wrong place,' I said.

A smile grew wide on his face. 'We are exactly as we should be,' he said encouragingly. 'Especially if you are doing nothing foolish.'

The accent was foreign.

'Force of habit,' I said. 'But I'll try to restrain myself.'

I don't know what I was saying. It didn't matter. I was concentrating on his face.

Mad? Desperate? Familiar? All these things may tell whether the shot is imminent or susceptible of negotiation. That's why you must fight the urge to look at the gun, and why you must read the face like your life depends on it. Which of course it does.

This bird wasn't mad, or desperate, or at all familiar. A fleshy, fortyish stranger, and very relaxed. As he could afford to be, being so perfectly in control of things.

In my odd, wandering life I've had more than my share of men pointing guns at me. Gentlemen in various places unhappy about some misunderstanding or other – whether political, sporting or female. The armed bandits that I seem to attract across southeastern Europe. (I attract them in the Levant and Africa too, but there they only run to knives.) Thousands of grumpy Boers in the war. The great thing is to know *why* the chap's pointing the gun, because then you know how much time you've got and what it's going to take for the gun to point elsewhere.

'What do you want?' I said. The note of alarm came easily; he was so comfortable, so certain. 'I'll – I'll give you anything you want! Money? I have money.'

Hands up and open – no threat, *stay comfortable as you like* – I took a step towards him.

'Actually,' he said, 'I am given to understand that you do not.' There's something about a German accent that makes you look for the firing squad. Was it German? There was a lightness – he was relishing the words – that could have been Austrian, or Swiss. Or perhaps he was just enjoying himself. 'It is of no consequence, as I want only to talk.'

'Oh.' I let my shoulders sag in apparent relief, as I took another step towards him. I glanced down at the pistol: I wasn't getting anything from his face, beyond his certainty that he was in control. A cheap brown suit, with a white ribbon pinned one lapel. No clues from the pistol, either. It was a revolver, and a sturdy one; a Webley, surely. Probably the most common handgun in England; I had one myself. 'Any chance we could exchange postcards instead?' Still pointing steady at my belly, the pistol looked vast.

I'd managed another step closer. The madness of the previous eighteen hours should have – what? Led me to assume this was linked? Left me too bewildered for assuming anything? Got me used to madness, at least.

As I got closer, looking for my moment, the movements had to be more careful.

He was watching me, and smiling pleasantly: the lips were wide in his face, and squeezed his eyes above the fleshy cheeks. 'That is correct, Mr Delamere. Come closer.'

It was all wrong.

'In fact, do please sit down here, at the desk.' He nodded at my desk, and then the barrel of the Webley gestured me that way too.

Keen to keep up the pose of co-operation, I took another half-step forwards, nearer to him and nearer to the desk.

The *Daily Mail* front page had been placed on the desk: 'SHOCKING SOCIETY STABBING IN SHIPYARD'.

'That is correct,' said my guest. 'Pick it up, why not?'

Doing so covered my movement a few inches closer to him.

And at last I understood, when it was almost too late.

'Sit down, Mr Delamere!'

I began to babble: 'I – I'd rather – look, d'you mind? – nerves, you know.' Obviously agitated, I began to move erratically away from him. 'D'you mind if I smoke?'

'Stop! Careful, Delamere…' My hand's movement towards my cigarette case couldn't have been any slower, but he was taking no chances. Very carefully, exaggerated carefully, I put two fingers into my jacket pocket and pulled out the case. One hand still holding the melodramatic headline, I lit a cigarette clumsily.

His arm was fully extended with the revolver. 'Sit down, now, Mr Delamere…' He was smiling again, all terribly pleasant, the most pleasant well-armed would-be-murderer one could hope to find in one's sitting room. I made a half-move towards the desk.

He wanted me sitting at my desk, the shameful headline in one hand, a bullet fired from very short range in my brain, and the pistol – standard issue for British officers in the Cape – artfully beneath me. He'd wipe it first, no doubt, and press it into my dead hand so there'd be no doubt about who'd last held it; if he was lucky, he might even get my dead fingers to clutch it. It takes the artistic touch, staging a suicide.

'Actually, d'you mind? I badly need a drink first.' I was stumbling across the room again, the Webley's barrel following me, and this time my assassin stood with it.

I made a fidgety mess of opening the decanter and trying to get some brandy into the glass. I turned towards him for a moment, so he could see how much of a fidgety mess I was making of it. Lord Northcliffe's latest contribution to English literature was still clutched in the hand that also held the shaking glass.

He glanced at the brandy, and I could see him calculating that it would enhance the effect. Artistic touch, as I say. 'Sit down now, Mr Delamere.' He was beckoning me back towards the desk. 'This won't take long, and then I will be leaving you in peace and joining my comrades outside.'

'Comrades?' I mumbled through my cigarette, decanter still rattling against glass and spilling more than it poured.

'Certainly,' he said. 'A man planning to overturn London may hide very nicely among men planning to overturn the world.'

I'd no idea what he was talking about. But I nodded agreeably, and turned away to finish pouring. With my back blocking his view, I stuffed the newspaper page into my glass, poured more brandy over it, and lifted the glass to my lips as if taking a first mouthful.

The cigarette ignited it nicely, and as it flared I spun and tossed the blazing bundle at him and ducked to one side. He got off one instinctive shot somewhere between me and my burning missile, and as he was beating that lot aside I hurled the decanter after it. Another shot, over my head as I ducked to the floor, and he was stumbling back a step – as you do, when a brandy decanter flung by a very angry man fighting for his life gets you in the shoulder – and I launched myself at him. My first punch got him hard in the throat, and only then I went for the gun. A Japanese I once met in a fencing tournament in Singapore told me some frightfully clever unarmed manoeuvres you can use on this sort of occasion, but I can't say I've ever been able to remember them in the heat of the moment. Somewhere beneath us, the brandy bomb was still burning. My hand was clamped over the hammer of the revolver – and that, now, is a clever manoeuvre – and I butted him in the nose with my forehead and while he thought about his choking and his watering eyes I got my other hand on the barrel of the revolver and twisted it round.

The shot roared. From a distance of six inches I saw my assassin's eyes go wide – damned surprised he looked, and no wonder. His lips gaped in one last ghastly grimace, and he dropped out of my arms.

The air was thick with fumes from the brandy; my late guest had been doused in the stuff from the decanter, and fallen on the burning glass, and now a dull blue flame was creeping up his sleeve.

There was a cough from behind me.

'Is everything in order, sir?'

7.

Quinn considered the dead man, flames still tickling the coat. Then he saw the bits of the dead man's grey matter spattered not-so-grey across the lace curtain. Then he saw the bullet hole in the ceiling. Then he noticed the broken glass beside him, and glanced up to where a bullet had smashed the portrait of the Princess Maria Teresa of Spain and her husband which I keep for sentimental reasons. My assassin's first shot had plugged Prince Ferdinand of Bavaria perfectly in the centre of his forehead; unfairly, for he's a nice enough chap for a hun. Presumably there was another bullet hole somewhere.

'About normal for today, Quinn, I should say.'

Quinn looked at me, at last.

'The carpet seems to be on fire, sir.'

'Yes, sorry about that. Is it ours or the Albany's?'

'You all right, sir?'

I gripped his arm, and it helped. 'I'm fair angry, Quinn.'

'Mm. Not ideal for making decisions, sir, as you always say. Is the gentleman dead?'

I glanced at my smouldering guest. 'I hope so. Bit of a clean-up job, I'm afraid. I'm sorry about the carpet.'

'Not at all, sir.' He didn't sound so cool about it. Quinn doesn't care about the fittings themselves, but he's a real puritan when it comes to minimising wear and tear.

'There's worse.' He waited. And before I could say another word, there was a hammering at the front door. 'Worse, as I say. It's the duty of a gentleman, Quinn, to stand up for what he's done and face the music. But personally, I've unfinished business. It's the back window for me. I'm leaving you in the lurch.'

'My pleasure.'

The door thundered again, and then there was a shout: 'Open up! In there!'

'I'm cutting loose. Jo'burg rules. Don't try to contact me at the club. Assume you and this place are watched.'

'Of course, sir. By whom, sir?'

'No idea.' I nodded at the body. 'But they're going to be unhappy. Use Dobbs's or The Pot for messages. Did you get any of what I asked?

'Table on the hall. Cash too.'

'The address?'

'Bayswater Road; Number 77.'

The muffled shouting again. 'This is the police! Open up!'

'Your pistol's in the usual place, sir; cleaned this morning.'

The door began to thump and strain; the police were breaking in now.

'Right ho then.' I nodded my thanks. As I left for the back window and the service stairs, my valet had picked up the soda syphon and was taking careful aim at the smouldering carpet.

8.

I came out between a pair of dustbins, glancing up and back and waiting for the sound of raised window and official shouts and whistles. I knew the pair of alleys that would get me out further along Piccadilly and hopefully clear of police interest, and set off at a trot. If it had only been the local constable who'd heard the shots and come to investigate, then my grumpy Cornishman and his soda syphon would give him plenty to be getting on with.

I needed a new base of operations, and I needed answers. I had to reckon myself fully a fugitive now. Either I solved this bizarre mystery, or I'd be on the run forever. I turned into the second of my alleys.

If, on the other hand, that wretched police inspector was for some reason lurking nearby and waiting for me to step out of line, then –

I was out into the brighter light and fresher air of Piccadilly, and I blinked and slowed to a walk. And immediately a body thumped hard into me and I stumbled back, clutching vaguely at whoever it was.

Whoever it was wasn't coming down easily, and I staggered upright still attached to his jacket, and was staring into a greasy smeared face under a flat cap. Two mighty hands shoved me backwards. 'Oi, ___ off out of it!' he yelled, and kept on coming like a man who planned to be well in it. I drove forwards into his stomach and he went stumbling back, then he clubbed me about the shoulders and I let him go. As I staggered upright I found myself surrounded by men like him: my assailant, and a dozen in the same rough jackets and caps and heavy boots, and all with the same dirty faces. And around us there was an immense yelling: by some nightmarish development I had found myself in an arena of street toughs, expected to fight on, and all of London was roaring for the other side.

It would have been the smart bet, too. I was bewildered and pretty groggy, and apparently outnumbered a hundred to one. More, I really didn't want or need this fight. I'd nothing against this chap or any of his mates, and no wish to dawdle and annoy yet another section of London society.

Breathing hard, I came instinctively to the defensive and waited for him to come, taking that valuable instant to look around me. Dozens of faces staring, and behind them placards held high. What madness was this? And he was coming in again, fists ready and body open and a grin on his face. 'Well look at this!' he called. 'Looks like I get me own blow for the workers, eh?'

He was relying on momentum and the fact that the sort of chap who wears a three-piece suit to a street-brawl wouldn't be much of a threat. So I took a worried step or two back as he got close.

It was a march: a protest, a political rally by workers. Rallies were ten-a-penny this season, and the papers were predicting bloody revolution on a weekly basis. And I'd barged into the middle of the class war.

I thought about trying to explain how the Delameres have been on the wrong end of every economic and social development in British history, but it's too long a tale. I saw his left shoulder flex and immediately I moved in towards his punch, blocking it with both forearms up and turning into him so that my back took his right and my momentum pushed him away, and as he went backwards I continued to turn and followed hard and kept him going with a wild jab of my left and then put him down with a precise right jab into his face. I really didn't want to do more than was necessary to get away. I turned to the side, ran at the two nearest onlookers and, as they hesitated, ducked down and pushed between them. I came up through a thicket of marching legs, and caught plenty of surprised glances, and worse as I started to weave and barge through them. Behind me I heard shouts, but I was through to the other side of the column of pro-testers and then I turned against the flow and ran, and I knew they'd give it up pretty quickly and get on with their marching.

I only ran for a couple of dozen yards, and slowed to a trot and then, as soon as I was sure that my posse of affronted proletarians had given me up and marched away towards the promised land, a walk. Concealment lay in normality. There was a loose string of spectators along the pavement, and I ducked in among them and continued sauntering eastward towards Piccadilly Circus.

'Delamere!'

With a last ounce of grip I stopped myself from turning to the shout, and walked on.

'Delamere!' and a whistle. Now I turned.

It was the damned policeman – Bunce.

I ran again. Another dozen yards got me to Fortnum's store, and I raced in like the last box of special biscuits was up for grabs. Immediately I slowed to a stride. In a crowd of protesting mechanics I was out of place and vulnerable. In here, in this temple of genteel grocery shopping and relatively good taste, I was on home ground, and even Bunce and his myrmidons would think twice about causing a rumpus. Pity their wine selection's so average. I made straight for the lift, pushed all the buttons, got out at the second floor, crossed to the stairs and came down again. Sixty seconds after I'd walked into the place, I was out the side door and across Duke Street and into my barber's and in another thirty I was under a cape and a faceful of shaving foam.

'A little late in the day for us, isn't it Mr Delamere?'

'Had rather a lively night, Thomas. Just getting on top of things now.'

9.

In a side street in St Pancras is a door with a small painted sign that reads just 'Dobbs'.

Dobbs's caters for gentlemen of limited or distressed means: travellers, and gamblers, and drunkards, and bankrupts and broken homers, and now at least one man wanted for multiple murders. It's clean, cheap, extremely discreet, and handy for the railway stations.

Dobbs is Lancelot Dobbs. He was once butler to the Fawcetts of Abingdon, until young Charlie Fawcett, last of the line, celebrated his inheritance of the increasingly impoverished title by selling his last and favourite horse to three different buyers on the same day with a promise to deliver tomorrow, then waving the accumulated cash under the noses of three different bookmakers with a promise to pay tomorrow, for a bet on an absolute certainty at Newbury. Marvellous plan, until the certainty tripped a furlong from home, and Charlie found himself being harassed by the police for multiple counts of fraud and debt. Fairly reckoning this the end of the Fawcetts, the poor lad walked out of the mortgaged house, said a fond farewell to the mare – I don't think he'd ever have given her to even one of the buyers – and blew his head off with a shotgun. Outraged by this collective failure of flexibility and good humour by the police, the buyers, the bookies, and the banks, Lancelot Dobbs the now-unemployed butler had gone into business as harbourer and guardian of disadvantaged young gentlemen, no questions asked and policemen be damned. I don't think the Fawcett creditors ever did find the family silver.

In one of Dobbs's spartan rooms, I slipped a thin package behind the empty wardrobe, a roll of bank notes into one of the metal legs of the bed, and more behind a loose bit of skirting board. I hefted my pistol in my hand for a few moments, in two minds. Eventually I stuffed it into the grey pillowcase and left it there. The way things were going, I'd be more likely to shoot a policeman than anything else. However tempting that was, it wouldn't help much.

Then I set off, back across London again, in the mild late afternoon. 'Westward, look, the land is bright', as the chappie wrote. But he probably wasn't talking about Bayswater.

10.

Without wishing to sound like a cad, I've been in various ladies' bedrooms over the years, and indeed passed some of my happiest hours there. But only when the lady herself has also been present.

To be in a lady's bedroom without the lady is not the behaviour of a gentleman, and a damn' sight less entertaining. I was particularly uncomfortable being in this particular lady's bedroom because downstairs her front door was being guarded by a policeman, so I'd had to come in the back way. Uncomfortable also because of certain aspects of our personal history which I need not detail. And because I was widely believed to have murdered her husband.

So I prowled pretty restlessly around Pamela Sinclair's bedroom.

Victoria Carteret had arrived at the front door with careful timing and much fanfare, great lady visiting her friend in her hour of grief and so forth, to allow me to arrive unobserved through the back garden. She was downstairs with Pamela now.

How do you find words for a woman whose husband has just been stabbed? And how do you find words to explain that you've installed his presumed murderer in her boudoir?

I hadn't told Victoria that I'd just shot someone else in my rooms. Even her patience is limited. We'd agreed this rendezvous with Pamela Sinclair before the whole burning foreigner debacle.

I needed to disappear, and this kind of meeting would become much more difficult – even contacting Victoria would become more difficult. I had to grab the opportunity while I had it.

It wasn't an entirely feminine room, I realized. For economy or modernity, the Sinclairs shared. Had shared.

David Sinclair's dressing gown hung on the back of the door

of the bedroom he had shared with his wife. On the dressing table there was a box of collar studs, and a tie-pin with a battleship design, to match the cuff-link that I'd found under his hand – and, I realized, still had in my trouser pocket. He would never again look at the things I was looking at. I felt even more of a swine.

The door opened. I took a deep breath.

She looked ghastly. Pretty girl, Pamela; but she'd aged a decade in a morning. For the first time, I saw the impact of Sinclair's death beyond its inconvenience for me. Her face was white, and waxy, where she'd wiped and wiped at tears that would not stop. Her eyes were rimmed an angry red.

She couldn't have looked at me with more horror and revulsion if I'd been holding the knife still dripping with her husband's blood. Her face shuddered as she gazed at me from the doorway, and her breaths came in great sobs.

'Pamela, I'm so sorry.' She pressed her eyes tight shut. It sounded like I was apologizing for having murdered him. 'He was a good man; he was a better man; and it's appalling that he's gone from you.'

Her eyes were still pressed shut, and now the tears came again. Victoria stepped closer behind her, and gently held her shoulders.

Her eyes flickered open, puffy and hot. 'Why are you here?' she gasped.

'Because I didn't do this terrible thing, Pamela, and I'm going to find out who did. Because I need to ask you some questions.' She shut her eyes again. 'Because even though I know I'm the last man you want to see, I won't hide from you.'

'Not in here', she said, and turned away. I followed her out, frankly glad to be out of the bedroom. But she was making for the top of the stairs – until Victoria saw my concern and took her arm again. 'We should stay upstairs, dearest,' she murmured into Pamela's ear. 'Best if no-one sees Harry here. That's why he had to come in the window.'

Pamela spun round, and gazed at me with venom for the chaos that I represented.

'Just like old times?' she said; the bitter sarcasm was weakened by her shaking voice.

Had Inspector Bunce had a little longer to put his papers in order, he'd no doubt have learned that when Sinclair and I had found ourselves digging in the same allotment, the object of our interest had been the woman whom Sinclair had later married. She had grown up in this house, and when her parents had gone from Bayswater to glory she and her sister had lived here together, and then it had become her marital home.

Victoria led her into a spare bedroom, which seemed to double as a dressing room for one or both Sinclairs.

There was a paper parcel on the bed. Pamela picked it up, and sat down on the bed clutching it close.

'He was better than you', she said. She wasn't looking at me.

'Yes.'

'You were wild, and unreliable.'

'Yes.'

'And he was decent, and serious, and hard-working.'

'Yes.'

'I was right to marry him.'

'Yes.'

'He truly cared for me.' Now she looked at me, and the tears were flowing again. 'More than you ever could.'

I just gazed back at her. Not a lot I could say to that.

It was true enough, almost certainly. I'd been fond, and enjoying myself, but as soon as I found out that Sinclair was serious about her and that she'd glossed over a couple of details about what had passed between them I'd been happy to step back.

Victoria sat down next to her, and put an arm round her

shoulder. 'We all get infatuated with Harry for a spell,' she said, looking up at me as she spoke. 'But then the champagne wears off, and he's just a headache.'

A bit harsh, but it wasn't the moment to explore the point. Pamela nodded. Victoria, head next to hers, went on: 'David was right for you; and you were very good for him.' Pamela nodded again.

'It's his suit,' she said, eyes closed again. 'I'm holding his suit.' She sounded surprised at herself. 'They delivered it just before you came.'

Victoria looked rather shocked at this. She'd not seen the body and the knife, and she'd no idea how torn or bloody the suit might be. 'I'll hang it up', she said uneasily. 'Where it belongs.'

Gently she pulled the parcel out of Pamela's arms, and turned away to unwrap it. As she turned I managed to catch her eye, and mouth the word 'pockets'. The look I got in return was not a happy one.

I crouched in front of Pamela, and took one of her hands in mine. 'Pamela, can you think of any reason why anyone would want to do this horrible thing?'

She shook her head, holding the emotion in with difficulty. Then she opened her eyes. 'Apart from you?'

I think she was trying to make it a joke. It didn't work.

'Apart from me.' She shook her head again. 'Was he… was he in any kind of difficulty? I don't know – money, that kind of thing?'

Again, the head shook. She pulled her hand away, and scraped a few wild strands of hair back over one ear. 'Oh no, nothing like that. He played cards – just with friends – for amusement; but he was very sensible.'

This, of course, was nonsense. Out of the corner of my eye I saw that Victoria had half-turned from the wardrobe and was frowning at the words. Sinclair gambled incessantly, recklessly, and badly. But if his widow didn't know now, then hopefully she'd never know. As news of his death got around today, the air above St James's would be thick with the smoke of burning I.O.U.s; chaps would quietly forget the debts. I'd already chalked off my thirty guineas as another lost hope for the family fortune. In any case, if his gambling had somehow led to his death Pamela wouldn't know about it.

'What about his work? Any problems there?'

This time she shook her head more slowly. Sinclair was foolish with a hand of cards, but serious about his work; he'd not have said much to his wife. 'No, I don't... He'd been – he'd been worried recently.'

'Worried?'

'I don't know. The last week or two. Preoccupied. Home late sometimes. There was one evening when he just sat in his chair and... I couldn't get through to him at all.' She was crying freely again. 'I know he was worried about the new ship. "A lot on my mind" – That's all he'd say.' Her breaths shuddered. '"A lot on my mind."' She took in a great sniff, breathed out unsteadily. 'There was a man – he'd been seeing a lot of him recently – something about international co-operation.'

'And... and this man was linked to what he was worrying about?'

'I don't know. They seemed to be becoming great friends. Go out together. But then sometimes when David came back...' She shook her head. 'Greenberg. His name.'

I nodded as if any of this was helpful. 'And last night? Did he say anything about what he was doing? Anything unusual?'

Victoria had turned away from the wardrobe, holding something which she'd got from Sinclair's suit.

'He was just going to his club. Nothing unusual.'

It was a slip of paper, no bigger than her hand. Pale blue, and thin; one end perforated. A printed number – 1536. 1536;

Tudor times, Henry VIII and Anne Boleyn and that business with the monasteries. Then, handwritten, Sinclair's own name, the date from a couple of days ago, and a longer number. Some kind of receipt, by the looks of it. I took it. 'Any idea what this is, Pamela?' She glanced at it; shook her head. 'Never mind; I'll look after it.' I slipped it into my pocket. 'He didn't say anything about what he might do after the club?'

Pamela Sinclair looked up at me straight now, the violent wounded eyes gazing at me. 'He said he hoped he was going to see you. He said there was something he wanted to have out. Something he hoped to settle once and for all.'

11.

I liked Hugh Stackhouse, as soon as I met him on his threshold and he showed me into his sitting room. Partly I liked him because he let me in at all, and had had the sense of discretion to keep the servants out the way. More I liked him because he was a quiet, steady, thinking sort of man. Solid chap; dark hair, strong features. It was frankly a pleasant change to meet someone who didn't try to assault me. But on top of that, his impression of calm and competence reassured and impressed.

Once he'd got me into a seat, he considered me for a moment or two, then offered me a drink, which I refused, and a very decent cigarette, which I took gladly. Then he sat himself, and considered me a moment more. 'It's my pleasure to meet you,' he said. 'You seem to be having rather a tough time of it.'

I took a long pull on the cigarette. 'Damned decent of you to open the door at all,' I said.

'Lady Victoria Carteret suggested that it would be sensible.' For a moment – some hesitation in there – I had the sense that he wasn't comfortable about it.

'I'll try to live up to that. Look, Stackhouse: for starters I should be entirely frank; the police still fancy me for the killing of poor Sinclair, last night, and there's been more trouble today. I'm a fugitive, and I should advise you that you're taking a risk by having me here at all. It's my assertion that if you give me three minutes' hearing you'll be doing something constructive as well as fulfilling Victoria's request. After that you'd be best locking me in the closet and sending your man for the nearest constable, or at least unlocking the back door and forgetting you ever saw me.'

Again the moment of steady consideration.

'My only concern is getting who really killed Sinclair. Whether that's you or not. And keeping the company going. You have your three minutes, Delamere. For Lady Victoria I'll make it five. Then we can review our options.'

'Fair enough.'

'Take another cigarette.'

'I will, thank'ee. So, as you'll understand, I have my reasons for wanting to find out who killed Sinclair. You do too. I happen to think it wasn't me. You're being a sport enough to keep an open mind, for the next five minutes at least. If it wasn't me, it was someone else, and they must have had a reason. I gather that you were close enough to the poor chap personally and professionally.'

He puffed at his own cigarette, and looked into the smoke. 'I cannot think of any reason why anyone would want to kill David Sinclair. Personally or professionally.'

'You'll pardon me for saying so, but – from my limited ac-quaintance – he wasn't always the steadiest with money.'

He considered me for a long time. Then a heavy smile. 'No. No he wasn't. But then... a creditor would be more likely to want him alive than dead. Which, I gather, is the main argument in your favour.'

'And my impeccable manners. Was he borrowing?'

'Not from anyone who'd use violence. He'd let a gambling debt ride for a while; with people he knew. And… well, he was happy enough to touch a friend if things got difficult.'

'And your business? The Thames Ironwork Shipbuilding Company, yes?'

'What about it?'

Still the dark, steady, reliability. 'Not wanting the commercial secrets, but – going well? Bitter rivalries? Impending disasters?'

'You seem to find my friend's death comical, Delamere.'

'I spent the night in a police cell, Stackhouse. That's how funny I'm finding this.' I puffed the last of the cigarette and stubbed it in a plain solid ashtray. Its plain solid owner waited. 'I'm a bit of a dullard at these business things: what were your roles in the company? How did Sinclair fit in?'

'There's a Board of Directors at the top. Great names; great beards. Meet once a year to nod at the Report. Below them are the tier of chaps who manage things day-to-day. Among others, that's me and that was Sinclair. We all have a general idea of what's going on, and we're each responsible for something in particular. I look after the finances. Sinclair did the legal side of things. Contracts, that sort of stuff.'

'And trade has been…?'

He left it a moment to see if he could wait me out. Eventually, he said: 'His Majesty's Government has commissioned us to build one of its newest battleships. That, of course, means financial stability for us. It's also proof of our reputation. And it means that even if there were trouble the Government would help us through it.'

'Sounds peachy. So why did Sinclair want to drag me to your yard in the middle of the night to talk about something terribly urgent?'

He thought hard about it. 'I have no idea. He didn't tell you any more?'

'He did not. No trouble at the yard?'

The handsome face hesitated, frowned, and then opened in interest. Then it closed again.

'Come along, man. I ain't a shareholder.'

He smiled heavily. 'You should consider it, given how involved you're becoming. I was going to say that I can't see how it's relevant, but we do have some labour difficulty at the moment. The yard's still working, but there are complaints, and demands for more pay – of course. There was supposed to be some march today.'

'I bumped into it. Or it bumped into me. You don't know more?'

He shook his head. 'Sinclair's business. I authorised an extra ha'penny a man when we got the contract for the *Thunderer*, and told Sinclair to camp on that; nothing more to do with it since then.'

'Who might know?'

'Yard manager, perhaps. MacNeice.'

'MacNeice?'

'Generally seen as indispensable. And, indeed, hard to miss.'

I was running out of ideas. 'Ever come across a chap named Greenberg? Sinclair mention him?'

'No... Wait though. Greenberg?' I shrugged. 'Samuel Greenberg. Bit of a crank. Runs an outfit called the... what is it now? – the Commercial Correspondence Confederation. Has romantic ideas about industrial co-operation across borders. Sort of chap one gets stuck next to at company dinners.'

'What was he to Sinclair?'

'God knows. I think Sinclair mentioned him once or twice. They'd probably bumped into each other at some business shindig, and Sinclair would have given him a more patient hearing than most.'

'Any reason why Sinclair should have been depressed after seeing him?'

He shook his head slowly. 'I suppose anyone who cares about international co-operation might be a bit down these days.' He frowned. 'Look, Delamere…'

'That's my five minutes, and I'm grateful for every one. Back door, or do you want me to wait for the police and see if I make a dive for the window?'

Again the heavy smile. Good looking chap, in a sturdy sort of way. 'Back door's not much use to you, unless you propose spending the night in the garden. Take the front door, and leave me to manage my relations with the police.'

As I say, I liked him.

'Listen, you should try to talk to MacNeice at the yard,' Stackhouse said as I was leaving. 'I remember Sinclair looking a bit rattled after a couple of his conversations with the workers' representatives. Ugly language.' He hesitated. 'Even the suggestion of sabotage.'

12.

I needed to clear my head, I needed to re-fill it with something considerably smarter, and I needed to lie low.

I disappeared into the steam of the Ironmonger Row Turkish baths, as into a magician's puff of smoke.

I was stripping off the last of my kit when I realized that the bathing wouldn't be wasted either. I'd been in the same outfit for twenty-four hours, with only a cold shave in a cup in a police cell by way of personal grooming, and my hygiene was in the same state as my reputation.

I jumped straight into the cold plunge pool – punishment for having let myself get assaulted, arrested or embarrassed by pretty much every single person I'd met. Then, pink and breathing hard, bare feet slapping on the stone, I stalked through to the steam rooms to wait for a massage.

In the real world of people who weren't hunted by the police for murder, it was supper time. The reputable clientele had gone home, where they probably hadn't been held up by foreign gunmen and set fire to their assailants with grenades of flaming cognac; the less reputable night-time patrons wouldn't be here yet. I had the place to myself.

I settled back on one of the white marble slabs. I felt it hard under my skull, my shoulders, my elbows and my ankles. A handy discipline, I've found: to take myself back to the very simplest of what I am. Bruised in body or spirit, in a dozen cities from London to Constantinople.

Time passed. Above me through the steam, the bare white vaulting of the chamber was the inside of my head, ready to be repacked.

David Sinclair had been distressed. Of a million possible locations, most of them more convenient and many of them more private, he had insisted I come to his shipyard. The shipyard was significant.

The hot air rasped through my teeth with each steady breath.

David Sinclair had been murdered. It was surely incredible that his distress and his murder were unrelated. There was something so wrong at or with the shipyard as to cost a man his life.

Heavy feet flopped wet across the floor near me. Through the steam and my sweat-bleared eyes, a vast flabby figure loomed. He was carrying a wooden bucket of soaps and sponges. Just the kind of brute I wanted for a masseur tonight.

'There's a tip for you if you really wrench me about,' I said.

He grunted. He put the bucket of soaps and sponges down

somewhere behind my head.

I closed my eyes.

Sabotage?

A flabby hand came down over my nose and mouth, and an enormous crushing weight on my chest, and there were hands on my legs too. For one stupid instant my brain thought this was the massage, and then he pinched my nostrils together and pressed harder and my eyes opened and I saw the great globe of his bald head and a gaze of remorseless murderous intent and I was struggling for my life. I was trying to struggle. I couldn't move. The brute had settled his monstrous bulk across my torso, trapping one of my arms under him and grabbing the other. Someone else seemed to be holding my legs. Pinned, there was nothing I could do to stop his careful suffocation of me. I was gulping at nothing under his palm; choking; desperate for breaths that wouldn't come; eyes gaping mad. And still he gazed down at me, and in the nightmare my body wouldn't respond. My shoulders were wriggling frantically, my hips, even my fingers clenching and straining. Futile. I was paralyzed, and the only thing that worked was my brain, and my eyes, watching my death.

I've been on the brink a few times and, take it from me, if you're expecting cool resolution and shrewd reflexes you'll be sore disappointed. It's bloody horrible and desperate and you panic, and anyone who tells you otherwise hasn't been there.

On the slippery stone my writhing became movement, and I twisted slightly under the weight. The weight came down again and harder, and the brute's grip on my arm bit like a claw. I felt one of my legs give a little, tried to find movement, but the other man got his hold back. I was being buried alive. There was nothing left in my throat to breathe, just the rattle of my tongue, and I felt the panic burning in my chest. The last screaming madness of fear filled my head, and I felt sleep coming, and I knew it would be easier than the horror.

The man on my legs adjusted his grip, and for an instant one of my knees was freer. The slippery desperate leg came up and he was clutching again but too late and I kicked out wildly and made contact and suddenly my legs were free. Now I had leverage, enough to get movement in my hips. The mountain of flesh on top of me realized something had changed, glanced round, tried to twist his bulk more completely on top of me. My right arm was numb in his grip, but from under his wallowing belly my left came free.

It was numb too. I tried to punch him, but could only slap ridiculously against his shoulder. I reached for his face, for those deathly eyes, but he twisted his head up and his palm pressed down on my mouth and nose harder still. My flailing hand fell away. It fell against the bucket behind my head. With the last movement of my life, I clutched at the bucket and swung it up towards the bald dome.

I didn't make it. The bucket caught his shoulder and was jarred out of my hand, and a burst of soaps and sponges bounced around us. Dimly, I saw him smiling, felt him moving to grip my arm again and resettle his body on top of me, felt nothing in my nose and mouth as his hand pushed me down into darkness.

Then I felt nothing at all. Not his hand, not the clutch at my arm.

He'd trodden on one of the soaps. As he'd shifted position, one foot had found a bar and he went sprawling. I felt a monstrous heave in my gut as his whole weight came on me, and then as he struggled for balance I was free.

So was his foot. It was beautiful to watch. The vast body cartwheeled backwards, the leg swung up in the best balletic style, and he dropped like a Dreadnought down a slipway. The back of his head caught a marble corner as he fell, and with one grim thump he was still.

I wrestled myself upright at last, gasping and euphoric. The accomplice had been knocked aside in the chaos, and was now staring at the fallen Goliath. He looked up at me, shocked, angry, just in time to get the bucket full in the face.

'Up yours you toe-rag!' I yelled triumphant. I tried to yell triumphant; actually it came out as a sort of croak. I staggered away. I think I did a full circuit of the chamber, stumbling and clutching at marble slabs and occasional taps, just trying to find the damned door. I was wheezing desperately, lungs on fire. I couldn't walk, and I couldn't see. The white glow of the walls was foggy, and lights flashed as I blinked.

I found the doorway, and staggered on. Another chamber of marble slabs and steam, then the corridor to the cold pool, and then the first hall with showers and lavatories. My breathing was coming more regular, but the gasps still sounded loud and hoarse. Here suddenly it was cooler, and clearer. A window up in one corner was slightly open, with the promise of fresh night air.

I took in one deep glorious breath, and opened the door to the lobby and changing rooms.

There were two men sitting in the lobby, coats and hats and clearly not interested in using the baths, and my appearance in the doorway stunned them. I might have been feeling a bit better, but I obviously wasn't looking it. I must have seemed a bit wild, and I'd lost my towel early in the fight. And they'd been expecting two men – two men reporting my death – and here was I instead.

They didn't stay stunned for long. They both came up and started towards me. I pulled back through the door. I wasted a moment wondering about trying to block it against them – me against two men who hadn't just dallied on the doorstep of death – then another moment remembering that they still had at least one accomplice somewhere on my side of the door, waking up with a bit of a headache and a strong sense of unfinished business. With a third wasted moment, I reminded myself that there really wasn't any other way out through the bath chambers, and so I was trapped.

It had to be the window. Vaguely aware of noise somewhere behind me, I was up on the bench, hands reaching for a showerhead and a cubicle wall, pulling myself up, getting a knee up, and there was the window. It was one of those that tilt horizontally, so I had to stick my head through the lower half and wriggle through, feet scrabbling for purchase on showerhead and wall behind me. Something grabbed at my foot, I wrenched free, and was through.

I slammed the window shut, and gazed down at my two pursuers. One now, because the other was disappearing through the door towards the street, while his mate considered following me up the wall.

I was at the bottom of a kind of well between taller bits of building: six feet square, blank walls on each side, no open windows. There was a fair bit of rubbish around my feet and, scrabbling with my hands, I found a piece of tile to wedge against the bottom of the window. It would slow my pursuer, now standing on the bench and testing his weight on the showerhead, if he summoned the nerve to try my window.

But he didn't need to, of course. At some point I was going to have to come back in; unless I planned to spend the rest of my life in the roof-well.

I began to explore the walls, and especially the corners of the well, hands slapping against brick and trying not to think about the moment when I'd tread on a bit of broken glass, or a dozing rat. I only had to get up one storey, before the roof seemed to open out.

I've been up and down a couple of drainpipes in my time. More often down, when I think about it: my sins have tended to be those one must escape from, rather than break in to. It's not as easy as it's popularly reckoned; determination, steady momentum and some forward-thinking about hand- and foot-holds are part of the knack. I've done it under what you might call competitive conditions too, with the hue and cry after me, and on one occasion a disgruntled French chappie throwing wine glasses and indeed a half-empty bottle at me. But I'd never done it in bare feet.

I felt for the holds as far up as I could before I started. Then I pushed my toes in behind the pipe, twisting the foot around, on the first bracket. A breath, as firm a grip as I could with my hands, and up. I gasped as my distorted foot took my whole weight. I scrabbled for the next bracket with my hand, found it, realized that I wasn't concentrating, forced myself to take another breath and try to ignore the pain in my foot, got my grip properly, and placed my other foot.

It can't have been much more than three or four yards to the top. Three footholds. I'm not sure I could have managed four. The last stretch, once I got my hands and then elbows on the parapet, I took entirely on my arms and shoulders, feet flapping useless below me. But at last I was up, gasping, toes burning, knees and elbows raw.

Rooves stretched away and up around me. Looking down, I saw that my pursuer hadn't yet got through the window, or had settled down with a cigarette and a good book to await my return. I had ways forward and, for a moment at least, I was free.

And naked.

13.

It was a glorious night. Absolutely clear sky, with the stars multiplying as soon as one looked up. The cosy glow of a million lamps stretching across the city, promising a million versions of life, of home. All the steeples ghostly in the darkness. Squat and queenly among them the dome of St Paul's; battleship of the mediaeval age. And the chaos of rooves, stone and tile and brick and wood, swooping and plunging like a sea in every direction.

And in the middle of it all, perched up high in the grand old city, one somewhat vexed gentleman standing stark naked on a parapet.

I hadn't, of course, thought this bit through. I don't think many would call me a conventional sort of chap; but I have some of the conventional instincts, and finding myself in the altogether, in an extremely public place, unsettles me as much as anyone.

Not to mention the fact – which I acknowledged as I stood there, hands on hips and considering the terrain with a certain frustration – that, with London's police and a murderous selection of London's criminals hunting me, my vital priority was to make myself inconspicuous. Loitering on rooftops with my essentials swaying in the night breeze, I was set fair to make myself the most conspicuous man in the city.

Something rattled beneath me, and I looked down. There was a shadow in the window. My pursuer had finished his reading and found something to stand on, and would be through into the well imminently.

Come along, idiot. The chase doesn't end until hunter or hunted is down. I didn't know if the chap had my experience of drainpipes, but I was pretty sure he had more appropriate footwear for the climb. *Come along.* I took a breath of the fresh night, and set off along the parapet to where, at waist height, a flat bit of roof stretched away. My feet ached fiercely – I didn't want to think what condition they were in after being wrenched behind the pipe – and I hobbled and hissed as I went.

I got up onto the flat bit of roof all right, and walked cautiously to what seemed to be its front edge. I had some instinct of look-ing for ways down, or away, which was stupid because the front aspect was the least likely to have outbuildings or a sloping roof.

Stupider still, and unlucky, because the exact moment when I stuck my head cautiously over the front edge of the building and looked down into the street below – so peaceful, so much normality, in the gentle rhythms of a few horses and pedestrians in the evening – was the exact moment when one of a couple of men who were arguing about something happened to glance up.

He saw me – I was rather obvious – and gaped for a moment. And then he was pointing, and yelling, and his companion was looking up too and shouting to someone else, and I pulled back and swore.

I'd got onto the flat roof at one end. One side was the front, and the opposite side ran into a sheer wall rising further up. I couldn't waste time hunting more drainpipes and I couldn't trust my feet to stand the strain. I looked back the way I'd come, and fancied I saw a head appearing over the parapet. My hunt-er's boots had carried him up the drainpipe well enough. *Come along.* I trotted towards the far end of the flat roof.

As I came near, I saw that the end of the next building had a double gable: there was a deep gully between two sharply pitched rooves. The gully was for me. I entered its darkness hap-pily, feet stumbling for their place in a gutter filled with the waste of storms and builders and birds.

Dark tunnels are happy places for the naked fugitive, and it was typical of my luck that this one ran out after twenty yards in a blank wall, the different profile of the next building along. One fond glance back along my tunnel, one sober thought of the hunter working out where I must have gone, and I started to scramble up the tiles beside me.

Immediately I slipped back down, into a heap in the gutter. Momentum, or I would never make it. I started up again, trying to keep low and scrambling with hands and feet and knees and not minding the slipping and ignoring the tiles that gave under me and just keeping the limbs moving and with a final lunge I had both hands on the crest of the roof.

I pulled myself up into a crouch. To my right, the direction I'd come from, there was only the gable end; no good. Left it had to be, where the crest of the next roof stretched away.

For a moment I gathered myself, poised in the crouch, catching my breath, aware again of my ridiculous nakedness, the most fantastical gargoyle silhouetted against the moon.

From somewhere – I felt as though it was nearby, but I also felt that everyone in London was staring at me so it could have been miles off – someone screamed. I started along the crest of the roof.

Again, not my first time. But again, my first time when completely naked. I was trying to walk, one foot either side of the crest, but the pain in my feet was throwing my balance and so it was more lurch than walk. Every few steps I would stumble and have to propel myself forwards on hands as well as feet, my moonlit arse surely the brightest most splendid target for my pursuers.

I settled into a goodish rhythm, scrambling forwards like a monkey trying to escape a leopard and determined to make a race of it, occasionally twisting my head round to spot the pursuit, and it was in this manner that I ran into a chimney. I should have expected one to pop up some time or another, but it was well-camouflaged against the night sky and I had been looking the wrong way. I went sprawling, which is a perilous manoeuvre on the crest of a greasy roof at midnight with one's vitals flapping. I pulled myself up, and took the opportunity to reach up and get a handhold on the chimney – its top was just above my head – and steady myself.

There was a noise from the darkness behind me; the leopard

was still coming on. With no choice, I started to edge round the chimney. Now the strain was all on my hands, not my feet. I could get a good grip on the top of the chimney but my feet, as I stepped off the crest and round the first corner, were on sloping tiles. My beleaguered toes took what weight they could, my legs were shaking with the attempt at control, and I unclenched one hand and moved it round and clutched at the chimney top again.

It brushed something that didn't feel like chimney and the night exploded in noise in front of me and a monstrous whirring rushed at the top of my head. I was becoming more sympathetic to those who suffered from unquiet nights, but assault by a bad-tempered pigeon – who I supposed had just suffered the avian equivalent of attempted murder by a fat man while he was clearing his head after a trying day and wondering about a massage – was shattering. My legs slipped away under me and I was left clinging to the chimney with my feet skidding for purchase on the tiles and the bird screaming in my ear.

At which point there was a shot, and bits of chimney spattered over my face and shoulders, and the pigeon went berserk.

I think it was this combination of the lethal and the ludicrous, the accumulated tension of twenty-four hours of chaos and danger, that finally destroyed my cool. 'Oh bugger off, all of you!' I roared into the darkness.

I suppose that if you're a frustrated assassin, deprived of the chance to get your man in the convenient warmth of a ground-level Turkish bath and forced instead to scramble over rooftops after him, it must be an immensely satisfying sight to see him hanging naked and immobilized from a chimney and wondering when a passing pigeon is going to take an interest in his genitals. A kind of mad anger at my ridiculous predicament was compounded by the thought of my pursuer's satisfaction, of the slow pleasure with which he must now be lining up a more careful shot, and I was away.

Two desperate lunges with my hands, feet scrabbling under me, had me round the chimney and dropping to the crest on the other side.

Except there was no crest. The profile of the roof was different: it was sloping down to the front of the building, and I dropped and began to roll, and kept on rolling.

You cover a lot of distance awfully quickly, on a slippery sloping roof with a jump-start. I had only begun to think of how to slow myself, had only begun to panic at what would happen when the roof ran out in a fraction of a second and I was catapulted out into the night – *Nude Baronet Makes First Unpowered Flight Over Clerkenwell; Flattens Orphan Matchgirl In Descent* – when I crashed into the parapet and clung on with every limb I could still feel.

The hunter must be closing again. Stunned, I scrambled more or less upwards. The parapet was half a yard wide and beautifully flat. I pulled myself up. Immediately there was a scream. My first swaying view of the street, three storeys below, was of a woman pointing up at me. Now there were more arms pointing, and shouts. Then two men running from the nearest corner, down to the right, following the pointing arms, pointing me out to each other. Presumably the ground-level party just in from Ironmonger Row. To the right the parapet ran out into nothing. I took a deep breath, tried to steady my throbbing head, and set off along the parapet in the other direction. Immediately there was another shot somewhere behind me, and my trot became a sprint.

I like to think that I made rather a fine sight, racing along that parapet, my naked form glowing in the moonlight. Ancient Greek Olympics; that sort of thing. In truth I didn't notice. Followed by the excited spectators of east London, at least one gunman, and probably the damn' pigeon too, I had to concentrate on that thin ribbon of parapet stretching out in front of me, and especially on when the stretching out would stop.

When I saw the end of it, just a dozen yards ahead, I slowed. To the left the upward slope of the roof, and somewhere the gunman. To the right the street. Ahead darkness: oblivion. The parapet stopped at the corner of the building, and beyond it was the drop to a side street. Slowing to a walk, I saw the other side. It wasn't more than an alley's width, really, but to me it looked wider than the Thames. There was no way, in my condition, that I – And then another shot, and I ran again, took three calculated paces and jumped.

I made the other side and kept on going. It was another sloping roof, but I was used to these now. I scrambled up on the diagonal, down the other side, and dropped a few feet to a flat roof beyond. Nothing either side of this, so I crossed it, and beyond it there was another small drop to another sloping roof. Down I went, and started more carefully across it. I risked one glance behind me. I couldn't see my pursuer. I had to hope he hadn't been desperate enough to risk the jump. I skirted a skylight – the only embellishment on this bit of roof. The other end of this roof came up against a flat wall. It rose a full storey above me, and there wasn't even a drainpipe.

The end of the road – or roof. Staring around myself, I knew that I couldn't be seen, not from the road or from the direction I'd come. But it might only be a second before the pistol appeared over the rooftop, and found me trapped.

The skylight. I started to contemplate the damage I might do myself if I dropped straight through it; wondered how thick the glass was, said a prayer for my poor feet, and other parts I was fond of. And then I saw it was ajar. I wrenched it upwards, wriggled through in the most ungainly fashion, and at last the naked roof-prowler of olde London dropped out of the night.

I dropped onto bare floorboards, and in the relief at relative privacy, and warmth, and the absence of pigeons and gunmen, I didn't notice the drop. I took in an enormous breath, and stood upright.

There was a gasp from behind me, and a female voice said: 'If you're Father Christmas, I'm blowed if I know where you've got my present.'

14.

I turned.

For a moment, neither of us said anything. I had nothing left. She presumably – and not unreasonably – was getting over the surprise of a naked man dropping out of the sky.

She was dressed in a burgundy-coloured corset, with all the trimmings, and she was damned handsome. But for the fact that every extremity I still had left was more or less out of commission, I might have responded more suavely.

She looked me down and up once. 'I suppose that'll have to do, present-wise' she said. 'Do you want one of my stockings?'

I managed a slight bow. 'Royal Aeronautical Society,' I said. 'Madam, I must apologize for dropping in so rudely. I imagine you'll want to call the police now, or at least scream the house down. If there's the slightest possibility of a brandy-and-soda before you do, I'd be eternally grateful.' She considered this. 'Oh, and I should say there's a reasonable chance that a man with a pistol will shortly follow me, so we might move away from the skylight.'

She looked at the skylight, and back at me. 'Is he...' – she gestured – 'also naked?'

'No, I think he'd stuck to the conventional look.'

'Oh. Well what's the use of that?' She stepped towards me, and reached up and bolted the skylight. 'Come along then.' She turned and led me out of the corridor and into the next room.

It was a bedroom-sitting room – on the basis that it was dominated by a bed, and much of the rest of the space was occupied by two battered armchairs. There was a ludicrously large lithograph of a church on the mantelpiece, and other bits of the bare plaster were covered by a pair of what looked like Gustav Dore prints, and some rather jollier playbills.

We considered each other again. She was certainly worth a second look, and not just because of the tight-bound undergarments. It was a fresher sort of beauty than I'd have expected of a girl in this sort of dive in that sort of corset. Not painted on – although the face showed the leftovers of thick make-up.

'Don't want to sound over-critical,' she said; 'but you look rather frightful. Did you climb up a chimney or fall out of a balloon?' Big eyes.

I searched for something witty, and failed. 'A fat man tried to crush me while I was bathing, and one of his friends has just chased me across the roof with a pistol.'

She tutted. 'Have you considered that you might be going to the wrong sort of parties?'

'I can't resist getting dressed up.' I took a slow breath. I felt deeply weary. 'Look, I don't want to get in the way. You know – if you're… expecting company.' I gestured in the general direction of her body.

'No, that's–' She turned pink, and then managed a little smile. 'Thank you for your delicacy, but I am not – er – the kind of lady who expects company. Naked or otherwise.'

'Oh, right ho.' I couldn't resist indicating the burgundy corset again. 'Just naturally stylish. I see.'

She looked rather cross. 'Will you believe me if I manage not to ravish you – or anyone else – for the remainder of the night?'

'You plan that far ahead?'

'You frankly don't look up to the job, anyway.'

'Please believe me that I really don't care. Perfectly respectable trade.'

'Well, that's not quite true, is it?'

'The conventional English hypocrisy is foolish on the point. Besides, I'm really in no position to get snooty.'

'That is certainly true.' She glanced at my body again, then looked deliberately up. 'Um – not wanting to give you the wrong idea again, but are you planning to stop, or are you just passing through?'

I hesitated. 'There is a real chance that if I leave now, the men who are after me will be waiting. The welcome would be… less congenial.'

'No manners, some people.'

'I wouldn't dream of exposing you to danger. But actually, there's more chance of that if I leave than if I stay.'

She nodded. I felt the weariness heavy on me now. 'Look, I should be candid. My name is Henry Delamere. As well as being a physical wreck, and some kind of magnet for every thug in London, I am also hunted by the police for murder.' I winced. 'Well, two murders.'

'Oh. I see.' She was keeping it light, but she looked worried now. 'No sense doing things by halves, is that it?'

'Seriously.'

She took a step towards me, and looked up intently into my eyes. 'My father believed that you could spot a lie if you looked closely enough.' Big eyes, as I say. 'But then he was extremely foolish, in his sweet way.' They didn't even blink. Her father must have got one thing right in his life, at least. 'Are you going to murder me tonight?'

I think it was the weariness convinced her. 'I really don't think I could.' What was left of my mind was elsewhere, wondering about the fat man lying in the bath-house. 'Actually, there's an outside chance it's three murders.'

She gazed a moment longer. 'Mm,' she said. Then she nodded, once, decisively. 'You'll be sleeping in the armchair. Mind Sir Henry Irving.' She turned away, while I puzzled at this. 'I've got some iodine.'

'A bucket of it'd do.' I was talking to her back now; in its cords and frills it was no less engaging than the front. 'I say: I don't wish to seem a prude, but…' – she stopped, and looked back at me – 'you being so pure, I mean – you haven't got anything I could put on, have you?' She nodded.

I glanced at the corset. 'Something at the looser end of the scale, if you've got it.'

The silk dressing gown – and it was silk; this girl spent her money very selectively, but well – barely reached my knees or elbows, but it covered my over-exposed essentials. It also made her more comfortable about getting close to me. I insisted on putting the iodine on myself, but found that the assorted strains of the previous couple of hours were now starting to burn in my shoulders, and I could barely reach one arm with the other. After watching me pityingly for a bit, she snatched the pot of iodine and took over.

'I do beg your pardon,' I said through exhaustion. 'I never asked you your name.'

She looked up into my face again. Big, big eyes, and a hand on my leg. A romantic moment, but for the fact that one of us was dressed like a Bedlamite and smeared in purple paste.

'Annabella,' she said. 'I'm Annabella Bliss.'

It was no less credible than anything else in that mad day. 'Naturally,' I said, and I think it must have been around then that I passed out.

15.

It was fully twelve hours later that I woke. Remarkably – for I'd never thought I'd know peace again – my night's sleep was not only in a conventional bed, but entirely uninterrupted. Apparently not a single violent assault in all that time. And from the indent in the pillow beside me, it seemed that I had after all – quite unconsciously – shared the bed with my lovely rescuer.

Waking started slow, and pleasant. And then I jolted awake, not knowing where I was, and then remembering, and remembering why. I started up quickly, and immediately roared in pain, as all of my abused muscles screamed their protest.

Her head appeared in the doorway. 'Did you scream?'

'Not at all. A glad cry to greet the morning; nothing more.'

'Bit late for that; it's afternoon.'

Teeth gritted, I fought myself into a sitting position. 'Look, I am sorry. I'd not meant to steal your billet. I must have passed out.'

'Don't worry. Your innocence remains untouched.'

'It's about the only thing.'

'Besides, Sir Henry Irving wouldn't have approved.'

I didn't follow this; I suppose the young people take their moral leadership where they can, these days. 'Pardon me, I seem to remember you telling me – What's your name again?'

Her face turned prim. 'My name is Annabella Bliss.' She waited. 'Any remark? Any humorous observation?'

'Not in the least.'

'Good.' She disappeared. She was back a couple of minutes later with a saucepan. 'Drink this. Broth.'

I pretended to protest, but set into it. 'I thought you probably needed it,' she said. 'You look terrible.'

I looked down at my legs. My knees, and my feet, and various patches between, were an appalling purple and yellow mix.

'You're famous,' she said, picking up a newspaper from one of the two chairs and tossing it beside me.

I continued to spoon the broth, glancing at the paper. 'Police Hunt Double-Murderer Aristocrat' ran right across the page. 'Public Outrage: Mad Baronet Lured Stranger To His Death'.

Hopefully Lord Aysgarth wasn't a regular reader of the *Daily Chronicle*.

I skimmed the first pages. As well as killing David Sinclair and the man in my room, I had apparently 'been responsible for a disturbance' during the workers' march. They only had a couple of facts, but cheerfully padded those out with the wildest speculations about my lifestyle and depravities. At the bottom of the second page was a smaller piece of late news: 'Naked Lunatic Sparks East London Uproar: Was It the Full Moon?' I didn't draw her attention to it.

'You were going to tell me all about it.'

I looked up at her. 'I was?' She was wearing a second dressing gown. It suited her better than mine; more conventional than her evening rig, but she still looked very fetching.

'Unless you want me to believe the version in the *Chronicle*.'

I nodded. 'Alright. But I refuse to hog the bed any further.' I swung upright with a groan, and made for the nearest chair. It only took me about five minutes to cover the ground. From the other chair she picked up what I'd thought was a cushion, but now turned out to be an enormous ginger cat. She sat, draped her legs over the arm of the chair, and settled the cat in her lap.

I took a breath. 'Last – No, two nights ago, I played cards with a man called Sinclair. Senior man in the Thames Ironworks shipbuilding outfit. They're building one of the new Dreadnoughts. An acquaintance; not a bad chap. He was… I'd not thought of this before – he was rather distracted. Lost pretty heavily, which I'd assumed was my brilliance at Baccarat, but might have been something else. He cornered me afterwards, said he had something frightfully important to discuss, and I had to meet him at his shipyard. When I got there I found him dead – murdered. The police arrived at that point, put two and two together and locked me up. I got out... yesterday morning. When I got home yesterday afternoon, there was a man in my rooms who wanted to fake my suicide. There was a struggle. He came off worse. I was trying to keep my head down at the Ironmonger Row baths, but a couple of chaps there tried to kill me. I escaped and – and ran for the nearest skylight.'

She was considering all of this, with a slight frown. She stroked the cat, and watched it purr. Then she looked up at me again. 'On the whole,' she said, 'I think I prefer the *Chronicle*'s version.'

'So do I,' I said. 'At least in the *Chronicle* I sound like I know what I'm doing.'

'And what are you doing?'

'I'm eating broth.' I did so, until I'd finished the pot. Annabella Bliss sat in silence, stroking the enormous cat, and it was as wise and generous a response as when she'd let me drop out of the night without screaming the place down or fetching the peelers.

'There's something wrong at the yard, or something wrong with the company that he could only prove at the yard.' I put the pan down on the floorboards. 'So I'm investigating the yard and I'm investigating the company.'

'Sounds clear enough.'

'Doesn't it? Perhaps I do know what I'm doing, after all.'

The cat yawned mightily. Its owner looked no more impressed. 'Why you, though? Why did this man Sinclair ask you?'

I started to say something hilarious, and then stopped. It was rather a good point. 'That's what's worrying, isn't it? I was probably the least reputable man within half a mile of St James's.' I thought a bit. 'Perhaps that's the answer. My only virtue is my vice – that I've knocked around a bit. For some reason, he needed someone disreputable.'

'Nice to be wanted.'

'Mm.' I drifted into thought again, and looked around the room, its dinginess and its bursts of colour. 'I've got it,' I said. 'You're an actress.'

She smiled. 'I would like to pretend so. Actually, I'm a singer. And a dancer if you're not too choosy. In the music hall; the burlesque.'

'Right. Hence the playbills, and the outfit.' She nodded. 'And hence the name. How did you get it?'

'From my father,' she said rather stiffly. She nodded to the table, where there was a formal photo of an elderly chap dressed up as a vicar.

'He was an actor too, was he?'

Now she looked plain cross. 'He was a vicar.'

I gave up. 'I need some way into those company offices. And I need to get into that shipyard.'

'Wearing a girl's dressing gown?'

16.

When he'd told me which of his Thames Ironworks Company colleagues to talk to, Hugh Stackhouse had said that yard manager MacNeice was unmissable.

He'd not been wrong. Patrick MacNeice was enormous. You couldn't have missed him with a harpoon. More aptly, you couldn't have missed him with a naval cannon.

A naval cannon would have had the advantage of keeping a goodly distance between you and him. And it might have had a chance of doing some damage. Nothing less seemed likely to bother him.

A pistol against him would seem merely ridiculous. A tiny toy against such a vast body; a feeble thing against his bulk.

I know this, because it was very much preoccupying me as I stood in front of him, in his office, with my Webley pointing at his stomach.

Quinn had retrieved it and some of the money from Dobbs's, and left them in a package behind the bar of a pub on the Strand whose landlord was a pal of his. I was going carefully. Annabella Bliss had collected the package from the pub. She'd also passed on my instructions for Quinn to find out anything he could about Sinclair's friend Samuel Greenberg and his Commercial Confounded Conspiracy outfit.

She was helping me. Something had convinced her: the ridiculousness of my story; the inherent credibility of my bearing even when covered in iodine paste and a Chinese-style lady's dressing gown; her dear old father's infallible test of innocence.

I thought I *was* innocent, of course; but I recognize that it couldn't have seemed very likely.

Miss Bliss had ransacked the costume room of Jolly's Theatre, to supplement the somewhat limited wardrobe she could offer me from her own collection.

Thus it was in the rough duds of an off-duty sailor that I had made my second approach to the Thames Ironworks Company Shipyard.

That was part one of my plan to avoid being picked up by any of the various groups after my blood: not to be noticeable.

Part two was simpler still: not to be noticed at all. Today was the next phase in the great labour agitation of that autumn: a march through London's East End, and a rally in the very yard where the latest war machine of the capitalist powers was being brought into its monstrous existence. (Not my own wording: I got it from a chap shouting beside me.) I would enter the Thames Ironworks Company yard among thousands of men dressed similarly to me.

Probably a healthy reminder to me of the positive power of the mob. But I wasn't feeling it. The necessary and tedious camaraderie of school and the army aside, I've never been much of a chap for crowds. I tend to pick and choose my company, and if he's a mile or more away that's fine by me. Now I was marching in a great throng of men, shoulders knocking between shoulders, a bobbing sea of heads in front of me and all around, the stamping of innumerable boots a continuous rumble underneath the banter, and the shouts, and the chants and the occasional song. It was a roaring, seething beast, this march, and I was bunched up in the middle of it.

The outfit wasn't helping. It wasn't, I should say, Bliss's first choice. She'd had a couple of attempts at putting me in something that looked fresh from the Jolly's Theatre's most recent Gilbert & Sullivan performance. And there'd been a rather frosty exchange when I resisted an eye-patch. But even though I didn't resemble Long John Silver or a French yachtsman on a spree, I still felt out of place.

I tried to match the rhythm and posture of the men around me. The lope. The slouch. We rumbled on along Commercial Road.

I restricted myself to grunts if anyone tried to talk to me: I wasn't going to fool around with proletarian accents, and an impression of grumpiness was the best deterrent against chat and questions.

The last time I'd bumped into this crowd I'd immediately got into a fight with one of them. The way my luck was going, that one man in thousands was probably tramping right behind me.

I didn't turn round. Even if that one didn't spot me as me, anyone might spot me as a fraud. And if they did that, they'd think I was a police spy. They'd probably kick me around a little, and then leave me for the police to pick up. Neither was attractive.

We rumbled on. Over the Limehouse Cut, trying to not to

breathe too deeply. East India Dock Road.

This morning's *Daily Sketch* had printed a photograph of me. An old and not particularly good image made during one of my previous appearances in the vulgar eye – a rather tiresome business, touching a lady's honour, that had blown up at a house party in Wiltshire – but good enough. Any one of these thousands of men might have read the *Chronicle* or the *Sketch* or presumably various others, and be able to spot me for the man who'd murdered their boss and 'caused a disturbance' during their march the previous day.

This was an angry crowd.

I've known the common Englishman on the parade square, and had to overcome his truculence and laziness. I'd never known anything like this. Organized labour had always been a phrase in *The Times*, nothing more; a concept intermittently troublesome but useful enough if the likes of David Sinclair and Hugh Stackhouse did their jobs right. Now I was among them, man after man after man, each physical and big and unhappy and bellowing his frustrations with the whole of society.

My little difficulty with the police seemed momentarily rather trivial.

Cotton Street. As if prompted by my thought, the chap next to me suddenly opened his slab of a jaw wide and roared 'PAY FAIR OR PAY THE PRICE!', and everyone around us picked up the words, and my ears filled with it like an explosion, and a fraction too late I tried to gasp out something that sounded similar.

In Poplar High Street I pretended to have pulled a muscle in my leg, and eased my way to the edge of the crowd, and slowed. I watched them file past me for a full minute, so many bodies and so many faces and so much unhappiness. I fell in with the malingerers at the back, and followed the column as it weaved through between the warehouses and through the great gates into the Thames Ironworks Company yard.

I slipped further back, and to the side, and away into shadow.

I took a moment to check where I was, relative to the direction of the mob and the layout of the yard.

The hesitation was unwise. Immediately my mind jumped back three nights, to the last time when I'd been on this exact spot, coming to meet Sinclair. The echo was uncomfortable. That moment, so recent but now the other side of an irreversible change, was the last moment when I could have turned around and headed back to the West End and enjoyed a life in which none of this nonsense had happened.

Instead, I'd walked on. I walked on now.

The yard offices were much easier to spot in daylight. They were a two-storey brick block running along the edge of the yard where it followed the road outside. The first floor offices were reached by an external stair and a walkway-balcony arrangement that gave a view across the great expanse of the yard.

The stair and the walkway had brought me to the yard manager's office: middle of the upper tier, neatly-painted sign, and big windows so he could look out on his empire. I hadn't hesitated, and I hadn't knocked. I was in and the door was closed behind me and my pistol was out and pointing at MacNeice before he'd properly focused on me.

Even sitting down, behind his desk, he was vast. Solid, not fat: a great bear of a man, across shoulders and around chest. No neck, to speak of, and then an open outdoor face and black curly hair.

He'd focused on the pistol now.

It hadn't seemed to impress him. I glanced down at it, to check that I wasn't holding it backwards.

He looked up at me.

'If you're after a job,' he said, 'you'll have to do better than that.'

The name hadn't misled. Patrick MacNeice spoke with the broadest Irish accent, a rumble that sounded like it was bubbling up with difficulty from the Thames.

'I'm not looking for a job. There; I'm doing better already.'

'You're not so daft you'd think there's money here surely?' He was considering me, head to foot. 'And you'd be a pretty fancy stick-up man to come armed with a Webley.' He smiled grimly. 'So you're one of the angry intellectuals from out there, are you? Come to strike a blow for the workers of the world by plugging one dumb Irishman.' He stood, slowly. 'Come along then, little man. Let's see if you've the potatoes for it.'

He'd risen with a gravity befitting his planet-sized appearance. I'm taller than most, but he'd half a foot more on me. And built like a ship's boiler.

And still the hard fatalist's smile, waiting for the shot. I'd have liked him considerably, if he wasn't making things so difficult.

'That's most impressive,' I said. 'Now sit down again. We're going to look ridiculous doing all this standing up.' I pulled another chair forwards, and sat down opposite him, and waited.

That made him more uncertain, which was a step in the right direction.

As he sat, he was examining me more carefully. Now he nodded. 'Gotcha,' he said. 'You're Delamere. Feller who killed poor Mr Sinclair. And now you've come for me.' He pulled his shoulders back. So steady. 'Picture in the newspaper doesn't do you justice.'

'Nothing does,' I said. 'Yes. I'm Harry Delamere. Come to continue my campaign of mayhem against the men of the Thames Ironworks Company.'

I considered the revolver, and considered the man sitting opposite.

I laid the revolver down on his desk. Nearer me than him, and pointing in the right direction.

'Or,' I went on, 'not.'

He looked at the Webley. Up at me again. And back down at the revolver.

One of the finest sleight-of-hand merchants I ever met was a monstrously obese Turk in Smyrna; needed two boys to pull him up from his divan, but could have the watch out of your waistcoat while he was asking you the time. Big men aren't necessarily slow men.

'MacNeice, I'd be obliged if you didn't try anything foolish now, you hear?' He considered this with the amusement it warranted. Nothing this man did would ever be foolish. 'I hold the unfashionable opinion that I'm not the desperate maniac that the papers present. But believe me that I am now desperate enough to do almost anything to stay out of the hands of the police and the other people who are hunting me. Make a grab for the pistol, and I'll make a grab for it. I'd rather not kill you, but I'd cheerfully take wounding you if it left me free to finish what I've started.'

'A sporting chance, is it?'

'Bullet'd probably bounce off you, anyway.'

Very slowly, he brought his two shovel-like hands together, and folded them in front of him on the desk – a foot or so from the Webley – and smiled.

Beyond his hands I noticed his watch-chain. I looked up at him again.

'Outdoor complexion. Military fob on your chain. You'd have made… what? Colour-Sergeant at least. Royal Engineers was it?'

'Artillery. Battery Sergeant-Major.'

I nodded. The only two arms of the British Army that require any brain – scientific, technical brain – are the Engineers and the Artillery. Building stuff and blowing it up again: both require intelligence. Certainly compared to what the rest of us were doing: digging holes, jumping into holes, jumping out of holes, running towards a lot of chaps trying to kill us, and – about the smartest thing we did – running away again. The only truly clever officers I'd met during my service – cleverness beyond that necessary for a superficially witty remark in Latin, anyway – were engineers and gunners.

MacNeice would have done twenty years. He'd risen from powder monkey to battlefield god, the embodiment of fear and justice to the soldiers under him, and an utterly dependable source of reassurance and authority for the officers notionally above him – who, if they'd any sense, left most of the command to those like him. A man used to calculating powder charges and elevations in his head while a squad of Boer horsemen charged at him with rifles blazing; no wonder I and my pop-gun didn't seem to shake him.

'Well, Mr MacNeice, here we are and ain't it charming?' Still the cold smile. 'I'm in a rush and you ain't, so allow me to short-cut your thinking. I'm hunted by the police, and by some other fellows who I don't know but seem to know me and not to be pleased about it. And one or two of the men out there' – I nodded back out towards the yard – 'don't like me either, I suspect. So you've no obligation to try anything desperate: my chances of staying alive until the police get around to arresting me are slim in any case.'

He considered this. He nodded.

'It's possible that I'm a homicidal madman, lulling you into your ease and waiting for the right moment to plug you; in which case we'll wait and see if the gunner eye has lost any of its sharpness.' He nodded again. This time with an appetite that I didn't like.

'Or I'm not. In which case I'm not going to try to shoot you, and I'm just going to ask you some questions, and you can decide whether and what you answer and I can't do much about it. Fair enough?'

From his furled fists, one finger emerged and pointed at me, cannon-like. 'Delamere,' he said.

'Yes. I thought we'd covered that.'

'Knew I'd heard the name before. You were in the Cape too. Brigade of Guards. Battle of Modder River, and so forth.'

'Happy days,' I said. It was no surprise; the professional grapevine among the senior non-commissioned officers of the British Army is one of the most powerful going. As trade unions went, the mob outside had nothing on them. 'What possible reason could Sinclair have had for coming to the yard here?'

'Normal run of things, nothing. His business with the contracts and the legality of things, that was all in the head office on Holborn. He might choose to come and check up on whether a delivery was right, but he didn't need to; I've fellows here for that. He might choose to call on me for a chat, rather than summon me to Holborn; but more often I was there. He paid the occasional visit just for the sake of it. Show the face, if you know what I mean.' He caught my eye, and smiled hard. 'Officer's tour of the trench, right sir?'

It was a good parallel. We all did it as Lieutenants and Captains: pretend we were raising morale and understanding the real conditions of the men, by getting under their feet for twenty minutes each morning and evening.

'Often?' I said.

'More than most. Every… week or two.' He thought more. 'Mr Sinclair was a – he was a worrier. About the details. About the men.'

I nodded. 'Type of officer that doesn't make any difference, and tends to frighten the horses, but the lads get sort of fond of him. That one?'

'That's the feller.' He leaned forwards a fraction. 'You weren't a worrier yourself, I think sir.'

'Bloody terrified. Especially when the champagne ran out.' He nodded, neutral. 'So there was nothing here he'd need to … to inspect? Records, that sort of thing?'

He gestured to his left. 'We've the drawings office just next door. The detailed plans that everything in the yard is worked from. Everything from… from the shape of the bow to the size of a bolt. But they're only brought in from the Holborn Office when we need them. If he wanted them he could see them while they were there, or call them back, or get duplicates.'

'You've had some trouble with the men, I think.' His face hardened. Battery Sergeant-Major MacNeice had never had trouble controlling men. 'Sabotage, I was told.'

'Told by whom?'

'By someone even more senior than you in the Thames Ironworks Company.'

He considered me for a moment. 'We've had our share,' he said. And then his shoulders dropped, and he leaned in, more earnest. 'It's a new time, Mr Delamere. I've known trouble in the yard before: bit of belly-aching, bit of barrack-room law; drunkards and hotheads; fights and shoddy workmanship and down tools for an hour or two. In my time I've had to kick a bit of discipline into the odd gobshite; you know how it is. Corporal's justice.' I nodded. 'But now… now it's political too. They're not just unhappy for they're poor; they're angry at the whole world.'

'So what's happened?'

He sniffed. 'This and that. The old Trade Union man here – nice old uncle called Merridew – well, they ousted him, and replaced him with a new man: Raikes – as vicious a little shit as ever settled in the mud at low tide. Then… Go-slows: organized – co-ordinated, yes? The whole yard, every single sod, working just 10% slower. Nothing specific you can spot or punish, and then at the end of the day you wonder and the end of the week you know. The mechanism on one of the big cranes' – he nodded over my shoulder – 'was got at; that department had to stop for two or three days before we got it fixed. One of my foremen got too angry with one of the riveting gangs; night-watchman found him that night – he'll live, but he got a fair going over.' The mouth twisted. 'Lines are being crossed, Mr Delamere.'

'If it turns out that it wasn't I who killed Sinclair – only an outside chance, I realize – could his death have been tied up with these protests?'

He puffed his cheeks out. 'Doesn't seem likely', he said. And it didn't. 'Not saying it's impossible. Surprisingly easy to kill a man, even if you don't mean to. But even the worst of them, even now, they'd think twice before a killing. Not a deliberate killing, of one of the managers. And anyway: how'd he come to be in the yard?'

'Could he have… I don't know, could he have heard about some act of sabotage? Come and find out who was responsible? Try to stop it?'

I knew the answer before I'd finished the question. 'If he knew something like that,' MacNeice said, 'why didn't he tell me, or the police, or bring someone else with him? Makes no sense.'

He was right. It made no sense.

We sat in silence for a few moments, reflecting on how little sense it made.

'On the whole,' I said, 'it's probably more likely that I killed him.'

He smiled, and nodded. 'That it is.'

Very slowly – fingertips only, and not touching the trigger – I picked up the pistol. MacNeice's eyes never left mine. I put the pistol in an inside pocket, and stood. He stood with me.

'I heard about what you did,' he said. 'At Modder River.'

'Long time ago, Mr MacNeice. I was more innocent in those days; and more stupid. Long forgotten now.' I opened the door.

'Soldiers don't forget, Mr Delamere.' He shook his head. 'You may be a rogue. But you're no coward.'

He stepped closer. 'Which may,' he said reflectively, suddenly distracted and looking past me into the yard, 'come in handy.'

17.

I stepped out onto the walkway and the whole world was staring up at me.

From where I stood to the water's edge was two hundred yards at the least. This area of the yard was about as wide. That whole expanse was a swarm of faces. God knew how many thousands of men. They'd decided to do their speechifying in the yard, not in public; they'd picked the shipyard offices – home of authority – as their backdrop. Looked like they were just getting warmed up. And I'd stepped out centre stage.

I think I've made my feelings about crowds and public prominence pretty clear.

'Well, Sir Harry, I enjoyed our little natter. You mind how you go, now.'

I don't know whether they'd been touring the yard while I'd been talking, or just gathering, but the speakers were only now starting up the steps towards my gantry: three in worker's best, two in smarter coats and hats, somehow unusual and oddly familiar. It was one of the latter who pointed up at me and said something, and now I caught a more general murmuring. The smarter-dressed pair each had a white ribbon pinned to their jackets.

Someone in the crowd shouted: 'It is him, too!' Well, what do you expect if you let working men read newspapers?

I turned to look at MacNeice. He was still taking in the size of the crowd.

Beside them was the *Thunderer*, a great dark hulk dominating the scene. The bow – where Sinclair had died – looked like you could reach out and touch it from the gantry. The stern was at the water's edge. I had the fancy that the swarm below me might pick the half-finished ship up and carry her away, ants with a stone.

The air was thick with the stink of oil and scorched metal.

'Hadn't realized they were going to come and preach right here', MacNeice said. 'I came to keep an eye and stop any of the enthusiasts breaking my windows or messing up the drawings next door. We'd given them the day and said we'd turn a blind eye to them coming through the yard, as long as they didn't smash the machinery or go for the ship.' He looked at me straight, and winced slightly. 'Um – chance they may not see you as company property, Sir Harry. Not covered by the insurance policy, so to speak.'

At the foot of the steps, a couple of sportsmen were shouldering their way past the platform party and starting up towards me.

I didn't even contemplate using the revolver. I'd be torn apart before I'd got more than a couple, and their blood was hot enough for any foolishness.

I glanced the other way along the gantry. It ended in a closed door, set in a partition wall. I looked at MacNeice.

He shook his head. 'Locked.'

'Key?'

'Not here.'

'That's a great help.'

I looked past him into his office. With its windows it wouldn't last more than ten seconds as a final redoubt. The advance party from below stairs was halfway up now and meant business, big lads with purposeful faces. I looked at MacNeice. Short of using him as a rampart, which I confess I did consider for a moment, it wasn't right to involve him.

'Right ho, then', I said. 'I thank you for your time, Mr MacNeice. See you across the river.'

He nodded. 'Sun on your back, Sir Harry.'

'Let's be 'aving you then!' It was the first of the lynch mob announcing his arrival at the top of the steps. I'm not sure what he thought he meant by the expression. Rather like Inspector Bunce reading me my rights, I suppose. Having got it out the way, anyway, he started towards me, and from below there was a cheer of encouragement.

I bowed slightly to the tough, and set off running in the other direction.

As soon as I moved there was a roar from the crowd, Derby Day excitement, and it echoed hollow and wild off the hull next to them. Halfway towards the door I had the Webley out and when I was a few yards out I fired three shots at where the lock ought to be, and I was just wondering what would happen if I'd misjudged it when I ran out of gantry and had to launch myself at the door.

I hit it full force with my shoulder and there was a shrieking of wood and glass and I kept on going, and somewhere in the mess my head made contact too. Then I was stumbling round and through and clutching for support and I was at the top of another flight of steps. Nowhere else to go, shouting behind me, and I started down.

At the foot of the steps, I saw bodies, faces, pointing arms, the flanking party coming in with perfect timing. I was already a few steps down as they started up; then I saw a girder stretching out beside me, a support for the stair and for the wall opposite. I brandished the pistol and yelled something equally pointless, and fired off a shot into the eaves to make them think a bit. Then I stowed the pistol and swung out over the bannister rail and dropped my legs onto the girder.

I came uneasily upright, and set off across.

A sitting baronet is not a sporting shot. Arms out straining for balance as I teetered along the girder, six rivet-pocked inches wide and leading me God knew where, I felt if possible even more exposed than when I'd dashed over the rooftops of the City. For one moment I made the awful mistake of adjusting my focus beyond the girder to what was below, and saw that the blur was in fact one seething mass of men. They were all shouting now, exuberant in the chase. And waiting for me to fall, baying for it. It's not the first time I've sympathized with the fox: the bloody hounds always get more gobby when their pea-sized brains finally work out how good the odds are.

I got across the girder with a sense of relief and immediately futility. I was going to run out of road sometime, and it might be right now. Vaguely I was aware of movement behind me, a bolder soul following me out onto the girder.

Blank wall: wooden slats built up to extend a lower layer of bricks. But just a couple of yards away a rough window had been cut in the slats. Deep breath. Step back along the girder towards my now more cautious pursuer. Then I turned and jumped.

My boot-tips caught the top of the brick half of the wall and momentum helped my arms reach for the sill of the window. Then my boots were scrabbling and I was pulling myself up and through the gap, and after the gloom there was breeze and light.

There was a flattish bit of roof below me – a shed built into the wall of the yard – and it was luxury for someone of my experience in these altitudes. Within seconds I was on it and off it and dropping into the street outside, and I even had a moment to look around myself and consider the options.

Just the one moment, and it left me only one option: a gate burst open – you don't need a revolver when you've got a couple of thousand men leaning on a lock – and the mob exploded into the street. I was already running hard for the corner.

As soon as I'd rounded the corner I started looking for

promising doorways, but there was nothing that didn't look like a dead end, and the hounds were too close on my heels for me to think I could hide.

Then, thirty yards ahead, outside a tavern I saw an omnibus. And at the front of the omnibus the driver was overseeing some business with the horses… Changing them? I ran harder, looked closer, and as I got nearer one of the horses came free out of the shafts. Then I was there, and vaulting up onto the beast and digging my heels in. Fortunately, it was a horse with pretensions – some worn-out old dray with fraternal sympathies for the labour movement and I'd been stuck for good – and it skittered and wheeled and we were away.

In a foot race with the average man – and I was in a foot race with about a thousand of them, fit youngsters all – I'm nothing out of the ordinary. On a horse I'm something rather exceptional. The mob dropped away behind, and I was left to work out where I was going, and to reflect on what MacNeice had told me about the head office and the yard and the workers, and to wonder who it was the two smarter-dressed speakers had reminded me of.

18.

I found Annabella Bliss in one of the dressing rooms at Jolly's Theatre, talking to Quinn. Buried in a warren of corridors beneath the theatre, it was spartan space of badly whitewashed brick and one long wooden bench facing some cracked mirrors. There was a rich smell of sweat and what must have been make-up paint. But Bliss and her comrades had brightened it with postcards and pots of make-up and cast-off feathers and biscuit tins crammed with mysterious feminine necessities. Biscuits, perhaps. At the moment I walked in she was quizzing Quinn about Methodism in Cornwall during his youth, and he was answering her with sober courtesy. When it's a matter of chatting with a pretty girl, Quinn's as ecumenical as they come.

My valet has naturally seen me in diverse states of dress and undress and, in the course of my somewhat eccentric career, some rather exotic get-ups. I still caught the faintest raise of an eyebrow when I sauntered in dressed *a la Wapping*. I'd regained my breath and composure during the ride on the borrowed horse, but I was still looking a little ragged and there was just a suggestion of disapproval in my valet's regard.

Miss Bliss said: 'How was your visit to the yard?'

'First tell me that you didn't arrive here together.'

'Different times, different routes, different doors, as you told me.'

I watched her a moment longer; I was trusting a lot to her good sense. 'Right.' I sat. 'Not altogether satisfactory. MacNeice, the yard manager, confirmed they have a serious problem with sabotage; worse than I'd imagined, indeed. But he also confirmed that there's nothing obvious Sinclair should have wanted or needed to drag me there to see that night. Even he can't have wanted just to show off his damn ship at that time of night.'

'At least you got away without being recognized.'

'I did perfectly, right up to the moment when a couple of thousand outraged dockworkers and their guests recognized me, and chased me across London.' I stopped. 'Guests, now...'

Bliss was looking genuinely shocked. She'd not got used to my fugitive habits; not by that point, anyway. 'I said you should have worn a beard, and a bigger hat.'

'So I could give 'em a couple of verses of 'He is an Englishman' while they beat me to death?' She looked sulky. 'How are you, Quinn?'

'Tolerable sir, thank you.'

'How's the old homestead?'

'Tidied as best I can, sir. A lot of policemen with too much time on their hands are still fooling around the place. Trying to find anarchist paraphernalia in your linen, or hidden maps on the back of the pictures.'

'Hope you've hidden the good port.'

''Fraid the carpet's had it, sir. What with all the police boots and… the, er,' – he glanced at the girl – 'the incident with the foreign gentleman.'

'Incident?' Bliss asked; no tact.

'Well, miss, Sir Henry was obliged to set light to a foreign person in the sitting room. The scorching was considerable.'

'Oh.' She looked at me then back at Quinn; I didn't care for the tone and direction of the conversation. 'Do these sort of strange things happen to him often?'

'No–'

'Yes, miss. Sir Henry has… an adventurous instinct.'

'How exciting. Must be rather trying for you sometimes, Mr Quinn.'

'Well, mi–'

'When you two have finished–' I managed to squeeze in. 'Quinn – anything useful to contribute?'

'Precious little so far, sir. Through a friend at the telegraph office I've tracked down that friend of Mr Sinclair you were asking about – Mr Greenberg.'

'Oh yes – the Confederation of Commercial Collaborators, or whatever.'

'I got an address for that office; place up in Clerkenwell. Went and had a nosey around. Place looks pretty shut up, sir. Post not been collected for a few days.'

I nodded. 'Keep at it. And what about the Thames Ironworks Head Office?'

'I'm afraid there's a police guard on the place now, sir. I did one walk-past, but I didn't want to risk a closer reconnaissance.'

'No, that's fair enough.' I thought for a bit. 'Well, it may have to be guile as well as stealth. Now, what else?'

'Guests, sir.'

'Eh?'

'You were talking about the dockers, and you mentioned their guests.'

'Yes, I did. They had a couple of guest speakers, and something about the look of them was a bit off, and a bit familiar. I think it must have been the outfits. Reminded me of the chap in my rooms, with his Homburg and a looser cut of suit. They had the same ribbon on their coats.'

'The one who – who had the incident?' Miss Bliss seemed to find all this fascinating. 'The one you set fire to?'

'He. I remember he mentioned joining his comrades outside; when that march was on. He was foreign, certainly.'

'Why on earth should a foreign Trade Unionist want to kill you?'

'Apparently I'm in season,' I said, with some heat. 'National bloody sport, now, isn't it, having a shy at old Delamere? Probably queues of the sods, stepping off the boat at Harwich and asking for a cosh and directions to Piccadilly. Any other useful tit-bits from your police pals, Quinn?'

'Not much, sir. Couple of appearances from that Inspector – from the court – Bunce.'

'Ah. Hasn't caught the fatal flu or been knocked down by an omnibus, then?'

'No, sir. Rather a persevering sort of body. Otherwise, they seem more interested in the naked lunatic – that ghost or whatever that people reported running over the rooves from Ironmonger Row.'

'Ah; yes – that reminds me, Quinn. I need you to go and collect some clothes for me.'

'Of course, sir. Where from?'

'From Ironmonger Row, Quinn.'

He gazed at me for a long time.

'We're not really on top of this business, sir, are we?'

19.

I met Joshua Merridew, until recently Secretary of the Thames Ironworks Shipbuilding Company branch of the United Society of Boilermakers and Iron and Steel Shipbuilders – God alone knew what he put on his visiting cards – in the middle of the evening in a private room in McArdle's chop house on Golden Lane. He was sitting stiffly upright, next to the sash window which wouldn't close properly.

He was a white-haired old lion. Nature had made him big, and fifty years of manual labour had toughened him, and a decade or two of speechifying had taught him poise and dignity. In the chop house snug with its cracked and greasy panelling, the occasional flaring of the gas light conjured weird shapes on the walls, and deep shadows in the face in front of me.

MacNeice at the shipyard had said that this Merridew had been ousted as Secretary by a new man, Raikes. With Raikes, I wouldn't know how to approach what I wanted to say. Given the instinct of his followers to tear me limb from limb, I wouldn't know how to approach him at all. The old regime seemed more likely to talk about what was going on at the yard, and fractionally less likely to try to murder me. So, Merridew it was.

I played it relatively straight. My name was Delmar, which was close enough to have been misunderstood if it became necessary to backtrack. Mercifully he hadn't seen my picture in the *Sketch*, and I didn't remember seeing him during my escapade at the yard. I didn't pretend to come from anything other than stiff-collared end of society, but I claimed I was interested in writing a popular book about the relationship between government and industry in the new century.

I opened with a rather wide-eyed and breathless picture of the power of the labouring masses as seen from Piccadilly. Voice low and rich and rolling, he came back with how societies have only achieved enduring stability and greatness when they have treated their working classes with dignity and fairness. This more or less set the framework for our discussion, and we batted it back and forth from there.

Merridew spoke with heavy eloquence. He was obviously better-read than I was, and more experienced at debate. But having been chased along Piccadilly by more than a few of the labouring masses, I could at least put a bit of feeling into my curiosity.

'But then,' I said, 'if your picture of the fundamental loyalty of the worker is true, Mr Merridew – his commitment to playing his full and equal part in society – how do you justify go-slows and strikes and so forth?'

'If the employer has broken his contract with the worker, the worker is no longer obliged to fulfil his duties within it. He finds himself in the same position as the American colonists who rejected the tyranny of King George, or the Parliament men who disproved in theory and in practice the Divine Right of Kings.' I remember a cockney corporal in my battalion who'd been taught to read late, and in his off-duty hours was working through the great historians. A regular Cicero, with 25 letters out of the 26 anyway, and the best-read man in the outfit.

'But this is more than just not fulfilling a contract: it's actively obstructing or even damaging the work.' He hesitated. 'Let's take your own yard. You and your colleagues are building Britain's newest battleship. That's a source of pride, isn't it?' He nodded, watchful. 'They're doing their bit to protect their country, their society.'

'Every man has his duties to his society, and he takes pride in meeting them. But conceive then his pain, when he finds that another part of society is taking his labour for granted; expecting his duty without giving him his due.'

'That's worthy stuff, Mr Merridew. But – sabotage? Dragging your feet's one thing; burking dock cranes and delaying a battleship is something else.'

'Sabotage is an extreme charge, often levelled and rarely proven.'

'I've talked to others. I can prove it.'

'These are grave times. The fundamental relationship of trust–'

'Can be fatal. Wasn't one of the company managers murdered in the yard recently?'

He looked genuinely shocked. 'But that was nothing to do with my lads.'

'Wasn't it? Mr Merridew, I'll take your word for it. You know your men and I certainly don't. But it seems rather a surprising coincidence, don't it? Trouble at the yard, sabotage – and then a manager gets killed.'

'I cannot conceive of any reason why any member of my union should want to do such a terrible thing.'

He wasn't saying it was impossible. 'Sinclair was–' I caught myself. '–Was that the name? What had he to do with the yard, and with sabotage?'

'Mr Sinclair had been preoccupied with the sabotage. He had even ventured to consult me once or twice – before I was – while I yet had the honour to represent the men. He agreed with me that it betokened some deeper breakdown of relations – a breakdown more fundamental and worrisome than any dockyard apparatus. We hoped to rebuild it.'

I didn't hide my scepticism. 'Sounds an implausibly enlightened attitude, from a senior manager.'

'Perhaps the limitation is in your imagination, Mr Delmar, and not his attitude.'

'Perhaps. What was Sinclair doing about it?'

'He and I had spoken once – casually – on the edge of another meeting. We then met privately, at his request.' He looked uncomfortable. 'And then – after I passed on the Secretaryship of the Union – he persisted in attempting a private meeting with my successor, Raikes.'

'How private was "private"?'

'Private. I received the impression that he had no authority for his conversation, and he knew that I – that Raikes – would be in an uncomfortable position were it known we were meeting a representative of the managers without the usual formalities and consultations.' He leaned forwards. 'His was a sincere concern. He wanted to know about relations, and arrangements, between the company and the workers. He was interested in attitudes among our workers towards foreign interests.'

'Foreign interests?'

'There are… some, in the movement, who would say that the interests of labour transcend these national boundaries. That national boundaries are only an artificial system of chains to divide a universal class who are naturally one.'

'I think I read that there's a delegation of foreign Trade Unionists visiting you at the moment.'

'That is so. There is a conference of Trades Unionists from all Europe happening in Birmingham, and the visitors will see London, and Glasgow, and diverse of our great industrial centres. In the century since their revolution, the French have refined the philosophy of the equality of man in practice. Germany has produced the most advanced thinking regarding the proper rights of the labouring class, as you may know.' He had an optimistic idea of my reading habits, but I let it pass. 'There are active groups from Belgium, and Switzerland, and a dozen other lands. Some rather... wild spirits from the Baltic – Latvians. As Secretary, I received a letter proposing that they visit our branch of our Union, in the Thames Ironworks yard.' Something flickered in his face. 'I own that I was cautious, sensing the tension between a man's natural loyalties to class and to country, but – well–'

'Good old Raikes took over the Secretaryship, and he got to send the reply.'

'A most auspicious visit. We may each learn–'

With a creak that was more shriek, the door of the snug swung open. We both turned. 'Well, well, well,' said the man in the doorway.

He was average height, and slender. Not an immediately impressive figure, until you looked at his face. Dark, strong eyes. They didn't give Merridew more than a glance, and then he was focusing on me.

'Well, brother Merridew,' he said, still not looking at the other man, 'it appears your devotion to our cause cannot be restrained. You fancied you'd help me out by having a meeting on our behalf. Load off my shoulders, was that it?'

Merridew's face was thunderous.

I can't think of a human I've taken a more instant dislike to. Which is saying something, given the number of people trying to murder me on sight that week. It was pretty clear who this chap was.

He half-turned and, very deliberately, pushed the door shut with his finger. Then he picked up a stool, placed it carefully at the head of the table, and sat as if he was now presiding over our meeting. He brought his hands together in front of him, fingertip to fingertip, and continued to consider me.

While the door had still been open, I had surreptitiously lifted my hand from my leg – a signal of calm, of confidence that I hadn't lost control of the situation.

As soon as the door clicked shut, I'd wondered if I had

miscalculated.

'This is Mr Delmar, Raikes,' Merridew said. Each word was spat heavily. He wasn't bothering to hide his anger. He'd have loved to beat Raikes to death, there and then. It was hardly surprising; St Francis of Assisi would want to beat Raikes to death after ten seconds in his company. But the proud old man had to swallow his bitterness, and I started to understand something of the power that the Secretary of the Union had, in their strange underworld of organized labour. 'Writing a book. Allow me to reassure you that this is none of your damned business.'

Raikes ignored him. He was still watching me.

He didn't blink. He never blinked. But the dark eyes narrowed, and then a thin smile crept up his face, like something he'd practised. 'Sir Henry Delmar, would that be?' He turned his head towards Merridew, but still the eyes stayed on me. 'Pity you weren't at the yard today, Merridew. Sir Henry gave us a demonstration of his acrobatics. Very spry, he is.'

Now Merridew got it: a frown, a flicker of shock, and then he was looking at me with fury.

'Well now, brother Merridew,' Raikes said quietly. Merridew was like an old boiler, steam seeping out of every crack and ready to explode. 'It appears we're both looking for reinforcements, does it not? Here's I coming to meet our foreign comrades. And here's you talking to… to someone who individually and generally represents the enemy of the worker. Curious, surely. Unfortunate.'

'He lied to me,' Merridew said. He wouldn't even look at me.

And Raikes laughed. It was a short, vicious yap. 'Oh he lied to you, did he? I suggest you need to do a bit of remedial reading, brother Merridew. A couple of pamphlets on the betrayal of labour inherent in the bourgeois economic system, that'll put you straight.' Still looking at me, still not blinking. 'Don't talk much, do you Mr Delamere?'

He emphasized the 'Mr' like the House of Lords had just blown up.

'Man of action, is that it?'

Let a talker talk.

'You'd like to kick me through the window.' The idea that the world hated him seemed to give him great satisfaction. 'You'd like to see me swing.' He glanced at our surroundings, then back to me. 'But you're at the wrong end of town, Mr Delamere. In the west end you could whistle up a dozen of your bullies and have me horsewhipped. Out here... my town; my terms. You'd just disappear. Another lump of flotsam, bobbing in the river and washed away with the tide.' He smiled. 'You were pretty active today, weren't you? What the hell did you think you were playing at? You – and Sinclair – what are these bizarre games you play? What do you think you'll achieve? What do you think you can change?' He leaned forwards, fingers still neatly together, manner mild and pedantic. 'Your world is dying. You will be swept away.' Said like the town clerk discussing the new sewage system. 'Nothing personal, Mr Delamere. Whether my colleagues had torn you to pieces today, or whether you get strung up next week, you're just a part in the machine, as much a victim of the system as anyone. Nothing personal.'

He leaned back, the tone pitying. 'But Mr Sinclair was so desperate to try to meet me.' He smiled. Every word was enunciated so carefully, one long elegant sneer. 'Hoped to persuade me to... what? Take another sixpence and help him start his war sooner? Play up, play up, and play the game? Such a problem for you, isn't it, that workers aren't gentlemen?'

The smile turned nastier again. 'But then, it seems that the gentlemen aren't gentlemen either. Did you knife Sinclair, Mr Delamere?' I waited. 'D'you know, I've the suspicion that maybe you didn't? You're a killing gentleman, no doubt of it. But that was a hot killing.' He gazed at me. 'And you're cold. I don't really care what you do to each other, but I confess I'm curious. Then you killed another man, didn't you? Perhaps you're going to kill me, too.'

I leaned forwards, and lowered my voice. 'I can assure you, Mr Raikes,' I said, friendly-like, 'that that would be entirely personal.'

The smile died, and the neat arrangement of his fingers became contorted. 'Make your jokes,' he said quietly. 'Play your games. Rome is burning.'

He stood, and left.

'There goes the new age,' I said, false jovial.

Merridew glared at me, wounded pride. Eventually, he said: 'You have ruined me.' He slumped. 'You have tricked me, you have mocked me, you have ruined me. I'll have no chance with them now; none. No respect.' He shook his head. 'I am finished, because of your damned games.'

I felt sincerely sorry for him. I preferred his version of trade unionism, and I'd take Attila the Hun over the odious Raikes. And in his way, he was a good man trying to do good as he saw it. 'You were ruined anyway,' I said. 'Raikes and his kind have made you as obsolete as the wooden ships.'

He pulled his shoulders up again. 'The worst of it is that they may be right. Their world of conflict between labour and owner – it is become permanent. It was unnecessary; now it is unavoidable. Satisfied, Sir Henry Delamere?'

'I'll be satisfied if I survive the week without one of your heroic artisans cutting my throat.' I stood. 'Get out of it now, Merridew. You've done your time, you've got your savings. Go and open a pub or play with your grandchildren. Otherwise the revolution will chew you up in its first turn.'

I left him there, in the tiny wood-panelled dining room, an old broken horse slumped against the farmyard wall.

I didn't even glance at the man in the public bar I'd signalled to earlier. But he waited a few moments and then followed me out into the evening.

20.

I ensconced myself in another tavern twenty yards up the street, and bought a pair of drinks. A few minutes later Quinn joined me.

'Clean?'

He contrived to look more sour than normal. 'Can't say sir.' He sat. 'No one followed you obviously. But they could have any number of static positions in this warren. Your health, sir.' He took a mouthful of brandy. 'Didn't like the look of the ratty fellow who shut himself in with you.'

'You and the rest of the human race. But I don't think he does his own dirty work.' I took a swig. 'Do you long for the revolution, Quinn?'

'Does it pay well, sir?'

I smiled. 'Well put. Seriously, though. Chappie back there's got it all worked out. Fellows like me are doomed – anarchist bomb or swinging from a lamppost sooner or later – and the working man's going to come into his own. I mean to say: you stuck in the Albany, polishing boots and haggling with the tradesmen – I've a terrible feeling I'm cramping your style.'

He was giving me the look he usually gives when I'm contemplating a 50-1 shot at Epsom or a red-head in the saloon at Deauville.

'I mean to say, his sneering at me, and at Sinclair: these wild errands we're on, all the other games I've been involved in over the years. Damned diverting for me, naturally, but don't mean a thing in the grand scheme of it all. And still scrabbling to win enough to pay the fees at the Albany.' I raised a glass at my reflection, and drank. 'To the fatuousness of the leisured life. I know what he means.'

'No sir.' Quinn took another mouthful of brandy. 'Begging your pardon, but no you don't. Real poverty's more than absence of money. Real despair is more than the absence of a job or a dream. It's when you're fighting every day just to stay alive, and to keep your kiddies alive. You remember the Cape, sir. Like that, but that's your whole life. When time itself has no meaning, because nothing can ever change. So what's the point of anything?'

I considered it. One of my valet's many virtues is a steady, deeply rational intellect. When he's in philosophic mood, and chooses to string more than half a dozen words together, I pay attention. Eventually I said: 'Which brings me back to my original concern. Why aren't you cutting my throat in the small hours? Not wanting to push you too much on the point.'

What passes for the Quinn smile creaked over the face. 'I'll bear the offer in mind, sir, thank you.' And as quickly the smile was gone. 'I'd be glad enough of a little more balance in the world. I'd be glad enough if those I was raised with weren't having to scavenge for seabirds to eat in the lean seasons. If the babies weren't dying in their dozens before they were out of the cot.' He took a swig of brandy. 'But I've seen the fast-lipped men. The smooth-talkers, and the dreamers. In a village meeting. On a boat. And they never brought more than chaos, and greater despair. You may tell your radical friends I said so.' He nodded out of the window. 'Your pal sir, I think.'

I followed his glance. Down in the street, outside McArdle's, the charmless Raikes was talking to another man and then apparently saying goodbye. They turned apart and went their separate ways.

The other man had an unusual cut of hat and suit. Same as

the guest speakers at the yard. Same as the man who'd try to murder me in my sitting room. I was leaning forwards, half out of my seat. Now the man disappeared out of my vision, off up the street.

By the time I got downstairs and to the door of the tavern, he was gone among the knots of strolling people and the dusk.

And then a woman screamed.

It came from the direction of McArdle's, and immediately I was heading back there. I felt Quinn's restraining hand on my arm – I assumed it was his – but shrugged it off.

A few steps closer and I heard a word screamed distinctly: 'murder!' By the time I was outside the chop house I was among a dozen curious loiterers, peering as best we could through the steamy bay window at the front. From nearby I heard a police whistle. Around me the busy empty chatter of the gawping crowd.

Sick, knowing, I shifted to the side of the crowd, to the alley which runs down beside McArdle's. The snug where I had sat with Merridew looked out onto this alley. I took a couple of steps down into its darkness.

The bottom half of the sash window was raised. Through it, slumped on the bench, I could see Merridew. His shirt front was crimson, and his face was white. His gaping eyes stared up into the ceiling. Joshua Merridew would never open his pub or play with his grandchildren.

Who could have got to him? What could Raikes possibly benefit from –

My heart kicked, and started to pump a very cold mixture indeed.

Presumably the last person known to have been alone with him was… I.

21.

I took a couple of instinctive steps back, out of the alley. I was still considering the window, getting my last glimpse of that old man, who had tried so hard to do his duty and eventually, somehow, died for it.

Assuming for the moment that I wasn't the murderer, in the bustle of the chop house anyone could have slipped into the snug after I'd left it.

Or could someone have stabbed him through the window? Someone he recognized, recognized enough to accept a whispered summons to the window, close enough to get a blade in the chest?

With each day, each outrage, I seemed to find new depths of anger.

'Get clear!' It was a low murmur, urgent, in my ear. I glanced round. It was Quinn, standing beside me but affecting not to be paying me any attention. 'Get clear, sir.'

It was probably sound advice, but he wasn't as angry as I.

I glanced further around myself, considering the options.

And I found myself looking into a face I knew too well. The face was on a man standing on the edge of the crowd. The very fair hair wasn't common, but that hardly showed under his hat, and to most people he'd have seemed unremarkable. Not to me. The face from the bathhouse lobby. The face that had hunted me over the rooves of London, almost to my death.

We gazed at each other for a long moment. I realized that my whole body was tensed, waiting for his move, anticipating the threat. Would he have the gun on him? Would he dare to use it in the street? Should I stand and fight? Where could I run? Still he stared.

And then he turned and, first at a fast walk and then at a trot, hurried away up the street.

Well, tally ho… I set off after him.

He hadn't gone ten yards before he glanced over his shoulder and saw me. His eyes widened and he broke into a run, and I did the same. *Let's see how you like it, you ___*.

He was a lively runner, but this time I wasn't barefoot and I about kept pace with him. We tore up Golden Lane. Behind me I heard a police whistle, and then another, and shouts. It was a mad race, weaving in and out of the drifting pedestrians and leaping out of the way of carriages that careered out of side-streets or wobbled wildly through the twilight. Beside a park my man crashed into an orange-seller and sent him sprawling and carried on, and I had to vault over the swearing hawker and through the scattering fruit. At the junction with Fortune Street there was an explosion and a motor car lurched out in front of me in a belch of smoke. I came up hard against its snub-nosed engine casing, pushed myself off and spun around.

Fifteen yards behind, a policeman was running hard towards me. For a stupid second I felt heartened that someone was help-ing me – and then his expression confirmed that of course he had no interest, no awareness, of the blond assassin ahead.

He was coming for me. I turned and ran again, now in the middle of a three-way chase.

We raced on up Golden Lane. I jumped left to avoid an old man having trouble with his pipe, and suddenly a horse reared up in front of me and sent me staggering back a step. Regathering myself, I realized I was right outside Jolly's Theatre.

I turned, looking again for my prey. Someone grabbed my arm. I spun round, fist up. I saw the helmet first, and hesitated: the policeman.

He was heavily-moustached, red-faced and breathing hard. 'You are Sir Henry Delamere,' he said, hoarse between gasps. *Damnit…* He had me tight. I could wriggle free, surely, and would I be seen escaping in the darkness? But I was static now, and he'd have reinforcements coming up behind. 'And you are under arrest.'

A hand tapped him on the shoulder. He turned, starting to speak, and caught a mighty fist in the centre of his moustache and dropped like a rock.

'Why Quinn,' I said, 'I'm not the best example, I know; but even I haven't started assaulting policemen yet.'

He didn't seem to find it amusing. I looked around the street, looking for the options, looking for –

And there he was. Just twenty yards farther up the street, standing still and watching me: my hunter-turned-hunted. From behind me somewhere there was another police whistle.

Our eyes met again. He smiled. Then he touched the brim of his hat cordially, and turned and began to walk away.

I was already starting after him when I felt heavy hands on my shoulder and collar. 'Come along, sir!' – and Quinn was bundling me up the steps and into Jolly's theatre. In the doorway I knocked into a young woman, made an instinctive apology, looked at her.

It was Bliss. She was in street clothes – presumably her act wasn't until later in the proceedings, and she'd popped out for a bit of air or a brandy-and-soda before getting togged up. Our eyes held a moment longer, but she made no acknowledgement and carried on down the steps, and anyway Quinn had given me another shove and we were inside.

22.

Quinn and I settled ourselves in one of Jolly's boxes. The theatre was hardly bigger than my sitting room (and the melodrama promised to be about as ripe). There weren't more than a dozen rows of seats in the stalls, from the front of the little stage back to the chap in the check suit sitting just below me; had check suit been more than five feet tall he'd have banged his head on the front of our box; my valet and I had to squeeze together on the box's two chairs like an over-friendly couple on the top deck of an omnibus. The atmosphere – the crowd milling around in front of me, waiting until the last minute to fold their legs into the stall seats, and my companions in the semi-circle of boxes, stooping and jostling to find their places – felt more like a rugger scrummage or the last stand at Stormberg.

A pocket orchestra, heavy on the brass and apparently skirmishing among the knees of the front row of the stalls, hurried through a cheerful rendition of 'God Save the King' like they had tickets for a better show round the corner, and the master of ceremonies trotted onto the stage and told the one about the French sailor and the pygmy princess.

I wasn't in the mood. I was even less in the mood when one of the side doors to the stalls opened, down to my right, and a man slipped in and pressed himself against the wall – in his defence, the alternative would have been to perch on the lap of the woman in seat C1 – and began methodically to scan the faces in the theatre.

It was my fair-haired friend of the rooftops: the man who'd invested a considerable amount of energy in trying to murder me, and now by an extraordinary coincidence happened to be on the spot when someone I'd just been speaking to had been murdered.

It didn't take him long to spot me. In a theatre auditorium barely bigger than a privy he couldn't fail to. Our eyes met for a fraction of a second. This time there was no courteous acknowledgement, no wry smile. As I watched, he turned and disappeared back through the door. There was a burst of audience applause, and a woman of the general proportions of H.M.S.

Thunderer steamed onto the stage and launched into 'I've got rings on my fingers'.

'Ever defended a siege from a theatre box, Quinn?'

Good chap that he is, Quinn considered the point seriously. 'Wouldn't fancy their chances trying to get through this little door, sir. But I'd worry about our supplies.' I nodded. 'You have your piece, sir?'

'Mm. And a full half dozen in the cylinder and an itchy finger. If this chap and his pals want to come on in I'll happily attend to them.' I touched the bulk of my revolver through my coat. 'But there's a snag, Quinn.'

'Of course, sir.'

'Several snags. One, I don't know how many they are: the fact that this chap went and came back suggests he's got reinforcements as well as new instructions. Two, they're probably not so obliging as to line up outside and knock. Three, they don't need to: they don't need to risk a massacre; they can just wait until we get start to get hungry or go mad from too much musical sentiment, and follow us out somewhere nice and quiet and finish the job at their leisure. Four... four, Quinn, time is on their side, not ours.' He frowned. 'Your policeman will have woken up by now. With a sore head and one thing on his mind. Won't take him long to find out where we got to.'

'I don't mind answering for putting him down, sir.'

'Good show. And so you should: guilty beyond question. Don't want to seem heartless, Quinn, but I'm more worried about myself. On top of my previous crimes, I must be their principal suspect for poor old Merridew. The longer I sit squeezed in this damned box, the more men Inspector Bunce can have waiting outside.'

Around us, the audience burst into wild applause again. We stood, as best we could in the cramped box, and I opened my coat just in case I felt the need for the Webley, and Quinn took a breath and opened the door.

The singer, having paused to take on more coal, started on 'The Glow Worm'. I closed the door silently behind us, happy to have escaped that at least.

The corridor behind the boxes was empty.

On the off-chance, we re-traced our steps towards the front of the theatre. But through the glazed door to the foyer, I saw fair hair talking to another man in the main entrance. If we left that way, they would track us easily.

I'd spent time in the dressing rooms of Jolly's, but not come at them from this direction before. We accosted an usher, who was well used to taking a shilling or two to point discerning gentlemen towards the actresses' quarters, and shortly we were through an anonymous door and heading down a spiral staircase towards the back-stage maze of the theatre. So far so good.

At the bottom I paused. 'Rules of engagement, Quinn. We do whatever it takes to get past these plain-clothes brutes. We do what we can to avoid arrest for our many crimes – you particularly, as the only man actually guilty of what he's suspected of' – Quinn smiled heavily – 'but we ain't shooting any policemen. Above all, this: if Miss Bliss can show us a way out of here without drawing attention to herself, well and good; but if there is any chance of endangering her, we stay clear and do as best we can ourselves, yes?'

'Of course, sir.'

Bare gas lamps lit our way along a brick passage.

At the end, another passage went left and right. We separated. I'd got ten yards when I heard a door from the other direction opening, and with it a sudden chattering of female voices. A beautiful dark-haired girl in a translucent wrap had stepped into the passage, to be confronted by a large Cornish valet.

Mercifully, she didn't scream. Nor, to his credit, did Quinn; I doubt he'd come across much like her in his God-forsaken fishing village. They chatted a while, while I loitered in the gloom feeling very exposed. Not for the first time, I wondered how numerous my enemies were; and – given that the policeman outside had recognized me – how quickly word would have reached the implacable Inspector Bunce.

Eventually my valet sauntered along to join me.

'No rush, Quinn; take your time. Friend of yours?'

'Not yet, sir.' He pointed ahead. 'There's a way out along here, according to Miss Francesca.'

'Miss Francesca, is it?'

There was indeed a way out, after a few more turns in the passage and another narrow staircase. But when we got there, we found a doorman arguing with someone outside. 'Nah, y'ain't comin' in! Y's can stay out like everyone else. An' keep yer damn' shillings!' A one-sided argument, to be honest. Whoever it was outside said something placatory and didn't push it.

The doorman was a stout line of defence, for now. But this clearly wasn't a way out for us.

We retreated down the staircase again, back into the gas-flickered brick maze of passages.

And through them we continued to prowl. Rats in a sewer. I didn't like the furtiveness of it, the sense that I was having to hide. And I liked even less the growing sense that we were trapped. Clearly, we were dealing with several opponents. They had methodically covered the entrances. Unless we decided to set up permanent residence with Miss Francesca and her company for eternity – and if that is what eternity looks like it'll be fine by me, but I've a few bits of unfinished business first, and I do like my fresh air – sooner or later we would have to break cover, and then these unknown hunters could pick us off.

Unless they decided to move in and flush us out; or finish us off somewhere among the tunnels.

Intermittently, from somewhere far above, I could hear the

muffled harrumphing of the Jolly's orchestra. A world of inno-
cence and cheerful operetta favourites.

We prowled on.

Once, as we trod silently along a passage, the figure of a man
crossed in front of us ten yards ahead, wearing a distinctive helmet. Pressed against the wall, we waited a minute or two before
we ventured on. The police were in the mix too.

Then, as we approached a corner in the passage, we heard
feet on the metal staircase beyond it. Quinn and I exchanged a
glance and, with rare prudence, retreated.

I knew there was at least one other exit, because I'd used it the
previous day. It wasn't even too hard to find, once we'd plotted
our way through the maze, endless and unchanging brick and
sick yellow gaslight, avoiding the shadows who hunted us.

But when we got to this other exit, walking quietly up behind the doorman who stood slumped in the opening smoking
a cigarette, I saw beyond him a man in the street leaning against
a lamppost, and watching. He saw me at the same moment, and
then he was gone somewhere into the gloom of the alley. All of
the exits were marked, by men who didn't hesitate to stab a man
through a window or stage a shooting in the middle of the day.

So back we went, down the nearest spiral staircase, into the
warren again.

'Plan B, sir?'

'B, Quinn? We're on about Plan Z now, I should think.'

'What happens after that, sir?' his normal growl was the faintest rasp in the gloom.

'Reckon your charming friend needs an understudy?'

We marked our journey by increasingly familiar landmarks:
a tea-chest half full of fabric; a broken and dusty violin, which
had obviously been lying in the dirt for a long time. Catching
sight of a shadowy figure at the end of a passage, still and waiting, it took me a full minute to realize it was a mannequin. We

walked on.

'Halt!'

I'd tried to check first. Perhaps I'd been distracted by the music from the stage, which seemed nearer now. I'd looked right and I'd looked left and then I'd turned right – and immediately the voice boomed behind me.

'No funny moves now! Put your 'ands up where I can see 'em.'

I put my hands up – enough that they could be seen over my shoulders, anyway. As I did, I pulled open my jacket with my thumbs. I wasn't fully clear of the side passage, and the open jacket enabled Quinn to reach in and retrieve my revolver and retreat a step or two.

I started to move forwards. 'Stop there!' I stopped. And then I took another couple of steps forwards. I had to hope that whoever it was behind me would want to see my face before he did anything desperate. Or at least that he'd want to be closer. Another step. Another.

I heard a thump behind me, and a faint groan, then nothing.

'Alright now sir.'

I breathed out, and turned. 'Who is – Quinn! It's another policeman.'

My valet was bending over his prey. 'Actually, sir, I think it's the same policeman.'

'That doesn't make it better. Quinn, they won't tolerate this sort of thing at the Albany.' He was bent down next to the un-conscious body. 'He going to be alright?'

'Should be, sir.'

'You realize they'll pin this on me, too?'

He stood, and smiled bleakly. 'Thought had occurred, sir.'

The shot roared in the confined passage, and Quinn hissed and clutched his arm. The shot had come from behind me, and I grabbed Quinn by the shoulder and collar and shoved him forwards and away down the corridor. The gunman could shoot me in the back at his leisure.

But he didn't, and I made the corner with spine intact and bundled Quinn round it to safety and turned, and peered back. Half way along the corridor a couple of chorus girls had emerged, hurrying for the stage. They'd blocked the gunman's view.

They were dressed as policemen.

Well, their top halves were, anyway; bottom halves were regulation dancers' frills. Of course. For a moment, they stood fluttering over the unconscious-but-real policeman at their feet, whispering in alarm. There was a clatter of cymbals and a fanfare of brass from behind me – they could set up a shooting gallery back here and the audience would never know – and one of the girls patted the other frantically on the arm, and they set off moving again, one away down the corridor and one towards me, brushing past oblivious as she rounded the corner.

We were by the stage. The corridor ran along behind the back of it. To my left, light was being funnelled off the stage by bits of scenery in the wings, and painting bright rays across the floor. I saw the girl grab up a policeman's hat from a box, there was another crash of cymbals and fanfare, and she and presumably her pal from the other side sashayed onto the stage in the Paris style to a roar of audience approval.

The cymbals made me think of our assailant again. I risked another peek around the edge of the brickwork. I fancied I could make out a pistol barrel protruding from the far corner of the corridor – by the other side of the stage, presumably. I withdrew, but then heard the same hurrying and hissing, and looked again to see two more girls in the same outfits going through the same performance, hesitating over the unconscious policeman then hurrying on. One, of course, came my way. She glanced uncertainly at me – I murmured a courteous 'evening, officer' at her and she smiled – and continued onwards to wait for her cue at the edge of the stage.

Treating his shoulders a little more gently, I turned Quinn so that the light from the stage caught him better.

'Really just a scratch, sir.'

'Clumsy ass.'

It really was just a scratch, mercifully, across the outside of his arm. There was blood, but it wouldn't bleed much more. I wrapped my handkerchief around the wound, and used my pocket pencil to wind the dressing tighter until Quinn hissed his discomfort.

'How does the land lie, sir?' His voice was almost normal volume, just to make himself heard over the crashing music.

'Rough, Quinn.' I finished tidying the dressing. 'Bad man at the opposite end of the corridor, with pistol and not afraid to use it.' I tapped his arm. 'Our options are limited.' I peered around in the gloom, trying to shield my eyes from the glare from the stage. 'Non-existent, indeed. There's no other way out, except the corridor, or the stage. Don't know any songs, do you Quinn?'

'None fit for public performance, sir.'

'We can either make a run for it down the corridor and hope that he keeps winging you.' I took my Webley back from him. 'Or we can exchange potshots with him, and wait until the rest of the constabulary arrives to arrest us.'

From the box which the chorus girl had used, I picked out another policeman's helmet. Holding the brim in finger and thumb, I slowly extended the helmet out round the corner into the corridor.

The shot was immediate, and the helmet was ripped out of my hand and clattered against the brickwork. I dropped to my knees, extended my gun arm and one eye round the corner and let off a snap shot towards the end of the corridor. A cloud of dust began to drift and settle where I'd grazed the wall. I stayed where I was, body shielded by the corner and pistol up, but he didn't re-emerge from his end.

What did emerge was another half-dozen girls, from the passage halfway along the corridor. They made the usual performance of bewilderment over the unconscious policeman at their feet – except this time he groaned and rubbed his head. He must have thought he'd gone to policeman heaven, bunch of pretty girls in regulation constabulary jackets fussing over him; he didn't see legs like those in the Bow Street washroom. Alas for him they had to hurry on, half one way along the corridor and half the other, as per. I lowered my pistol and stood as they came past me.

'What act are you?' one of them murmured.

'Er… Hotshot, er, Harry,' I said. 'Catch bullets in my teeth, that sort of thing.'

'What's up with him?' hissed another, nodding at Quinn's bandage.

'He fails to catch bullets in his teeth.'

Another verse or two had passed, and there was another fanfare and clash of cymbals, and the girls donned their helmets and followed onto the stage. God alone knew what the sketch or dance was; I was almost regretting having ducked out of our box so early.

I pushed the Webley back into Quinn's hand. 'Another option has occurred to me,' I said. 'Use the helmet and the pistol barrel to keep him interested. Try not to get shot this time, old fellow.'

'I'll keep my head well back, sir.'

'Not the head I'm interested in, Quinn. Your trigger finger is much more important.'

'What about you, sir? Off to join your lady friends or something?'

I smiled.

Then I picked up another helmet from the box beside us, put it on, and took a deep breath and a long step forwards.

I rather fancy that on the madness of that stage, behind the line of charming young ladies doing some sort of can-can business while half dressed as policemen, not a single member of the audience noticed a chap sauntering across behind them with a policeman's helmet and an occasional attempt at a sort of rhythmic two-step shimmy. I can't have made the performance any less interesting or more bizarre, and the audience were the least of my worries. Halfway across I heard what I thought were shots – the noise from the band and the audience and the girls was deafening, and I couldn't be sure – so it seemed that Quinn was holding the gunman's attention nicely.

I escaped off the stage and into the darkness of the wings with considerable relief. I took a moment to remove the policeman's helmet – in general I'm reluctant to sail under a false flag, so to speak – and for my eyes to re-adjust. Two steps brought me nicely behind the gunman.

I tapped him on the shoulder, he spun round and I punched him in the face.

'I've no idea what you're up to,' I said as he staggered back and I caught him with the sharp left jab, 'and I might not have cared,' – another sharp left – 'but no-one' – I concluded with the swinging right and he collapsed into a hat-stand – 'no-one shoots my valet.'

Groggily, he started trying to clamber his way out of the wreckage of the hat-stand. Quinn was making his way towards us along the corridor. I turned and retrieved the pistol, which the gunman had dropped with my first punch. He'd made it half-upright now, fell against a wardrobe, wrestled his way round it, and staggered on towards Quinn.

For about three seconds I really felt, for the first time in days, on top of things. I had a live miscreant under my control, and with him I had a much better chance of finding out what was going on and a much better chance of clearing my own name.

For about three seconds, as I say – until the policeman stood up.

He must have had one hell of an evening, what with getting lamped twice by a well-built Cornish valet, repeatedly stamped by some lady policemen, and then waking up to find himself in the middle of a gunfight. Presumably now he had quite a headache, too. But he was obviously a determined sort of chap, and he'd had a breather to regather his strength, and the inspiring vision of all those dancers' legs hurrying over him, and so he was looking in reasonable shape as he came upright.

It couldn't last. The first thing he would have seen was Quinn, Webley in hand, advancing towards him. The second thing he would have seen, and felt, was our assailant, who was still stumbling along the corridor and now collapsed into his arms.

The third thing the policeman would have seen would have been me, but he didn't, because as I saw his face turning dazed towards me I ducked into the wardrobe.

Mine was the only face he knew, and I had no doubt that collaring me would make his whole evening worthwhile. He'd almost got me twice, suffered both times, and badly needed to restore his pride. So the wardrobe it had to be, before he clocked who I was.

I'd one bit of luck: the gunman, equally bewildered, had pulled himself up and found himself staring into the face of a policeman. He'd shoved the policeman aside, and lurched off down the side passage. I had to hope that the policeman would see him as the more interesting threat, and follow, and that Quinn would see the importance of keeping tabs on him too.

And so it worked out. In my wardrobe I could hear the thump and blare of the orchestra from the stage, but the corridor seemed to have gone silent. After half a minute, I risked opening the door. I stepped out, gun in hand.

Right in front of Annabella Bliss. She gave the slightest gasp, and recovered. 'Looking for a new costume?' she said.

'You… You cannot begin to know what—'

'Save it.' She was curt. 'Inflict yourself on me as you like, but never get in the way of my performance.'

I nodded. She turned, and I watched her go, that tight-strung back pale in the gloomy corridor as she made for the stage. I needed to get after Quinn and his policeman and the gunman and sort out that muddle somehow, but Bliss was a momentary glimpse of another life.

I was still focused on the far end of the corridor, when my vision filled with Inspector Bunce, stepping out of the side passage in front of me.

'Well well,' he said. He looked awfully pleased with himself.

I took an instinctive, weary step backwards. The gun was still in my hand, and he saw it, considered it, and took a step towards me regardless. I took another step back.

I surely couldn't shoot him, could I? I retreated, back out of the corridor and into the darkness by the side of the stage. A dead end.

I kept the gun level, an automatic reaction to the threat, pointing at his chest. And still he walked on towards me.

This damned policeman had made himself my enemy, the embodiment of the mad injustice of recent days, and a pain in the backside. Somehow both infuriating and dangerous. But in that moment, as he stood there alone and willing to face down an armed man whom he knew to be a multiple murderer, I had to admire his nerve.

'Come along then, *Sir* Henry: you'd better add me to your charge sheet, or throw in your hand.'

If ever a pestilence deserved shooting, it was Inspector Bunce in that moment.

'Ain't that the way of it? So much easier in the back, eh?'

The pistol wavered, as I considered shooting him in the leg, as much for his impertinence as to get him out of the way.

'No? The hangman it is, then, unless you'd like to save him the trouble.'

There was an explosion of applause and cheers and squeals and a cloud of helmeted tutu'd girls burst out in front of me and engulfed Inspector Bunce. I last saw him flailing and wrestling among them, trying to get at me while they with giggles and scolds hurried past him for their next costume change. Not a bad way for a chap to go, all things considered. While he couldn't see me, and with nowhere else to go, I stowed the pistol and made for the stage. There were various props and bits of light scenery in the wings. I grabbed up an urn with a large plant in it and strode onto the stage, face full of leaves, placed it carefully in the centre and carried on and off the other side.

The orchestra started up, piano and violin, something melo-dramatic. I glanced back across the stage; Bunce didn't seem to have seen me go.

Something stabbed hard into my spine.

'Don't move. Don't turn.'

I didn't move. I didn't turn.

'I'm afraid my man's got my ticket,' I said.

'I would prefer your pistol.' The voice was quiet, calm, and close behind me. 'Finger and thumb.'

Finger and thumb only, I pulled the pistol out of my coat.

'Just drop it.'

This chap knew what he was doing, unfortunately. No chance of a scuffle; not a move I could make before his bullet would shatter my spine.

The stage in front of me, and a man with a pistol behind. My eyes were finding it hard to make anything out in the gloom of the wings with the glare of the stage still dominating. A ladder going up. Umpteen ropes. A rickety set of shelves, with assorted props on them no doubt, but I couldn't see anything useful and couldn't have reached it anyway.

The stage went dark, and I knew it had to be my chance. But immediately the pistol jammed harder against my spine, and the lights came up again, and as I blinked in the glare I saw that Bliss was standing on stage.

She was alone, next to a wooden lamp-post; poised ready to sing. If she was surprised by the potted plant sharing the lime-light, she hid it like a pro.

For a second, I forgot the killer behind me and saw just her.

Then a flurry of whispers and feet nearby – the chorus coming our way – and again the pistol hard in my back, and a hand on my collar. He hesitated; he was almost as short of options as I was.

'Up!' he hissed, and pushed me forwards.

In front of me was the ladder: a simple wooden thing, leading up into the gloom. The pistol stabbed into its familiar position. I started up.

As I climbed, I heard the voice of Annabella Bliss, helping me heavenwards. Jolly lovely it was too, and I'd have enjoyed it in other circumstances – any circumstances, that is, other than my imminent death. If I'm going to go, let it be in the arms of some-one like her, not plugged by some scoundrel. And dear God let the accompaniment be something other than Marie bloody Lloyd.

I came level with a walkway: a wooden affair hanging in space somehow, two planks wide with no obvious hand-rail. I glanced down. My fair-haired angel of death was climbing steadily after me. It wasn't easy for him to keep the pistol out, but he was do-ing well enough. He used it to beckon me onwards; upwards.

I went on upwards.

I was climbing into a strange forest of the stage: dozens of ropes, and painted backdrops ready to be lowered on the ropes, and sandbags at various heights acting as counter-weights for the backdrops. The only light came from the glare of the stage below.

I was climbing out of options. I considered dropping onto my assassin; easy enough. But he had less far to fall than I did, and he'd be doing it without a bullet in his arse.

I came level with another walkway, the path of boards stretching away narrow and dusty in front of me. I glanced down again. This time he gestured me forwards, onto the walkway.

I swung on, and steadied myself. Normally I've no particular problem with heights, but the rickety planks were not inspiring, and it was damned peculiar to be perched up in the darkness, with the glare of the stage far beneath.

'*The boy I love is up in the gallery…*'

I watched him come. I looked for the chance to kick his head off as he came level, but his mind was at least as devious as mine. He came on cautiously, pistol steady on me all the time, and as he reached the walkway he gestured me away.

Gingerly, I worked my way backwards on the walkway. Around me the forest of ropes, and the occasional sandbag where something had been lowered to the stage, sending its counterweight up into my gloomy heaven.

Fair hair swung himself onto the walkway, and it shuddered, and we both staggered for our balance. I saw that he'd wrapped something around his face – a scarf, perhaps. If he had to bully his way out they'd find it hard to identify him.

We faced each other on the walkway, eight or ten feet between us.

'*… The boy I love is looking now at me,*
There he is, can't you see, waving his handkerchief,…'

What was he planning to do? He couldn't hope for subtlety: a gunshot, or me falling to my death on the stage far below, there was no… Then I saw his eyes.

He didn't care. These people had proved themselves game

101

for any outrage, if it achieved their ends. Right now, all that he cared about was my death. And there was nothing to stop him succeeding, and within a very few seconds.

Gazing around me, I saw a sandbag suspended near my ankles, its rope running up beside me to some pulley above. And so I stepped off the walkway. I grabbed the rope, found a vague foothold on the sandbag, and clutched on desperately as a pulley above me creaked and turned, and rope and sandbag started to swing and lurch, and I dropped slowly below the level of the walkway. Whatever was on the other end of the pulley was lighter than me and my sandbag, but enough to keep my descent steady. Clinging to my rope, I looked for the lower walkway. As I gazed around, I saw the wooden lamp-post rising to meet me on the other end of the rope. God knows what the audience thought. The lower walkway was getting near now, and I waited for my chance to catch it as I dropped.

I never reached it. I was still a few feet above it, my leg starting to swing out ready for the step, the lamp-post looming beside me, when my descent stopped with a jerk. Fair hair must have... But then, slowly at first, and then more briskly, I started to rise.

The lamp-post dropped, and I rose. My assassin had done as I had done, but on the other side of the pulley. Scoundrel plus lamp-post being heavier – as Archimedes would have put it – than distressed baronet plus sandbag, he was now coming down and I was on the up. Except that he wasn't actually dropping. He must have been quite the athlete, for he'd obviously pocketed his pistol and was climbing the rope as it dropped. So he stayed level, while the lamp-post returned to the stage.

Which meant my chance had to be when I regained the upper walkway. If the rope was suddenly free of my weight... As soon as the walkway was at my waist-level I started to scramble on to it, one hand and foot, and the other foot flailing, but it wouldn't come free of the rope, and the sandbag was dragging it upwards as I clung to the walkway, and I struggled wildly with my face full of dust and splinters and eventually got loose and pulled myself forwards and further along the walkway and wriggled round.

He hadn't fallen. A yard or two away, thanks to the wild swings of the rope and our desperate scrambles, my killer had managed to regain the walkway during my escape from the rope, and now he was getting to his feet. He stopped in the crouch, and saw me. His hand went instinctively into his jacket, and he liked what he found there.

Somewhere far below me, I heard laughter. The lamp-post had just landed serenely on the stage beside Bliss. Gamely, she sang on.

I came up clumsily, desperate, looking for the last chance, and lurched into a sandbag hanging nearby. It swung away from me, as I came upright.

And now he was upright too, just six feet away, the pistol levelled at me. The heat was fat around us.

'...*As merry as a robin that sings on a tree.*'

I'd nothing left. He couldn't miss. From his eyes alone, I knew he was smiling.

I hope he enjoyed it. Because in the next moment the sandbag swung back in, on the gentle arc on which I'd sent it, and caught him on the side of the head. The gentlest knock, but it was enough to send him off balance and as the walkway started to sway I dropped and clung on and he toppled away. His scream went on forever, as he plummeted down towards the stage, but at last it reached a crescendo as, with an explosion of woodwork and chords, he smashed into the piano.

23.

I have, I'm afraid, killed more than my share of men in my time.

For all his thoroughness, Inspector Bunce didn't know the half of it. Or perhaps he'd been saving the good stuff for my trial.

A few in the war in the Cape, of course. With time, some of the memories fade. But so, with time, does the comforting certainty that we were fighting that war for a good reason. There are faces that don't fade, and as with age one becomes aware of one's own corruption, so the faces of those dead boys become more innocent.

And as – Bunce's phrase – no stranger to hot water, I've added a few in the miscellaneous, peacetime column of the ledger too. They've all seemed necessary at the time. But you'd oblige me by not pressing the point now.

In the chaos caused by my latest victim dropping out of the sky into the middle of 'The Boy I Love Is Up In The Gallery', and a costume which I don't care to describe, I made it out of the theatre at last. Quinn came out safe too, with less need for disguise – which I thought unfair, given that he was the blighter who kept assaulting policemen. He'd pushed off home, to try to maintain the pretence of normality at the Albany.

The evening had been a shambles, but we were all in one piece; in the circumstances, I thought that was rather positive.

Bliss was having none of it. She was *livid* – fuming at the interruption of her performance. I had one attempt at pointing out that the only alternative outcome had been me instead plunging to my death during the final chorus of a rather hackneyed music hall number, but it didn't help. She sat with the obese cat on her lap, murmuring into its ear my many crimes against the drama. The cat regarded me smugly.

'And after all I did for him last night…'

'Right. Yes. Eh?'

She looked up. 'Your fair-haired friend. The one you'd started off chasing. The one you killed before he could tell you anything. Well, when you had to come and hide in the theatre because you'd attacked that policeman–'

'Quinn, actu–'

'I followed him. Before he came back to the theatre.'

'You what?'

'He went off up the street, and I followed him. He gets round the corner, and has a conversation with someone in a carriage. Smart business: four-wheeler, two horses.'

'You could have been killed!'

'Least I'd have gone quietly.'

'Yes. Good point. Beautifully put. Any markings on the carriage?' She shook her head. 'Did you hear any of it, or see who was inside?'

'I came up too late for that. Just at the end, when they were finishing, I walked past them. I got sort of a glance inside, but nothing I could describe. I did hear the voice of the man inside.'

'What was he saying?'

She stopped scratching the cat's tummy for a moment. 'He said "Kill him".' She smiled grimly. 'Meaning you, I suppose.'

I nodded. 'Usually means me.'

'Suppose you've got what you need now, anyway.' I looked the question. 'You've enough to go to the police, surely.'

'Enough to get hanged, certainly. Even if I could prove myself innocent of the deaths of Sinclair, and Merridew, and clear up the business in my rooms and the business in your piano – which at the moment is unlikely – they'd have me banged up for days first. No good.' I shook my head. 'I'm still in the wind.'

She gazed at me with something between despair and scorn. Then she buried her face in the cat's fur. 'It's not very impressive, is it?' she said into its neck. 'No, it certainly isn't.'

The cat purred its agreement.

I spent the next morning grouching around Bliss's rooms, in enforced and uncomfortable idleness. She was on necessary missions of reconnaissance and logistics for me, and I wasn't fine company in any case.

I slumped in one of the armchairs, in the increasingly battered trousers of my evening suit – the only non-ludicrous male legwear available to me – and the dressing gown, arguing with the cat. The cat was unmoved.

Among other things, I reflected on the various attempts to close my account permanently during the recent days. At first I replayed them with rather unproductive bitterness; but with time on my hands I got myself to review them more coolly. What seemed most striking – besides my obvious unpopularity with some of the most vindictive elements active in London – was the difference in style between the business in my sitting room and the businesses at the baths and the theatre. The first had been elaborate, and considered; the assassination *de luxe*. The others had been hurried and clumsy. On the first occasion, they had felt it worth their trouble to try to set up a suicide. On the second they'd risked questions being asked: Inspector Bunce wasn't a stupid man and, however satisfied he might have been by my death in a bath-house, he'd probably have thought it unlikely I'd throttled myself. Something was different by Round Two; something had changed. I felt it might be important to know what.

Sometime in the small hours of a fitful night, Annabella Bliss and I had bumped into each other, and nature had taken its course.

There are faces that don't fade, and as with age one becomes aware of one's own corruption, so the faces of the girls become more innocent.

In the morning, I found that I'd made the newspapers again. Twice, in fact, and neither alas recalled the luxuriant self-assured vitality of Miss Bliss.

I featured anonymously in the *Mail*'s front page story: MURDEROUS OUTRAGE IN THEATRE: Desperate Death-Struggle Of Masked Bandits.

I got top-billing in the second page feature: SHOCKING NEW DISCOVERY IN PICCADILLY ASSASSINATION. The police – still, apparently, fooling around my rooms in The Albany and attracting the macabre West Country curses that my valet had picked up from his mother – had finally discovered something. I don't say it was shocking to me, exactly – a gentleman doesn't betray that sort of emotion, and in this business nothing was surprising any more. But it was certainly curious.

In a development 'described by Inspector Bunce as "highly significant"', 'police thoroughness' – instinctive light fingers, more like – had found a cufflink somewhere in my rooms. A single cufflink: one with a unique battleship design made only for senior personnel in the Thames Ironworks Shipbuilding Company.

Curious, certainly, as I worked out how it must have got into my rooms.

And then somewhat vexing, as I checked, and confirmed that its companion cufflink was still, at that very moment, in my trouser pocket.

24.

SCENE: The Thames Ironworks Company Head Office on Holborn. The curtain parts – well, two horse-drawn omnibuses cross, pass each other and go their separate ways, one top-heavy with unshackled clerks heading west for the railway station or a pint of beer, the other rather emptier and returning east to collect another load, and the gap between them widens – to reveal the pavement bustle of Holborn, and through it a discreet doorway with a brass plaque to one side. The attentive viewer may read on the plaque the name of that august shipbuilding enterprise.

A scream, obviously female, from somewhere inside the doorway. Then a pause, and after a few moments the thunder of boots as a POLICEMAN hurries down the internal staircase from his post at the inner, first floor entrance to the Thames Ironworks Company office and finds a YOUNG WOMAN swooning on the bottom step. Perhaps the policeman glances towards the face, but it is veiled. If he is a policeman of regular instincts, perhaps his glance is more naturally drawn to the considerable disarray of the young woman's clothing in the area of her bust.

YOUNG WOMAN: *(gasping, distressed)* Oh – help me sir, please. The brute! He attempted... *(points along the street, swoons some more)*

The POLICEMAN notes that the young woman is still conscious, casts one last look at the pale plentiful promise of her décolletage, and hurries along the pavement in the direction indicated, blowing his whistle as he goes. As he starts, he notices a SOLID FIGURE disappearing down an alley.

From the other direction, another FIGURE IN POLICE UNIFORM appears, and enters the doorway. The YOUNG WOMAN emerges, crosses the street and exits.

This had been the relatively easy bit of the business. Quinn had been a bit windy about framing himself as an assaulter of women and getting chased by the constabulary, but I'd cursed him for having the easiest bit of the job, and Bliss had fluttered her eyelids at him and talked a lot of guff about characterization and said how wonderful he'd be, and between us we talked him round.

She, of course, was in her element. My only worry was that she'd be determined to overdo the thing, and start reciting Cleopatra or bits of Shelley. I felt sorry for her: her Sarah

Bernhardt moment at last, and it was just to help a wanted fugitive with a bit of breaking and entering. But we had to have another to-do over costume. She wanted to be a duchess or a flower-girl; I observed – with, I regret to say, more asperity and coarseness than was appropriate – that as long as she opened her top-hamper it wouldn't matter if she was dressed as Kaiser bloody Wilhelm. She did as told, but I didn't entirely relax until she was well out of the door and away.

Even my own part – in this first phase – wasn't so hard. I hadn't really done anything wrong, yet. The costume might take some explaining, but given the remorselessly lengthening list of serious crimes for which the police were hunting me, a few minutes of impersonation wouldn't make it out of the miscellaneous etceteras at the bottom of the charge sheet.

Quinn leading the police sentry into the back streets, and Bliss across the road and clear, I had the stair to myself and a moment to breathe.

Assuming the reconnaissance was to be believed, the plan ought to work. But we hadn't had time really to establish the routine at the Thames Ironworks offices, and it would only take a variation in routine or a bit of bad luck and-

-At which point a door opened beside the foot of the stair and a tubby fellow in clerk's coat was immediately under my nose.

For a moment we stared at each other. I tried to look imposing, restrained the urge to say something. He gazed up at me. Eventually, he mumbled 'Oh – the Thames Iron – of course… Er, thank you', and squeezed past me and out into the street.

I breathed again, and started up the stairs.

Quinn and Annabella Bliss had – separately – watched that front doorway at closing time and well past. If our understanding was right, once the last of the managers and clerks was clear, it was just the cleaner left in the offices – and of course the policeman on guard outside. That extra snag had to become my way in.

I trod up the stairs with deliberate pace: sturdy; unflappable; not an impostor. As I turned the half-landing I saw the closed door up ahead of me, and as I reached the first floor I saw another brass plaque confirming that this was the inner entrance to the Thames Ironworks office.

The other deduction from the reconnaissance was that – unless the shipbuilding chaps had bladders the size of rugger balls or were in the habit of pissing out the window during working hours – their office had to have a lavatory in it.

I knocked.

This, I realized as I stood there, essentially trapped in a dead end, was where the plan could most easily go wrong. At any moment the policeman would be back, having lost Quinn in the undergrowth and recognizing that he'd deserted his post with nothing to show for it. If he got onto the stairs before I got off them into the office – or before I gave up the madness and hurried down and out again – I'd be done for. I was the very man he'd been posted here to watch out for, and I'd have nothing to say and nowhere to run.

I knocked again. Harder.

From the bottom of the stairs, I fancied I heard boots.

I tried the door. Locked, obviously.

Definitely feet on the stair. Hopefully Quinn had exhausted him in the chase. Hopefully he had bunions. I glanced around me; the stairs went no further, and there were no other doors. Hopefully he'd collapse on the stairs and suffer some kind of –

The lock clicked and the door opened, and the cleaner stuck his head out. He was uneasy, and more so when he saw my policeman's uniform. 'Mind if I use the thunderbox?' I said, pushing the door open and stepping past him. 'Long shift today.' I closed the door behind me, and locked it.

He led me through a front lobby of desks to a corridor, and

pointed out the privy. 'Thank'ee', I said, and jerked my thumb back towards the entrance. 'I'll let myself out when I'm done. Lock her up after me, soon as you're passing that office again. Have to be extra careful, with this madman on the loose.'

He nodded, and lolloped off to wherever he'd been sweeping. I took the chance to use the facilities – verisimilitude's the thing in these affairs, and more importantly I knew I'd have to hole up somewhere for a good few hours – and to remove my boots. Then I cautiously came out into the corridor again, alert to where the cleaner might be, and hurried for the front door again. I unlocked it as quietly as I could: to my anxious mind it sounded like a rifle shot, but I had to hope the policeman on the other side was a little less nervy than I. Now the cleaner would find it unlocked, and conclude that as promised I had let myself out, and lock it again as I had asked, and everything would be in order.

I was already moving swiftly back through the front office, boots in hand and hunting for my hide-out. It had to be big enough to take me for a couple of hours, and it had to be something that the cleaner wouldn't want to come and clean. Almost at once I got lucky: a door in the corner of the front office proved to be a walk-in cupboard for the coats of the junior clerks, and I was in there immediately and closing the door, and settling myself into as comfortable a sitting position as I could manage.

I've had a goodly share of vigils over the years, often in darkness and occasionally in much greater discomfort than this. One learns tricks and habits to get through them without going batty or reckless.

If at a truly loose end, one keeps the bean ticking over healthily by recalling lists. Kings and Queens of England. Horses on which one won a bundle. Women.

If wanted for more murders than one can keep count of, one gives one's bean a cold shower and takes the opportunity to run through the problem.

In this case, and still, the problem of how David Sinclair had ended up dead in his shipyard. And, consequently, what I was supposed to do about it, having got myself cornered in the company offices.

Time passed. At least, I reflected, this would be the last place the police would look for me.

What upsets a man about his business?

Fraud? But why the yard? Sabotage? But what would Sinclair have known about it – and, as MacNeice and I had agreed, what was he doing on his own at the yard? What possible proof of sabotage could he have hoped to find or deal with on his own?

Of course, he wouldn't have been on his own, would he? He'd invited me to meet him there.

Was he looking for something there? Or something *missing*?

That was a fool's errand, surely. Unless someone floated the *Thunderer* off downriver in the middle of the night, Sinclair couldn't possibly hope to spot something missing, not in that vast warren, not in darkness.

Time passed. Harry Delamere, legendary *boulevardier*, spending his night in a cupboard.

In any conceivable scenario of criminality, Sinclair would have had half a dozen people in his company to talk to, and all the forces of law on his side to investigate it. This was the nation's newest battleship: the government would give him an army of policemen and detectives – they'd give him the army, indeed – to keep it protected.

Sinclair wasn't sure.

He suspected something, but he was so uncertain that he had to go to the yard to check… something.

Something at the yard that was… what? An object or a fact? There or not there?

It was still – however much I tried to make it make sense

– nonsense. MacNeice would have spotted that kind of thing long before the company lawyer, and he'd have been the man to find –

MacNeice?

I replayed our conversation.

Surely a man of MacNeice's character… But that was naive of me. Old soldier sentiment.

Was MacNeice a secret revolutionary? Was he selling off rivets on the side? Swapping out quality parts for cheap?

I couldn't believe it. By force of character and talent he'd won himself an excellent billet managing the yard; status, good salary no doubt, and probably a fair pension too. No shabby fiddle on the side could be worth jeopardising that.

And what of the mysterious Samuel Greenberg, Sinclair's frequent acquaintance in the period before his death? The Cabal of Carefree Cat-burglars, or whatever his damned shop was called. What did he mean to Sinclair? What might he know, if I could track him down?

Had he been Sinclair's *informant*? What might he have known about what was happening at the yard, and why would he have wanted to share it?

A door thumped. For a moment I thought it was my cupboard door, and for another moment – snatched from my reflections – I was about to reply.

It wasn't the cupboard door. The reconnaissance conducted by my mixed squad of valet and burlesque dancer had shown that at eight o'clock the chief clerk of the Thames Ironworks Company offices would conclude his supper in the public house round the corner, and return to the office to turf out the cleaner, check that he hadn't damaged the portraits or looted the glassware, and lock up finally for the night.

I assumed this would be a pretty brisk business, abbreviated by habit and complacency. I hoped, anyway.

I heard footsteps, and then a lock. The cleaner opening up from inside. He'd be keen to be off, surely; thirsty for a refresher with the lads and then home. He'd be waiting ready. Unless the chief clerk was particularly picky, in which case the cleaner would make sure to be caught with broom in hand trying to do an especially good job.

Muffled voices.

Come on, chaps. All ship-shape, and off home with you.

Another voice now. *Oh lord…* That would be the policeman. He'd be trying to show professional efficiency to the chief clerk; the chief clerk would be trying to show that the company was efficient enough without the police.

A miscellaneous selection of boots clumped into the outer office. They could be here for hours.

As long as they didn't feel the inexplicable need to check the coat cupboard.

Surely not. After all, only a madman would want to spend the night in a coat cupboard.

The voices got louder, a nice chorus of tenor, baritone and bass murmur. The boots got louder too.

Very slowly, I shifted my weight. My cramped muscles screeched. I reached up and carefully wrapped one hand and then the other around the door's inner handle.

The boots had stopped. Voices – no, boots again, just one tread, moving away. The clerk, perhaps, off to do a quick check of the office valuables.

Voices now, just the other side of my door. The cleaner and the policeman. *You're not the policeman who was here earlier, are you? Stopped in for a piss, he did.* The most casual, innocent enquiry could betray me.

The door rattled and instantly my muscles gripped hard. I felt the pressure from the other side for a vital second, and then I heard the cleaner distinctly: 'Just for coats. Nothing in there.'

And the pressure was released.

I let my breath out very slowly.

Silence. The shuffling of boots.

And then, a few minutes later, more movement and a door closing hard and the key turning.

25.

Something else was troubling me – besides, I mean, the indignity of being found dead of a heart attack in a clerks' closet.

Sinclair.

Up until now, I had focused on what other person's guilty secret could possibly have brought the innocent Sinclair to the yard that night, and to his death. What if I'd been looking at it the wrong way around?

I'd been searching for something suspicious. And the person behaving most suspiciously had been David Sinclair.

I gave them another quarter hour to get well clear, before I risked opening the cupboard door. Even then, I was half-expecting them all to be sitting there in the office, in a little semi-circle, policeman and cleaner and chief clerk, all waiting for me; probably Inspector bloody Bunce too.

They weren't there. Sometimes one's luck holds.

I left my boots in the cupboard, and in return borrowed a scarf that someone had helpfully forgotten in there. I turned on my electric torch, muted as best I could against my palm, and walked to the front door. I thanked the lord for parquet floor; a more old-fashioned outfit would still have had floorboards, and I'd have been tip-toeing all damned night. I stuffed the scarf along the bottom of the door. If the bobby was at his post, a crack of light under the door would set his boots agleam immediately. I had to risk the sides. Fortunately, the only natural light to this office came through an elaborate skylight: had the office given onto the street this whole nonsense would have been impossible – even the sleepiest policeman on the Holborn beat would spot me wandering around by torchlight and bumping into things.

I turned on the lights.

There was no immediate hammering at the door, alarm bell, or lightning bolt from heaven.

I took a better look at the outer office now. Half a dozen desks, each with ink stand, blotter, and plain chair pushed neatly under. Along one wall, a line of glass fronted cupboards, containing ledgers. A glazed partition and a doorway separated a smaller office space; that, presumably, was the lair from which the chief clerk ruled the juniors. Then the door into the corridor. In the corridor, I tried a couple of the other doors; they were locked.

A waist-height wooden cupboard fixed to the wall in the chief clerk's nest looked like what I was after. The keyhole suggested a modern lock, and the catch was shielded, so I didn't waste any time on it. Fortunately, having spent lavishly on the lock they'd run out of money and ideas on the hinges; these were simple, and external, and I set about the screws with my pen-knife. Not exactly a scintillating quarter-hour; but at the end of it I had the cupboard ruined and the run of the Thames Ironworks Company offices.

Which would have been splendid, had I possessed rather more time, more ease, and more of an idea what on earth I was looking for in all those offices and drawers and papers.

During my vigil in the cupboard, I had of necessity decided to narrow down the search. I would look for correspondence about the state of the company. I would look for Sinclair's particular affairs. And I would look for material about the management and supply of the yard.

A selection of larger keys proved to be for the office doors along the corridor. The Thames Ironworks being efficient sorts of chaps, each key had a neat label on the fob, which handily corresponded to the plaques on the doors: 'Chairman'; 'General Manager', 'Mr Stackhouse', 'Mr Sinclair' and so forth. All shipshape. With the light in the corridor turned off, I tried a couple of these.

These confirmed my pessimism: the Managers' offices – considerably more lavish than the space for the clerks – had windows onto the street. Through them I could see the other side of Holborn, a row of dark windows reflecting these ones – and, dimly somewhere within, the reflection of my ghostly self. The offices also had their own desks with drawers. I'd be fooling about on my hands and knees all night if I started going through that lot.

Sinclair's I had to explore, though. I crawled across it, and sat against the wall under the window looking back at the room.

Despite the impressive panelling, the big desk and the comfortable chair, it was rather a spartan place. A framed print of St Paul's; a framed print of a battleship. A pen and ink set with a battleship motif; the manufacturers of novelty nautical trinkets must have been euphoric when the Thames Ironworks Company won the contract to build the *Thunderer*.

From where I was sitting, on the floor, I could see a flat central drawer in the desk. Inside it was Sinclair's desk diary, a big leather covered business.

I think a small part of me hoped it would be a journal, page after page of detailed analysis of the crimes of the Trade Union, or a signed confession of something. But of course it was only his appointments. Times; names of people or companies.

Several times in the weeks before his death, there appeared the initials S. G., usually for an evening appointment. Samuel Greenberg, presumably. Once again, I wondered at Sinclair's relationship with the elusive Mr Greenberg and the good old Carthorse Counting Collective.

The day before his death, Sinclair had written two things in the margin of his diary. 'H.M.S. ??' Would this be His Majesty's Ship *Thunderer*, or did the question marks imply speculation about a different battleship? Then a four-digit number at in the margin of his diary. The start of a calculation?

1536.

The number was familiar.

I replaced the diary in the drawer. I had a peek in the Chairman's office, just to get a sense of how the other half live, and the Chief Cashier's, just in case he'd left anything lying around that might help Quinn with the housekeeping. The next office was 'Drawings'. Curiosity led me in.

It was double the size of any of the other offices. This was a working space. The inhabitants had less fancy furniture than their neighbours along the corridor. There was a drawing board in the corner: I guess they don't do all of their technical drawings at the head office, but they could dash one off if the mood came upon them.

And all along one wall were metal cabinets. They were out of place. Instinctively, I compared my collection of keys with the locks. None fitted; none looked even likely. In these sumptuous old-fashioned offices, these cabinets were an alien modern intrusion; and the regular inhabitants of the offices couldn't open them. More than the affairs of the chief cashier, more than the affairs of the chairman, the technical drawings of the Thames Ironworks Shipbuilding Company were close-guarded.

I returned to the cupboards I could get at. Some of the smaller keys in the Chief Clerk's cabinet let me into the glass-fronted cupboards of ledgers in the clerks' office. And here the fastidiousness of the servants of the Thames Ironworks Company, pain in the arse though it might be to a man hiding in a cupboard and waiting for the coast to clear, proved more helpful to the man ransacking their correspondence. The ledgers were all named and indexed, fully and neatly.

In twenty minutes or so I was able to skim through 'General Correspondence T.I.S.C. January – June 1910', as well as its sequel, the similarly engaging but as-yet unfinished masterpiece 'General Correspondence T.I.S.C. July – December 1910'. Even assuming I knew what to look for, I could see nothing to indicate a company in anything other than steady satisfactory health.

Two recent letters did interest me. The first was from the Chairman to the Home Secretary. It summarized recent incidents of sabotage in the Thames Ironworks yard and more or less asked the Home Secretary what he proposed to do about it. Fairly high-handed stuff: where most citizens confronted with crime had to roam the streets hoping to find a policeman (and fat chance of that they had; most of the police were now in my sitting room rummaging through my French magazines for artistic pictures), the Chairman of the Thames Ironworks Shipbuilding Company went straight to the top, and didn't mince his words when he got there.

The second letter was in similar style: take the opportunity to inform the Home Secretary that, following our recent conference, and noting your reassurances about security and the Foreign Office's on the diplomatic issues, and in spite of German and other protests, the Company will not protest against the visit of German Trade Union representatives nor impede their meeting with Company workers. And when it all goes to hell in a handcart, it'll be your fault as Government and good luck trying to scrounge campaign contributions for the next election. I paraphrase, but that was the thrust.

There was a third caught my eye, chivvying McKenna, the First Lord of the Admiralty, about getting in early with a follow-up order for Dreadnoughts beyond the *Thunderer*, but I assumed that was standard practice, like when the fellow tries to sell you a second pair of boots.

Useful colour, but nothing specific. I went looking for Sinclair's side of the business. The Chief Clerk had thoughtfully labelled one of the ledgers 'Legal Correspondence'. I had even less chance of spotting anything out of place, but I went at it dutifully. I didn't spot anything out of place. Working back through dozens of recent letters signed by David Sinclair, there wasn't one suggestion of concern; not a single legal eyebrow raised.

I was losing heart a bit. I hadn't known exactly what I was looking for when I contrived to get myself locked into the Thames Ironworks offices for the night, but I'd hoped for at least some indication of something awry. Now I felt I could spend a week in here going through ledgers and I wouldn't find a damn' thing. The night was passing, there was always the chance that the policeman outside might have a key and might feel the need to come in and put his feet up for ten minutes, and my involvement with Sinclair and his company was leaving me more and more trapped.

I ran my finger along the spines of the ledgers, looking for inspiration; or, if not inspiration, at least something to do with the yard.

I didn't find either. I went all the way to the end of the line of ledgers – these last were labelled as receipts, and such things – and back again and the yard didn't seem to have a ledger of its own. There'd been sets of ledgers on 'Supply' and 'Contracts' but it would take me months to make anything of them, even were there anything to be made. To make up for not finding what I really wanted, I had a quick look at the recent entries in 'Labour': some stuff about predicted manning needs and work-rates that might have fascinated my Trade Union pals but didn't do as much for me, and a couple of recent bits of correspondence with the Union about their regular meeting with management. Other than the sheer fatuousness of the management world-view – essentially that the workers should work harder for the same money because it was their patriotic duty as free-born Englishmen, an approach never calculated to have much impact on the impoverished Irish who probably made up most of the yard – there was nothing of note.

I turned away, and started to scan the office, wondering if there was another cupboard or cabinet somewhere.

But my subconscious, a tad more methodical and sure, stopped me. Something among the apparently trivial administrative ledgers. Something had caught my attention. Something had resonated. One of them…

The edges of the pages of one them were pale blue.

I'd seen paper that colour before. Recently.

The same blue as the slip of paper Victoria had pulled out of Sinclair's suit.

The ledger, squatter in shape than the others, was labelled 'Drawings Log'. I opened it. It was a book of receipts: all the same colour and shape as the one that had been in the dead man's pocket.

Pretty routine, presumably, but after hours of fooling around in the office it was the first link I had with what had happened in the yard, so I gave it a few more seconds' thought.

The ledger was mostly made up of stubs of paper, with perforated ends: the slips that had once attached to them had been torn off. It had been one of these slips that Sinclair had been carrying when he'd been murdered. Each stub had a serial number printed on it, and a handwritten name and date and reference number, and each had then been stamped 'Returned' with some initials and another date. There were then several stubs with the slips still attached: the stubs had the same details on them, except they hadn't been stamped and initialled; the attached slips repeated the serial number, and the name, date and reference number. The rest of the book was made up of blank stubs and slips.

The ledger was for drawings, it said. So it presumably recorded drawings that had been taken out of those metal cabinets in the Drawings room down the corridor. If they were special enough to need their own cabinets, it made sense that there'd be a system for keeping track of any that were taken out. And presumably those doing the actual building would need to consult the drawings occasionally – check they hadn't put the guns on the wrong way round, or missed off a funnel. And when such a person borrowed such a drawing, the details of both went onto both stub and receipt slip – I saw MacNeice's name a few times, but there were a couple of other names that came up much more often, presumably those responsible for particular bits of construction, or perhaps the men who couriered between office and yard. That way the office could see, from the slips that were still in the ledger, which documents were out and who had them. When the drawing was returned, the stub got stamped to close the story, and the borrower got the slip for his scrapbook and to prove that he'd handed the drawing back rather than leaving it in a tram or selling it to the Frogs.

The slip in Sinclair's pocket had had the serial number fifteen hundred and something – I remembered I'd thought of Henry VIII.

1536. The same number I'd just found written in his diary.

I skimmed through the early 1500 stubs; sure enough, serial number 1536 had Sinclair's name on it. The stub only, of course, not the slip that had once attached to it. That was in my pocket, in the bedroom of a music hall artiste in east London.

There was one inconsistency. The tearing out of the slip, presumably for Sinclair, should have meant that the document had been returned. But, uniquely, this stub hadn't been stamped 'Returned'.

Trying to make sense of this probably trivial bit of bureaucracy, I walked back down the corridor to the Drawings Room. Perhaps the handwritten serial number would tell me something.

I was standing in the open doorway of the Drawings Room when, from behind me, back down the corridor, apparently in the clerks' office, there came the sound of breaking glass.

26.

If you ever fancy a really good laugh, get Jacko Hart-Dixon to tell you about the time he was on the run from the Boers after they'd cut up the convoy he was escorting at Heilbron. Skirmishers from the Boer commando were tracking him, and he'd had to shimmy up a tree. Despite them rootling around beneath him, he was cosy enough for an hour or two – until the call of nature became increasingly urgent. Very uncomfortable moment. And then he realized he was about to sneeze. Funniest thing, the way he tells it; gets better every time, too.

Funny in hindsight, anyway. Well, old Jacko was much in my mind as I hesitated in that doorway in the Thames Ironworks Company offices. There I was, a wanted murderer on the run from the police, a conspiracy of unknown assassins, and the restive proletariat of Europe. For reasons that were increasingly elusive to me at that moment, I'd chosen to secrete myself in a set of offices that were under 24-hour police guard. And now, bizarrely, and unless I was much mistaken, someone was trying to break in after me.

Thank God I'd used the privy when I'd had the chance.

The sound of breaking glass had been short and faint. Not the crash of something heaved through a window, but a subtle, controlled sound. If my predicament prowling around the offices hadn't got me at my most alert, I mightn't have heard it at all.

I stood still; listened.

Nothing more.

It hadn't been a whole window, surely. And only a lunatic would have put a ladder up from Holborn to one of the office windows, anyway. There was no glass around the front door, nothing that one would break to try to get at the lock.

Had I disturbed something? Had one of the ledgers fallen against one of the glass fronts of the cupboards?

Above all, how alert was the policeman standing guard outside the office door?

I crept back along the corridor, towards the clerks' office. Fortunately I'd left the corridor light off, for my forays into the larger offices. Ahead of me, light from the clerks' office spilled into the corridor.

Keeping out of it as best I could, pressed into the shadows against the wall, I peered round into the office.

I couldn't see anything amiss. The glass fronted cupboards were as I'd left them.

I shifted back along the corridor a couple of feet, to get a different perspective through the open door and around the desks. Now I could see the centre of the parquet floor, and on it a few shards of glass.

My glance shifted slowly upwards, to the multi-paned skylight.

Projecting down through a hole in one of the panes, hanging as if from sky, was a boot.

As I watched, it waggled slightly – deliberately – and dislodged another few fragments of glass.

Peculiar, to say the least.

I mean to say, I was in no position to sneer at the odd things people did on rooftops – at least this chap had boots – but it seemed a particularly inept way to go about breaking in. It had to be a tricky job, balancing up there on the frame of the skylight trying to kick delicately at the glass.

He seemed to think so too, for I heard an urgent murmur. And then someone, presumably the boot-fellow's accomplice, turned on an electric torch. Its glare illuminated the shadow hanging over the skylight, foot dangling through the glass.

It also illuminated me. I backed away but the accomplice had obviously seen me: there was a shout, it startled the chap on the skylight, he swore and slipped and his whole leg plunged through the glass. That, now, was a proper shattering sound. Shards clattered down onto the parquet, the burglar was scrambling desperately up out of the skylight again, dislodging more of it as he went, and I watched from the shadows.

A hammering at the front door. 'Oi! In there! This is the police!' With the key in the chief clerk's pocket in the suburbs he couldn't get in immediately, but it had good dramatic effect. I heard hissing and scrambling from the roof above, and the intruders were gone. My curses went with them, for they'd queered my pitch properly now; I wished on them the biggest most vicious pigeons in London, and no right of parapet. From the other side of the door I heard the unmistakeable squawk of a police whistle, and then boots thundering down the stairs, as the policeman bustled off to summon reinforcements.

Where exactly was the nearest key to that door? Had it gone home with the chief clerk, or was there a spare somewhere? Would the police contemplate breaking down the door? The policeman wouldn't have to go farther than the foot of the stairs before a comrade would be running to the whistle.

There are times when the gentleman runs out of options. I did the only thing I could, under the circumstances: I locked myself in the lavatory.

Half an hour later, I heard the front door opening, and voices and boots hurrying into the outer office. They'd have plenty to look at, what with the shattered skylight, and what I'd done to the chief clerk's key cabinet. I'd dropped the keys amid the glass on the floor; the only door they couldn't open was mine.

Halfway to the privy I'd remembered my boots, and hurried back to the coat cupboard to retrieve them.

Once I was sure there were a handful of voices milling around, and once I got the sense they'd dispersed around the building doing whatever policemen do at a crime scene, I unlocked the door and slipped out into the corridor. Helmet pulled down hard, at first glance I was just one more policeman. The curious business at the skylight, and the consequent arrival of a posse of police among whom I could disappear, was a welcome improvement on my original plans, which had involved a reversal of the lavatory scenario or trying to pass myself off as the postman.

I think I passed Inspector Bunce on the stairs as, trying to not to run, I hurried down into the street and away.

27.

I'd passed my whole life more or less unaware of the existence of the Thames Ironworks Company Shipyard. Now I seemed to spend most of my time in the damned place.

My first visit, just a few nights ago, had led to my arrest for murder.

My second visit had led to my fleeing for my life from thousands of outraged dockers. But I had at least got a better feel for the lie of the land.

My third visit surely couldn't be any more chaotic. I'd a clearer idea what I was doing this time, too.

I'd slept for much of the day, with wild dreams of infinities of policemen and ledgers. With dusk I was heading east again. And once it was fully dark, midnight long struck and the streets of Poplar silent, I reversed the steps of my melodramatic exit via flat roof and girders and was soon back in the heart of the shipyard, climbing the steps to the walkway where the offices were. I'd not brought my Webley – unless you really know whom you want to shoot, a pistol's just an invitation to trouble – but I'd borrowed a few tools from the theatre.

Over my shoulder – and you may call me fanciful if you wish – I could feel the *Thunderer* looming over me, watching my strange games.

Yard Manager MacNeice's office door had a good solid lock on it, befitting the man and his importance. His office window, on the other hand, had a miserable little catch that I jimmied in something under ten seconds with a screwdriver I'd brought along.

I stopped, and turned, and gazed around the yard below me. No sign of the night-watchman, but I was hellish exposed up there. My ears strained for imagined noises; my eyes wondered at what filled the great pockets of shadow, out of reach of the few lights.

Nothing. Just the immense blackness of the battleship, darker and vaster than the night itself.

I pushed up the lower sash of the window and scrambled through. Not elegant, as such, but the watchman wasn't there to offer comment.

The Yard Manager would surely have a set of keys for the other offices, and they were probably thought more secure in the yard, and if they were in the yard they were in here, and that could only mean his desk. Wooden desks in shipyards aren't built to the finest engineering standards: the lock on the drawer was small, and my screwdriver was rather large, and I levered enough of a gap to be able to slip the catch. I was hoping not to draw attention to where I was really going, and I preferred to do damage where it just might be less obvious. There was a chance

MacNeice would think he'd left the drawer unlocked; and I was frankly past caring.

It was a goodly set of keys, on an old-fashioned gaoler's ring; very satisfying. The only key that wasn't on there was for MacNeice's own door, of course, so after another careful scan of the yard I went back out through the window onto the walkway.

Again I stopped, crouching low; again I checked. Still the silence, and the impassive *Thunderer* above me.

The drawings office, next to MacNeice's, showed the same insistence on extra security as the drawings room in the company's headquarters. Its single window, and the window panel in its door, were barred. The lock was more elaborate than the Yard Manager's. Which didn't concern me particularly, as I wasn't going through the window and had the key for the lock. But once again I felt the importance of the drawings. I slipped in, and closed the door behind me.

It was a simple enough layout. The moon, and the glimmers from the yard's minimal night-lighting, showed a bare flat desk running from under the window to the back wall, and taking up fully half the space. On an extension of the desk against the back wall was a cabinet, reaching as tall as I am. And that was about it for the decor. A working room; a place that personnel visited, but not where they were based.

I was fiddling at the cabinet with the smallest keys on the ring, when I found the door was unlocked anyway. Which was handy, because it didn't look as though MacNeice had a key for it.

Inside the cabinet was a rack, and the rack held perhaps two dozen leather tubes. Their round ends stared back at me: each was four inches or so in diameter, showing a cardboard label with a handwritten number.

For the first time in days, the world was functioning with a glorious consequence and logic. I gave thanks to the engineering brains of the shipbuilding industry. They even kept the tubes arranged in numerical order of label. It was a sight to make Quinn's heart sing: along with my sock-drawer it was about the neatest vision of administration I could think of.

The number on the pale blue slip I'd retrieved from David Sinclair's pocket was 1536. Sure enough, in the third row down, between tube numbers 1481 and 1883, was a neatly-labelled 1536. I was doing splendidly now. I had the tube out – it must have been three feet long – and on the desk and open with a rare sense of enthusiasm.

There were five large sheets of technical drawings rolled inside, and I couldn't make head or tail of them. The mystery was supposed to be becoming clear, and instead it had just got worse.

I don't consider myself exactly stupid, but these drawings apparently so significant to David Sinclair might as well have been blank, for all they meant to me. Some sort of machine or apparatus, certainly – I saw wheels; I saw wires. But the dimensions marked in the drawings suggested the real thing had the size and approximate shape of the average table or desk, which in the context of the *Thunderer* was rather a disappointment. I suppose I'd expected something vaster, or more obviously weapon-like. This looked like a lathe, or a sewing machine. What strange apparatus was this?

My blood cooled. I felt the isolation and vulnerability of my position, staring down into those pages I couldn't understand, in the office I'd broken into in a quest that now seemed futile. And what could I have expected, after all?

Perhaps it worked out for the best. Perhaps it was stepping back from the desk, trying to reopen my focus from the damned drawings, feeling the vastness of the silence around me, that meant I heard the boots outside, making their way along the walkway towards me.

28.

For a foolish instant I started to roll up the documents. That nonsense didn't last, thank God. The boots were thundering on the boards outside, and in a second I'd stuffed the cap back on the tube and shoved the tube back into the cabinet and shut the cabinet and grabbed up the documents in my arms and dived under the desk. I hunched back as far as I could and against the front wall of the office, stuffed the drawings behind me and covered my face with my arm as best I could: I had to become part of the darkness.

The boots stopped just behind me, at the window.

I've been in this sort of scenario a few times. Your hearing plays tricks – or, rather, your brain plays tricks with your hearing, amplifying things that are negligible and muffling things that are crucial. The knack is to concentrate on what could really give you away: a breath that becomes a gasp; an unconsidered movement of a finger that knocks something over.

I heard a key in the door. Unnecessary, of course. As whoever it was immediately discovered, the door had been unlocked for them. All part of the good old Delamere service. My deft scouting – shimmying through windows and breaking desks – had cleared the way for them nicely.

It was a them. The door was opened slowly, and two pairs of legs stepped in beside me.

The nearest boot was within reach of my left hand. I pulled my left hand back under my body. The papers stuffed behind me made a sound like a tree falling in a forest.

The two pairs of legs walked away down the office, to the cabinet. I heard it opened.

The unusual depth of the desk made it harder for me to be seen – but likewise harder to see anything myself. All I got was the two pairs of legs. For all I could tell, the top halves could have been a couple of Red Indian chiefs or Chinese cooks or Mr and Mrs Asquith carrying banjos. Or a pair of dancers from Jolly's, given their usual style.

I don't think they were any of those things. There's something very distinctive about the sound of liquid in a metal canister: a kind of sickly sloshing echo. I heard it now. And then I smelt something very distinctive, too. Solvent, or perhaps motor spirit. I knew what was coming next.

The opposite wall flared orange, and the two pairs of legs stepped back quickly from the cabinet. Another moment as they checked that the fire was taking properly – if a thing's worth doing, and so on – and then they were walking past me and out.

I heard the door lock. I was trying to decide whether I'd seen the end of a document tube under one of their arms when I heard another sound, similar but duller, like a second turn of the key.

29.

That was a long thirty seconds.

Four or five times during it, I checked the ring of keys in my pocket. And I watched the flickering on the wall.

How long might they wait outside, checking their handiwork? Surely not long, not with the start they'd given it, and the possibility that the night-watchman would see them up on the walkway.

After about twenty seconds I saw the flames, creeping down the cabinet to the level of the desk and into my sight-line. Now I had to risk sticking my head out from cover. As I emerged, I could feel the fire hot behind my shoulders.

They weren't waiting outside. They'd no need to, and every incentive to hurry off home, job well done, time for a whisky and soda. At last I turned to see the fire.

The front of the cabinet was a wall of flame. Near it, on the desk, they'd left the can of spirit. The heat, in that small office, was ferocious.

I turned back to the door, key ring ready. But the key wouldn't get into the lock. I swore at it: the usual clumsiness of haste. Tried more calmly. Double-checked it was the right key. Tried again.

The key really wouldn't go into the keyhole.

That second, duller sound had been my efficient companions jamming their key in the lock.

ow the security of the drawings office seemed more impressive. The lock was impenetrable. Those bars were anchored deep in the window frames. The lower half of the door was panelled; still half an inch even at its thinnest. I could feel the flames behind me. The office building was brick. It wouldn't catch fire quickly. But the walls between the offices might, and the ceiling, and the floorboards. It would be seconds before the flames spread to the wooden desk, and then they'd spread quickly along to the front wall. The heat and smoke would get me before that. Already my throat was feeling it.

I snatched the screwdriver from my pocket and went at the door hinges. There were only two of them; six screws was all. My wrist and shoulder strained; I added my other hand, felt my palm burning on the screwdriver.

Nothing. Fifteen seconds, thirty, and the first screw hadn't shifted. I coughed violently; whorls of smoke were rolling along the ceiling. I made another desperate attack on the screw, mind full of the image of the enormous navvy whose strength had driven it in years before. Nothing.

I dropped the screwdriver, gazed around me. The far end of

the drawings office was an inferno, the heat off the blazing cabinet making me flinch yards away. Beside the cabinet, the desk was starting to smoulder. The metal can of spirits gleamed in the light of the flames.

One arm shielding my face, half-crouching below the smoke, I took two long steps towards the furnace and grabbed at the can. I gasped, swore, dropped it; the metal was scalding hot. I grabbed it up again, roaring my anger at the pain. There had to be some spirits left. They couldn't have used all of it on that tiny cabinet. I could not die in this appalling way. Stumbling, retching, hissing with the pain in my hand, I dropped to the floor by the door.

There was liquid still in the can. Two-handed, with desperate focus, ignoring the pain in my fingertips, I splashed some of it on the lower panel of the door. I snatched up the sheaf of drawings from where I'd left it under the desk, screwed it back into a rough roll, and scrambled back with it along the floor to the fire. It caught instantly, and I scrambled back to the door and held the flame against the panel. As soon as the first flickers of blue appeared, I stamped out what was left of my makeshift torch before it ignited my sleeve.

I watched the flames start to spread on the inset door-panel, trying to ignore the terrific heat from behind me, breathing thin through my teeth in that increasingly rancid atmosphere.

I had to gauge this right. I wouldn't have too many second chances. Even if there was anything left in the can, and even if my torch would take a second use, my lungs wouldn't stand this much longer.

I waited, watching the flames spread across my way out. I waited, my breaths shallow and rasping and hot. I had to weaken the inset panel, that half-inch thickness of wood. If I left it seconds too long, the thicker frame of the door would catch and I'd never get through. One chance.

The panel was fully aflame. I waited. The flames started to flicker beyond the panel, onto the frame. I waited. I was alternating feeble breaths and great hacking coughs. In one spasm, I saw that the desk above my shoulder was burning fast.

Lying on my side, I took a mighty kick at the flames on the door.

The wood held. My foot throbbed with the impact, there were wisps of smoke on my trouser leg, but the wood held. I kicked again, and this time the panel smashed in a cloud of sparks.

I had successfully got my foot stuck through a burning door. I wrenched it free, leaving my shoe on the other side, and kicked frantically around the hole with my other leg. As the panel gave way and cleared my path, the flames died away too, or fell as smouldering shards of wood on the other side. In another moment I was scrambling through, with smouldering shoulders and scalded breaths.

I lay broken on the walkway. I rolled my head round, out over the edge, and took in a vast breath. It was clear and beautiful; mountain spring, the first dawn. So I took another one. Then I set off along the walkway, hands and knees. After a couple of yards I shuffled back, retrieved my shoe, and had another go.

My journey down the steps involved falling as much as walking, but the effect was the same. At the bottom I put my shoe on, looking around, wondering when the night-watchman might wake up, getting my breath back to normal. Then I staggered more or less upright and set off, aiming for the first bit of complete shadow.

In the shadow, I found the night-watchman. I tripped over him, indeed. He was lying in the darkness, stabbed to death. I was crouched by him, fingers tracing the outline of his body and the knife in his chest, when the shipyard came alive with light, and from behind there were shouts, and whistles, and boots converging on me.

30.

'Oh dear. Oh dear oh dear oh dear.'

Forget your Greek Gods and your grand sculptures. If ever humanity has produced a model of triumph, it was Inspector Ernest Bunce in that moment, sitting in his vile green interview room, gazing at me.

I wasn't much to gaze at. My clothes were a mess, my face – from the glimpse I'd caught in a mirror as I was pushed through the front room of the police station – was smeared and greasy with soot and dust, and my hands hurt like hell.

Don't tell me, *Sir* Henry: you and the night-watchman had your tea together at the Ritz, then he invited you to the shipyard to give you a tip on a horse. Like that, was it?'

I was very tired.

Old pal of yours from Eton, was he?'

The wearying sarcasm was undercut with something else. He was spitting the words out. Inspector Bunce was, I realized with some concern, steaming angry.

He gazed at me some more. 'Anything to say? Any funny remark?'

'Will this take long, Inspector?'

'A man is dead, Delamere! Not an especially remarkable man, not a gentleman. An average sort of fellow. John Tulliver; guess you didn't even know that, did you? Just another anonymous innocent, and you don't care.'

'And when I'm swinging for it, Inspector, and you're leering at your triumph, and you find out that I was innocent after all, what then?'

He leaned in close. I forced myself not to recoil from the proximity. The big, battered, pock-marked face was in alarming detail. He hissed: 'I'll take that chance.'

I won't deny I was worried. Even if they couldn't get me all the way to the gallows on coincidence and a bad habit of bumping into bodies in shipyards, the next days – weeks – Gods, months even – were going to be hellish inconvenient. Even Victoria Carteret couldn't get me out of this. And all the while, the real killers – and though I had some idea of the sort of thing they were up to now, there was so much more I had to find out – would be jogging along unhindered.

There was no point saying anything to Bunce, and he wasn't wasting any more time on me. I was in my old cell not fifteen minutes after I'd arrived at the police station.

And now my situation was even more grim. I might have been confident in escaping a murder conviction because there wasn't conclusive proof I'd done it, but not four murder convictions. Four – I thought it was four, but it was becoming hard to tell – four times I'd been on the spot, four times I'd a kind of motive, and now the police had caught me.

Five murders. I kept forgetting the fat man in the baths. Perhaps the police would never have the witnesses to tie me to that one.

And what the hell did it all mean?

The paperwork showed that David Sinclair had ordered some very special drawings to the shipyard. At the shipyard, less secure than the company offices, murderers had come to steal those drawings.

In the morning – after another uneasy night – I was woken by an argument from somewhere along the corridor. For a moment I thought it might be Quinn, trying to bully his way in with a change of smalls and a pistol hidden in a pork pie, but he wouldn't be making that kind of noise.

It went quiet for a time, someone swore again – it sounded like Inspector Bunce, for some reason – and then there were footsteps in the corridor. A policeman opened the cell, and a stranger stepped into the doorway, and considered me.

Good boots. Smart suit. Expensive-looking tie pin, elegant 'tache.

'Delamere', he said. Drawled. 'Time to go.'

I can't say I liked the look of it.

'You really don't' he said firmly, 'have any choices. Out you come.'

I didn't like the look of it at all. I stood, put my jacket on, and out I went. I didn't have any choices.

Inspector Bunce was at the front desk, and he had another go at protesting. He barely glanced at me, and when he did it was with pure hate. I didn't meet his eyes. I wasn't at all sure what was going on, I could see his fury and I guess I could understand it, and antagonising him couldn't make things any better.

We were sitting in the carriage outside – a neat affair, two horses and closed – before I said anything. 'Pardon my curiosity, but who in hell are you and where in hell are we going?'

The dapper stranger glanced at me. 'It doesn't make any difference,' he said. Then he tapped on the roof with his stick. 'And I ain't saying.' We rattled off westwards.

31.

I've never particularly liked the new Admiralty Arch – building a set of offices into an arch over the road is pure swank, and it's played havoc with the traffic going up – and I was in no mood to have my opinion improved.

The building wasn't what was making me uneasy. What was making me uneasy was that I was being marched into the building when it still wasn't finished. They'd started it a few years ago, as a tribute to the late Queen from her respectful son and heir; but now Eddie the Elephant had followed his mama across the great divide – if they'd ended up in the same department, one of them must have been sorely surprised – and the memorial arch was still a building site. The structure was done, but they were fitting the place out: there was scaffolding up against the facade, and I was marched between piles of wood that would become panelling, and the door was a temporary business of planks and cloth. No workmen; no watchman. All wrong.

I'd been bustled out of the cab too fast to do more than glimpse where I was, and to see how my escorts arranged themselves to limit my lines of escape, and then I was inside. The dandy was at my shoulder, all the way up a flight of stairs and tap-tap along a stone corridor and through a doorway. Everywhere was bare plaster, and dust, and the debris of abandoned work. Everything was a pale grey.

Except in this one room.

In this one room, amid the paleness and the dust, three elegant hard-backed chairs had been arranged in an arc. Three elegant men were sitting in them.

There was a fourth chair in front of them. I looked once round the room, and sat.

'Well, Delamere, is it? Run out of rope, have we?'

I didn't say anything – tempting though it was to suggest that if I wasn't Delamere they were going to feel pretty foolish.

The chap who'd spoken was sitting in the centre: a stately, solid worthy in his forties, formal suit, stiff collar, I guessed official rather than commercial, and sure of his own importance.

The second, to the left, was older: a gaunt and weathered ancient, somehow so grey that he hardly seemed there.

The only good news was number three. It was Hugh Stackhouse – the shipping company director who'd given me a second cigarette and put me onto manager MacNeice at the Thames Ironworks yard.

'Been having rather a lively time of it, have we?' The politico again.

I still didn't answer him. I considered each of the other two, and nodded to them.

'What d'you think you've been playing at?'

Now I looked at him again. 'First, trying to keep myself alive. Second, trying to work out what in hell's happening at that shipyard.' I leaned forwards towards the big cheese. 'What are you playing at?'

He didn't like it. He looked a little more pink and stuffed, and said nothing. Stackhouse was clearly too junior in this company to speak. It was the old man who answered me at last. 'Trying to work out what in hell's happening at that shipyard, Sir Henry,' he said, and the voice was as dusty as the speaker. 'On your first point, I confess that we are… indifferent, to whether you stay alive.' There was a lightness in the words, as if he wasn't so concerned about this world.

It was honest enough, anyway.

I was gazing at the big cheese in the middle. 'You're properly worried, aren't you?' I said.

'I beg your pardon?' I might have accused him of robbing the collection box or pushing urchins off Westminster Bridge for fun.

'Sir… Percy something. Savary. Sir Percy Savary.'

Now he looked as if I'd caught him red-handed. 'I hardly think—'

'Sometimes I trip over the political pages on the way to the racing; seen your face. Don't worry, Savary. The police and the press think I'm a murderer and a scoundrel; they'll hardly believe me if I tell them I'm having secret meetings with the most powerful fixer in London, will they?'

He still didn't like it.

'But I should probably be flattered, shouldn't I? Or worried. If the man who guards the stability of the Government suddenly takes an interest in one errant baronet. For you to take a hand, and to dirty it with me, this business must be something.' I sat back. The chair creaked. 'So what do you want?'

Savary glowered at me. 'We want your co-operation on the business at the yard.' He was more comfortable making demands.

'And in return?'

The old man, of course: 'Work with us on your second objective, and perhaps we can make things a little easier for you on the first.'

'And if I refuse?'

'The door is open, Delamere.' Savary. 'All London is yours. Somewhere out there are the police, and apparently they're the least of your troubles. Good luck trying to claim this meeting ever happened. We'll watch the chase with interest.'

I considered him, without warmth. 'A wash', I said. 'Something to eat. A drink.'

32.

'Know much about ship-building, Delamere?' A fatuous question, obviously. 'After your recent experiences?'

I waited. Dousing my head in cold water and bolting a sandwich had left me significantly livelier, but hardly jovial.

Sir Percy Savary leaned forwards. 'It's a war in itself!'

This rather startling statement made, he sat back, inviting me to consider the grandeur of his pronouncement.

I considered it rather foolish, but I was trying to behave myself so didn't say so. He gestured impatiently to Stackhouse.

'It's like this, Delamere. A battleship is actually a thousand different technologies, synchronised; brought together and co-ordinated. About the most complex organism you can imagine, even before you start trying to organize the men to run it. And in every one of those thousand technological areas – the engines, the quality of the oil, the umpteen different scientific skills that make an effective gun – there is a race for progress.' I waited; it was clear enough. 'A competition. We are temporarily strong in one; one of our rivals is temporarily strong in the other. By and large, everyone is aware of new technological developments. But a small improvement can have a decisive impact on the overall performance of a battleship taken as a whole machine. Anything from a new material or shape for the propellers, to the modernisation of the fire-control table.'

Now it wasn't clear enough. 'The what?' I said.

Savary looked pretty scornful – clearly, any truly patriotic Englishman should be an expert on this particular piece of furniture – but he wasn't the sort to bother with details himself. He gestured impatiently to Stackhouse.

I took another sip of brandy. It was poor stuff, but it did.

Stackhouse took a moment to compose an answer fit for those too imbecilic to be up to date in naval warfare – or for those still too disreputable to be trusted with specifics. 'The capacity of modern naval guns makes it possible to throw a shell many miles. But that, plus the speed of modern ships, makes it dashed hard to aim.' His was a good voice for explanations: steady and sensible. 'You're trying to hit a moving target from a moving base, at long distance. You're having to compute the interaction of three different moving bodies: your ship, the enemy ship, and the shell on its parabolic trajectory between them.' Sir Percy Savary's face twisted faintly: he could make or break a Cabinet Minister's career with a single telegram, but he didn't know what was going on here and he didn't like it. 'A fire-control table – and its base has the size and look of the average table – is a mechanical calculating device that does the mathematics for you. You set a couple of dials to reflect the course and speed of your target, and your own, and it tells you how to aim. Rather an extraordinary business: an apparatus more capable than the human brain.'

Well now, I was thinking, maybe Delamere ain't so ignorant after all.

But even if I'd been tempted to brag, Sir Percy cut in first: 'These machines are one of the areas where Britain has a considerable edge, I think I'm right in saying.' He half inclined his head towards Stackhouse, but Stackhouse was too sensible to suggest otherwise. 'We're well ahead. And we intend to stay that way.'

He stopped. Apparently under the impression that he was addressing a public meeting, he seemed to feel this was an adequate conclusion.

'Rule Britannia', I said heartily, and I think I saw the old man suppressing a smile.

Stackhouse hurried on. 'Naturally we're very nervous about any attempt to slow our progress. If we lose our advantage in any one area, then the relative strengths of our rivals in other areas – explosive propulsion, for example, or the technology of armour – become even more troubling.' I nodded.

'The preponderant strength of our Navy, Delamere,' – Sir Percy Savary was still on his public platform – 'its power not only to defeat the enemy but to so overawe him that he dare not dream of defying us, neither on the high seas nor in the farthest Asian inlet, lies partly in its true strength, but more in the reputation of its strength.'

I nodded again. My radical comrades like Raikes would have proposed a simpler approach, and rather cheaper, but within the mad logic of imperial rivalry this all made sense.

I yawned, and pretended to try to hide it.

Stackhouse politely pushed on. 'The recent trouble at the yard – the stoppages and so forth – is beginning to look like something even more serious. The murder of poor Sinclair. The burning of the drawings room last night. It's as if someone wants the *Thunderer* badly delayed.'

Savary piped up. 'There have been a series of incidents at or around factories involved in the manufacture of components for our Dreadnoughts.'

'A bit of industrial espionage is normal form, I should say.' It was the old man. He spoke like it was normal form for him. 'Any of three of four countries might be up to it, including those we consider allies.'

'And no doubt we're doing it to them', I said.

The old man merely smiled. Sir Percy was ploughing on, full of alarm. 'We've reports over recent weeks of various suspicious persons lurking around the Thames Ironworks yard.'

'Besides yourself', the old man said pleasantly. I smiled back.

'Then, two nights ago,' – Savary leaned in confidentially – 'there was a break-in at the Thames Ironworks offices on Holborn.'

'Gosh', I said. 'What effrontery.'

'Damned outrageous', Savary said. I saw the old man considering me curiously.

'Anything taken?' I said.

They looked at each other. Stackhouse was clearly uncomfortable. Presumably pretty embarrassing to convince the nation you can be trusted to build a battleship and then fail to manage your front door properly. Eventually, the old man said: 'We're not quite sure.' A lie, presumably. 'They made rather a mess of the place. And now the diaries of Sinclair and a couple of his colleagues can't be found.'

Savary said: 'The police are closing in.'

I hurried on. 'So the question, then, is: who are the "they" you keep talking about?'

The old man again: 'We were rather hoping, Sir Henry, that

after your recent investigations and adventures you'd be able to tell us.'

33.

I took a large mouthful of brandy.

'Let me start by offering you two possibilities. Possibility number one: I am some kind of traitor or lunatic, who murdered David Sinclair as the prelude to a trail of death and chaos over the last few days. Possibility number two: I am not.' I paused, to try to make possibility number two sound more weighty. 'As soon as you decide to accept number two–'

'Temporarily.'

'All I can ask. As soon as you consider possibility number two, then certain points become clear.' I paused, to recollect and arrange the conclusions I had drawn in the cupboard at the Thames Ironworks offices, in the cell last night, and at various other occasions. 'Firstly, we are speaking of a substantial and organized group, with resolve and resources. I have met a few of them. There must be more, in order to trail me as they have. They are well-informed and well-supplied. Secondly, they are linked to a series of crimes. I take it for granted that Sinclair's murder is part of this. They have attacked me in my rooms and then in a bath-house. One of the men involved in that attack was also on the scene of the murder of the moderate union leader Merridew, and then tried to kill me in the theatre. Then this, er, appalling business of the break-in at the Thames Ironworks offices, and the attack at the shipyard last night.' I checked. The three of them were watching me, considering. I wondered how much they were still debating between possibilities numbers one and two. 'Finally,' I said, 'they are somehow connected with the group of international trades union delegates visiting England at the moment.'

Three pairs of eyes widened, and very satisfying it was.

'Anarchists!' said Savary. Stackhouse looked worried. The old man was frowning; perhaps his grasp of labour politics was a little sharper than the grandee.

'There were two attacks on me in one day. At the time it seemed rather remarkable; I'm more used to it now. Anyway, the first of them, in my rooms, was carefully planned to look like suicide. I was suspected – at that point', I added heavily, '– of the murder of Sinclair, and I'd have been found with all appearances of having put a bullet through my brain. In one elegant *coup* they'd have tidied up both Sinclair's death and any possibility that I had learned anything from it, and no-one would ask any more questions. Later that day they tried again, in the bath-house, and this time they made no attempt to stage something plausible.'

I still had their attention, no doubt about it. 'So what changed? They must have worried that I'd have learned something from the chap in my rooms. That – assuming I was seconds from death – he might have let slip some clue as to his real purpose.' The three of them were waiting. 'He didn't so much, but he was clearly a foreigner and he did make a reference that made me think he was associated with the trades unionists who were marching that day. One of the foreign visitors was with the British labour man, Raikes, when Merridew was killed, and one of the killers from the bath-house was there too. And they seem to be able to come and go at the Thames Ironworks yard pretty freely.'

Sir Percy Savary was nodding heavily. Nice when one's prejudices are confirmed. 'And these outrages – at the offices, and at the yard – all designed to interrupt the work on our new battleship.' He made it sound like he was paying for it out of his own pocket. 'Hell of a mess, Delamere. And you were there – what, investigating, were you? – at the same time as these ruffians were attacking the offices at the shipyard last night. Stackhouse, what is the effect of the destruction at the yard?'

'To be honest, sir, it's not that bad. We lost a couple of dozen sets of technical drawings, but there are duplicates for them. The damage to the offices looks dramatic, but it shouldn't slow us down too much.'

The old man had woken up again. 'There is a more worrying possibility', he said softly. Savary paid attention to him; that told me something.

The old man had also spotted immediately what I'd had to learn painfully: the real reason for the attack on the Drawings Office at the yard. 'Not to destroy. Rather to cover the theft of something.'

'Well now,' I began. Delamere the intrepid – intervention saves the Empire; about time I made myself popular with the authorities. But then I felt that increasingly familiar chill of concern in my blood.

This was all very cosy, but they still weren't convinced by me. And the whole show was clearly nine kinds of mess. And if, as seemed entirely likely, it ended badly they'd be looking for a scapegoat. And who better than the man who, as well as tripping over every corpse, had been in the drawings office when it burned? Not to mention – and I didn't plan to – the business at the head office.

They were all three looking at me expectantly.

'What's the plan, then?' I asked, feebly.

It seemed they didn't have a plan.

Predictably, it was the old man who spoke first. 'We have now, I understand, taken precautions to safeguard the offices and the yard.'

Sir Percy jumped in. 'Detectives guarding the Thames

Ironworks head offices around the clock, and the offices of other critical manufacturers likewise. Extra guard on drawings and other confidential material.' Stackhouse nodded. 'Extra guards at the shipyard, and a platoon of soldiers from Woolwich ready to deploy in the event of trouble.'

'Most impressive. But we have still to identify the responsible persons.' The old man looked at me. 'There's to be a grand meeting of British trades union representatives with their foreign guests this weekend, in Birmingham. Part of the visitors' tour of the country. On the fringes of the Birmingham meeting, some of the more presentable of the foreigners will participate in a conference, and a couple of them will be invited to a dinner given by the President of the British Federation of Industrial Development. He'll have quite a number of government and diplomatic guests at his country house for the occasion.' Again the pale, penetrating gaze at me. 'Assuming we can make you presentable again, Sir Henry, I was thinking that we might get you an invitation to the house party, and let you sniff around the foreigners and see if you recognize any of them.

'Delighted,' I said, not feeling very delighted. 'Who is this Federation President?'

'No doubts there!' Sir Percy said jovially. 'There's no man more respected. It's Magnus, Lord Aysgarth.'

34.

My public and official reputations were still pretty ropey, not to mention my reputation with the almost-father-in-law whose house party I was going to crash. But I badly needed comfort and relaxation, and my club was the place to get them. My reputation's always been ropey there anyway. And on the plus side, the inbred intellects of most of the members were incapable of reading more than the sporting pages, and the few others would be too polite to mention my recent public notoriety.

At about ten in the evening I was enjoying a gentle hour of whist, a second cigar and some barley water. I don't drink when I gamble; partly it keeps the head clear, mainly it annoys the hell out of the opposition.

There was a murmur in my ear: 'A person is calling for you, Sir Henry.'

I finished the hand, wondering who it might be. The 'person' was meaningful: the staff at the club have the nicest sense of who's a gent and who ain't.

Whatever kind of person he was, he was certainly calling for me. As soon as I got to the top of the stairs, his voice was roaring up out of the lobby and shaking the statues.

'Delamere!'

For a moment I hesitated. Was just one evening without confrontation really so difficult?

'Delamere! I see you!'

It was Inspector Bunce.

I sighed, and started down the stairs.

'What the hell are you playing at, Delamere?'

Weatherby the doorman was trying to catch hold of this obvious anarchist or lunatic and eject him, and Bunce wasn't having it, and staff reinforcements were hurrying to the scene, and some of the members were getting interested too.

'Delamere, if you think you can – Get your hands off me, will you! – Delamere, you're an arrogant, patronising – If you even think about touching me, boy… I'll take you all on, then! I'll leave this place in rubble!'

More doors were opening. 'Sir Henry–' I had visions of a pitched battle between a squad of policemen and the frock-coated ancients of the Club staff here in the lobby.

'Delamere, if you can't control your guests, you shouldn't–'

'Bugger off Tarlton, would you? You belong in prison more than anyone.'

'I'm not his damned guest!'

'If you'll just step this–'

'Oldster, if you grab my arm one more time – Delamere, what did you say to the Home Office?'

'There are rules about–'

'Sir Henry, this gentleman–'

'I'm no damned gentleman!'

'Well that's obvious! Delamere, he shouldn't be at the front–'

'Any more discourtesy from you, Tarlton, and I'll put you in the river. He's my guest.'

'No I am not!'

'The Committee will hear of this, Delamere!'

'My regards to the Committee, but they couldn't agree on a trip to the privy.' I'd reached the ground floor, and was face-to-face with a hot and dishevelled Bunce. 'Let go of him, would you please Weatherby? Thank'ee. The gentleman is here at my wish.'

'I told you, I'm no–'

'Getting into the Club and getting out depend on whom you know, Inspector. Just like Wapping police station, though the food's a bit better there.' I considered the face a moment: proud, and angry. 'Will you take a drink?'

'Here? No. From you? Never.'

'You clearly have something to say to me. And I've one or two things to say to you. I don't propose to conduct the exchange like a couple of Smithfield porters on a spree.'

In the Blue Posts round the corner, we sat opposite each other over a pair of whiskies.

'Guess I've queered your pitch with your Club,' he said, with a suggestion of malice.

'They actually kicked me out a few weeks back. I forget why.'

'Yet you still go and they still tolerate you.'

'Clubland is like the British justice system, Inspector, and the faeries at the end of the garden. As soon as people stop believing in the thing, it ceases to exist. Cheers.'

'You're trying to call a truce, is that it?'

'No.'

'You're trying to draw me off.'

'No.'

'You want to work together somehow.'

'Emphatically no.'

'Late this afternoon I was hauled in by the Assistant Commissioner. The Ass-ist-ant Co-mmissioner. That meant it had to be my knighthood, because if they were kicking me out they'd use someone much more junior.' The words were spat out in his usual South London rasp. 'He recited my many failures in this case, very helpful, very constructive, disappointment to the Force and so on and so forth, Bunce to be taken off the case and put to harassing tarts or checking bicycles where he can't do any harm.' I was watching carefully. As in our previous conversation, in the middle of the night when he'd arrested me in the shipyard for the second time, Bunce's sarcasm was undercut by clear anger. 'But, he said, lucky fellow that I am, I am not being taken off the case. Oh no. Because, Sir Henry ber-loody Delamere himself, God bless him for a noble and public-spirited soul, has personally requested that I be kept on. Christ I hate the British system.'

I nodded.

'To hell with you, Delamere.'

'Likewise, Inspector.'

It served as a more appropriate toast, and at last he drank.

'Bunce, believe me when I say that I'd be delighted if I'd never met you, and I'm sure the feeling's mutual. I've been wishing you under an omnibus all week. But I need you.' He looked revolted, and took another mouthful of whisky. 'That bunch of politicians or officials or whatever they are – a set of men who seem to have more perspective than you, Bunce, but whom I trust even less – they've decided that for now I'm better inside the tent pissing out, than outside in. As part of the deal, they did, indeed, offer to muzzle you. I refused, damned tempting though it was. Two reasons:'

He was watching dubiously.

'One. Holding the unfashionable belief that I am innocent, I'm determined to find the real murderer of David Sinclair. Holding the unfashionable belief that you're competent, I'm judging that your damned stubbornness and perseverance might be rather useful to my aim. Secondly,' – I leaned in – 'when I do find the real killers, I want you there, so you know the truth and know I'm innocent for sure; and know how much of a pain in the arse you've been.'

A grim smile spread over his face.

'So this isn't some foul posho fellowship thing, all pally-wally and have another cocktail old chap?'

'It is not.'

'You're not expecting me to be grateful or anything?'

'I am not.'

'You don't mind that I still think you're a wrong'un and want to see you locked up?'

'I do not.'

'Well that's all right then.'

35.

The train journey heading out of London was a useful opportunity for a council of war.

We were three, in a First Class Compartment. I can't afford First Class, but can't abide elbows and cheap cigarette smoke in my face either, so usually force myself to pay the extra; strange how one's more tolerant of roughing it when abroad.

It was Bliss's first time in First Class, as she kept reminding us.

Quinn's normally in Third, with the convicts and the livestock, because once I've splashed out for myself I definitely can't afford First Class. But Bliss wasn't going to approve of that, and I felt I could do with his steadiness and sense. And given what I'd seen of the forces ranged against it, the revolution would probably triumph sooner rather than later and I was feeling I should get in a good word for myself before the blade fell. Quinn was looking pretty comfortable in the opposite corner, and with him there I had to behave and keep my feet off the seats.

I hadn't told the Government chaps that I was bringing Bliss along for the excursion.

Nothing to do with her *demi-mondaine* reputation. That was about the single biggest point in her favour, as far as I was concerned. No, something was far wrong at the heart of this business, and I felt that the fewer people who knew who she was, and what she'd seen and heard in that night, the better. But if I could bring her along relatively unnoticed, perhaps she'd recognize someone.

On reflection, there was quite a lot I hadn't told the Government chaps. Bliss, and her encounter with the mysterious figure in the carriage while I was undergoing my trials in the bowels of Jolly's Theatre. Quite a few of the details of my trials in the bowels of Jolly's theatre. Exactly what I'd been doing in the shipyard. And of course anything about breaking into the Thames Ironworks offices. Oh – and having done most of this in fancy dress; one has one's pride.

It was vaguely reassuring to feel that I was playing for the home team again. But the reality was that I was still, to the official perspective, guilty of diverse mischiefs and as soon as they got impatient they'd be reaching for me. And wouldn't Inspector Bunce be pleased?

The narrow brown brick canyons of north-west London housebacks eventually released us. Soon enough we were in the pleasant countryside of the Chilterns, the easy hills and the cattle and the freshly cut wheat fields.

In the course of the journey, I talked through the whole business: from the mysterious death in the shipyard to… well, to the next mysterious death in the shipyard. The murder of Sinclair to the murder of the night-watchman. And I rehearsed my speculations about Sinclair before his death.

I'd hoped that this logical re-examination of the business, on top of a good breakfast and with a bit of fresh air coming in through the train window, would prompt some new clarity. It didn't.

Half-way through, Quinn shifted as if to speak, and then let me talk myself out. They both waited expectantly for more. I didn't have any more. 'Something to add, Quinn?' I said at last.

'Something to add, sir. Been waiting to tell you. That friend of Mr Sinclair's – the foreign gentleman, Mr Samuel Greenberg.'

'Ah yes. The Corduroy Cloth Co-operative.' I certainly hadn't forgotten him. Sinclair's mysterious friend, and probably my best chance of learning Sinclair's secret. 'Tracked him down?'

'I've been back and forth to his offices, and they're still shut up. And I finally got hold of his landlady.' He shook his head. 'It's been several days, sir. He's proper disappeared.'

36.

Magnus Carteret, Lord Aysgarth, has more houses than I do rooms. And he doesn't like seeing me in any of them. His place at Shulstoke is his main country residence, a vast Regency barracks with a couple of unwise add-ons; sort of thing people built while waiting for the invention of the ironclad battleship. With Victoria at his shoulder, he welcomed us in the hall – a room bigger than any house I've ever had.

I say he welcomed us. It would have been inconceivable to him not to receive a guest with basic courtesy. The Lords Aysgarth have been dispensing haughty hospitality for umpteen centuries – usually while rustling their guests' sheep round the back or shifting boundary markers. It's what's made them the Lords Aysgarth. But, a man barely civil even to his oldest friends, he wasn't exactly jovial at my arrival. Someone significant – Sir Percy Savary, or someone even more distinguished – had quietly explained to him that Delamere was temporarily on the side of the angels and that it was in the national interest – his patriotic duty – to tolerate me on the premises for a night or two. He couldn't have been less chirpy if the King had ordered him to walk naked to Paris and miss the shooting season in the process. I've got used to it, and the brief period when his attitude meant anything to me has long passed.

'Delamere', he said, as if noticing that the drains had backed up.

'Thank you, sir,' I replied. I can do courtesy too. The Delameres only ever stole enough cattle for that night's dinner; that's the difference between us.

He grunted. Miserable old sod. After all, he ought to have been grateful to me for not marrying his beloved daughter.

He thawed a degree or two when his eyes turned to Bliss. He may be one hundred and fifty and a sour inbred ogre, but his male instincts are sound enough. 'Lord Aysgarth, let me present Miss Angela Joy,' I said. 'We just met on the train.' He thawed even more when he heard that she wasn't anything to do with me. 'Writing a book, you know.'

To get Bliss onto the guest list I'd managed some sleight of hand between Victoria and the Home Office, and neither really knew who she was or why she was there. There'd be dozens of guests in the house this weekend, and no one – least of all Lord Aysgarth – knew everyone.

'Oh,' Aysgarth said. It passed for rapture, by his standards. 'Writer, eh?' He didn't understand women who did things.

Bliss had taken the offered hand, and held it, and contrived a rather breathless curtsey. It was masterly. 'A hobby, really,' she said. 'The effect of modern labour relations on the family.' Aysgarth was nodding vaguely now. Hobbies, and families, were much more the sort of thing for women. 'Hutchinson's asked me to write something accessible for them, and one likes to do one's bit in these unsettled times. Lord Aysgarth, you're rather an extraordinary man, bringing together such a unique and important gathering of people from across the continent.'

Victoria was watching this performance with some interest. I moved on to greet her, with our standard brusque affection. Bliss followed, and there was the usual moment one gets when two attractive women meet for the first time, and sort of size each other up, and you wonder if the world might just explode.

Beyond them – across the hall, not more than half a mile off – I saw two other figures, observing. Other guests, presumably. One of them might have been English, a thinnish chap dressed in country standard. The other, a contrast in every way, I suspected wasn't: a vast person in a vast and unseasonal three-piece, with a vast bald head on top.

My focus shifted back to the ladies. The world had survived – surprisingly, in my company – and we were in.

37.

I've seen chaos in my time: the great bazaar in Constantinople; the retreat after Magersfontein; Frenchmen trying to put up a tent. They had nothing on the collected trade unionists, radical philosophers and anarchists of Europe on their annual ice-cream-and-conspiracy jamboree to Birmingham.

I hadn't known Birmingham at all – I tend to avoid cities and, as much as possible, Britain – but they've done a damned impressive job of it. Grown ten-fold in the last century – Bliss had read this from a guide book during our train journey – and there's solid business prosperity wherever you look.

Raikes's Army had felt the need for a parade, and the city had agreed. Presumably it was a good chance to show off their grandeur, and to get a bit of credit with the workers whose work had paid for it. And because Birmingham was determined to show its modernity, they had laid on motor cars for all the foreign delegations. The parade started up at the Law Courts building, where they'd have been better finishing. It's one of the jewels of the new city apparently, a great red fairy castle of a building, and when I wandered up to have a look there was an enormous scrum of bewildered radicals outside. They were milling around the cars, and joking a bit, and arguing a bit, and flustered union officials were pushing through the mob with handfuls of paper shouting for their lost Luxembourgers or ticking off the Germans for trying to get too many people into a 40/50 Rolls or swearing at the French for refusing to get into one.

Eventually, everyone was squeezed in, and the convoy set off down Corporation Street. That's another of the wonders of the city: they cleared acres of slums to create it, and now it's a grand boulevard of Edwardian splendour: gothic facades and high-end ladies' underwear shops wherever you look. What they haven't yet done is work out how to fit in all the different kinds of traffic, and the addition of a couple of dozen motor carriages over-filled with excitable foreigners brought the whole business to a standstill. Fifty yards along there were two cars and a tram jammed into space enough for one of them, because the French delegation had decided that the universal promotion of the rights of the worker didn't extend to letting a carful of Germans in ahead of them, and in the middle of Old Square I found half a dozen Swiss sitting haughtily in a Darracq while their chauffeur wrestled with the driver of a milk cart. Between the unfamiliar motor vehicles, their increasingly grumpy local drivers, the delegations shouting bright ideas from the back seats in any of a dozen languages as yet another tram threatened to crush them, the regular traffic of horse or foot, and the throng of local workers who'd wanted to escort the foreigners the whole business was more like the charge of the Light Brigade. Anarchy it may well have been. A new order it was not.

Then, miraculously, all was transformed into order. They got down past the railway station and round into Victoria Square. And there the motor vehicles stopped, crashed or blew up in one great scrum and, with the old Queen gazing down pretty grimly from her plinth, everyone filed into the Town Hall – a grand Roman-looking business. Suddenly they were quiet, and dignified. The delegations stood in murmuring groups, exchanged polite greetings across the hallways, waited their turn to be guided into the main chamber.

And I watched them all. A small part of my brain was guessing nationality, from face and dress and speech. It was a pretty rich mix: the richer skins of Spaniards and Italians; distinctive collars that meant French and jackets that meant Austrian; accents Latin, Teutonic and Slav. One tight-bunched handful of men passed in front of me like a beacon, tall and pale and blond: presumably Scandinavians, or perhaps the Latvians someone had mentioned.

I went pretty carefully. I didn't think I was in danger here, not in such a public place and event. But I didn't want to cause trouble unnecessarily. And as I lurked in stairwells and shadows, I was also looking out for any of the diverse groups who might have it in for me. There were men here outraged because they thought I'd murdered their employer. I was pretty sure there were men here vengeful because I'd killed one or two of their number during the bizarre goings-on of recent days. There might be some fired up enough to have a go at me because I represent the oppressor class. There was probably the chap I'd knocked down during the street rally, fancying he had unfinished business.

I was looking for familiar faces – anyone involved in the diverse recent attempts to do me mischief, whose background and associations I could then investigate – and trying to spot anything that suggested this extraordinary gathering was more than what it claimed to be. I wouldn't have a better opportunity: all of them here on display, conspiring with each other in the corridors and on best behaviour. It was a splendid plan, as long as I saw my men, and the various unhappy parties didn't see me.

And at that moment I bumped into the appalling Raikes, and I knew that the sudden order of this building was his doing, his will.

I literally bumped into him. I'd been watching one of the lobbies from the shadows and elevation of a staircase, and as the lobby emptied into the main chamber I stepped down after them and hit someone coming round the corner. We each took a step back, started to offer a token apology, and then recognized the other.

An eerie gleam came into his eyes as he saw me, and he actually smiled. '*Sir* Henry Delamere,' he said, soft level sneer, and somehow the smile was hungry. 'Truly your interest in the plight of the international worker is remarkable.'

I contrived a smile in return. 'If you're involved, Raikes, they're certainly in bad trouble.' I glanced at the scene around us. 'You put on a good show. I don't suppose there's any chance you'd be persuaded to become a British Army staff officer after all.'

'A pretty compliment, Delamere, coming from you. But thank you, I have a greater movement to lead, with a nobler purpose.'

'Jolly good. Well, you'd better not let me hold you up.'

Again the thin dead smile, and very slightly he shook his head.

We each turned away at the same moment, and I found myself confronted by half a dozen men. Some looked like British workers. A couple were clearly foreign. Now they were standing in a semi-circle, facing me.

Then from behind me, there was a familiar voice. 'If only you'd something to say to the workers of the world, Delamere, you'd find these occasions less fraught.'

It was Raikes again. I didn't bother turning. If he wanted to crow while his heavies beat me to death, I wasn't going to give him the satisfaction of an appeal. My eyes continued to move slowly between the men in front of me, gauging them, looking for the intent, watching for the first movement.

'Mr Delamere is a man of action, brothers.' His voice was nearer behind me. 'Not a philosopher, as we.' Their expressions didn't pick up his sneer.

And fought fairer for a better cause, damn' you all, I was thinking, but I knew it wouldn't mean anything to them; and it probably wasn't true.

You learn to read the faces on sporting occasions like this. The professional toughs about to thrash you on instruction, they're hard to read: the expressions don't change much, and you can only watch for the slight flexing of the shoulders, the adjustment of balance. Nervy amateurs and angry men, you'll see what's about to happen in their eyes.

There was a short solid chap second from right: I'd clout him first. Put down one of the professionals, and you make the amateurs think twice as well as evening the odds. And sending that one sprawling would slow his neighbour down too, and for a moment I'd only have to worry about my left.

I made it obvious that I was looking to the left, while out of the corner of my eye I checked where his throat was.

'You'd better come along, Delamere,' Raikes said. Come along where? 'Mr Delamere is my guest, brothers.'

Now I half turned, trying to read the cold face, while keeping an eye on the mob. What the hell was he talking about?

Then a bit of light came into his face, an idea. 'In fact, I'd be honoured if you'd join me on the platform.' He was amused now. He looked like a snake about to strike. 'You might say a few words to our General Assembly.'

38.

Thus it was that the latest and probably the last of the Delameres, a family of some distinction back in the day, found himself an honoured guest on the platform at an international convention of revolutionaries.

Probably the Delamere stubbornness running true to form, I suppose. We have, on the whole, been on the wrong side of every single fight in British history. Whenever there was a misguided, muddle-headed, futile rebellion during the last thousand odd years, there was a Delamere, sitting proud on a borrowed horse and waving the family sword and angry about something. Whenever there was a shrewd, well-led, successful rebellion, the Delamere was off sick, or sulking in his tent, or visiting his tailor. I exclude a couple of occasions when the Delamere of the day contrived to be on both sides. Good gamblers, in our way.

Mind you, it looked like I might have gone against tradition and backed the winner this time. The global fraternity of Down-With-The-Delameres were a serious outfit.

I've not much experience of these speechy occasions; being a deeds rather than words sort of chap, I tend to avoid. But in my thirty-something years I've not heard or read a single solitary political speech worth a damn. These fellows, though, they knew what they were about. Speaker after speaker spoke briefly, respectfully, logically, and very earnestly. Not a one had been to a school you've heard of, but every one intelligent and articulate.

And I had the same uneasy sense I'd had when marching with the fraternal mob towards the Thames Ironworks shipyard, shortly before the fraternal mob tried to lynch me. There was a real, deep anger in this hall. Not idiot's anger, incoherent or plain drunk. Not affronted anger, cheap pride and silly dignity. No, this was a carefully-considered, carefully-nurtured anger. It understood itself, and it had purpose.

I thought of my club companions the previous evening. I thought of Aysgarth and his houseful of gentlefolk. Against Raikes and his army of relentless thinkers, they wouldn't stand a chance.

And so once again – as I sat on the platform feeling somewhat exposed, and watching the line of neat thoughtful speakers delivering their quietly effective destructions of the current social structure, of the price/wage relation, of the arrangement of European powers, of organized religion, of contemporary gender identities, and of much else that I didn't really follow – I wondered why on earth these lads were bothering to interfere with a battleship. One Dreadnought more or less wasn't going to stop them, not even if the Navy started shelling libraries, working men's clubs and grammar schools full-time. And I couldn't for the life of me see what kind of a threat David Sinclair could have been to them, or to any plan they might have.

My mind was distracted with this, when I realized that the

whole hall was staring at me.

Last time this had happened I'd had to pull my revolver and take to the rooftops. I was unarmed now, and all of my exits were blocked by sturdy philosophers. So, a bit of a jolt.

'… gained a certain notoriety,' Raikes was saying in his usual nasal drawl, presumably about me; impertinent sod. 'And in many ways precisely the enemy of all that we stand for, the enemy of true equality and the enemy of the working person's rights and the enemy of a fair and fairly-earned wage.' *I fought off waves of Boer cavalry for six shillings a day*, I was thinking, *so less of your cheek*. But then Raikes probably didn't consider that proper work and, looking at the faces in the hall during the speeches, I'd guessed that a few of them must have worn the khaki themselves. And here they were.

'But ours is not a spiteful movement, brothers and sisters.' *Tell that to poor Sinclair*, I thought. 'The upheaval in society, which we all seek, to which we have all devoted ourselves, it will be achieved as much by the patient nobility of education and the earnest passion of persuasion, as by the regrettable necessity of force.' There was a burst of applause at this little homily. 'He has the courtesy to present himself here alone, as our guest. As our guest, accordingly, I have the honour in your name to welcome him. Henry Delamere, would you *gratify* us with a few words?' And he turned to me and he actually grinned; evil little so-and-so.

Stubborn, the Delameres, as I say. Not inclined to back down. I stood. I walked slowly to the lectern. I looked at Raikes for a long moment, holding his eyes until they flickered. Then I turned and took in the enormity of that audience. God knew how many hundreds of them, mostly as surprised as I was to find me there, and at least as unhappy about it.

I had to address my company of infantry, before they made the bayonet charge at Graspan. I once talked a bunch of Bosnian bandits out of cutting my throat, using only mime and snatches of Tennyson I remembered from school.

'I thank you, gentlemen, ladies,' I said, 'for your courtesy.' I glanced at Raikes again. He was gazing at me. I hadn't realized I was so fascinating. 'Mr Raikes here has given you a typically clever introduction. As he hints, I suspect that my idea of what British society should be like is rather different to some of yours. But if two ideas are both based on a sincere concern for the good of others, they can probably work out their differences. If not, well, then we've a problem. I've no match for Mr Raikes's rhetoric. But then I've seen rhetoric used too often for ill purpose. I'll just say this.' I hesitated. 'I'm a killer, ladies and gentlemen.' They sat forward at this, and there was a very satisfying murmur. I knew Raikes would be staring. 'Ten years ago now. I killed a bundle of Dutchmen. At the time it seemed like the grandest thing. Now, ten years on, I haven't the first idea what it was about.' I had them now. They were silent, and watchful. There were a few nods. 'If one of them had got lucky, he'd be making this speech instead of me. And I doubt he'd understand either. My tip to you: be sure to ask why, when someone's encouraging you to jump off a cliff, and be sure to know what's at the bottom.'

I nodded to them, turned and nodded to Raikes, and walked off the stage. There was an uncomfortable silence behind me. As I said, I've never been one for speeches.

As I pushed my way to the door, I heard Raikes starting up again behind me. As soon as I was out of the hall in the corridor I took a deep breath. I've always mistrusted crowds.

'Sir Henry Delamere!'

I turned. Tallish chappy coming along the corridor, foreign accent, dapper suit. Something about his face was familiar. He was flanked by two others, more normal height, but making up for it in width. From the way they filled the suits, they were clearly a pair of very solid individuals. The *ensemble* had the general impression of a country squire with a pair of prize mastiffs.

"Fraid you've missed my speech,' I said. 'Probably be in the *Times* tomorrow.'

He smiled. Where had I seen him before? 'We are determined' – like all foreigners he had trouble pronouncing that W, but the rest was smooth as silk – 'not to miss you again, Sir Henry.' Never has a clumsy threat been more elegantly delivered.

They weren't hiding anything anymore. The association with the international world-changers' luncheon society was open, and so was the intent to kill me. And I still couldn't prove any of it.

Country squire went on. 'I wanted only to present you to my two companions. So that they know you... when the time comes.'

I smiled without warmth at the two toughs. 'I hope I don't disappoint. But you haven't introduced yourself, sir.'

He actually looked embarrassed. Well brought-up, these foreign assassins. 'Your pardon, Sir Henry. My name is Hertenstein; of the Swiss delegation to the conference.' He could see my uncertainty. He doffed his hat elegantly. 'I think, perhaps, that you met my brother.' And he smiled ice.

Under the hat I saw the blond hair, but I'd already remembered where I'd seen the eyes.

Hungry-looking, as they hunted me around the backstage of Jolly's Theatre. And then somewhat surprised as they fell to destruction.

And he had a brother.

He didn't look the turn-the-other-cheek sort. 'Your brother gave quite a performance,' I said. 'Most remarkable debut in the history of the London stage, but alas only a one-night stand. Or rather fall.'

He smiled at this cheap hilarity. 'We will see you very soon, Sir Henry.'

39.

I was fairly sure they wouldn't try anything there and then. It would have drawn too much attention. And, unlikely though it seems, I felt that the protection of Raikes's hospitality actually meant something.

Fairly sure. I decided it was time I was away.

But then I felt a hand on my arm. I turned, ready to swing and run. But it was a flustered face I saw, some kind of junior official, desperate to grab me back for something. I went warily.

And thus it was, that my participation in that strange gathering was memorialized for posterity. It should be possible to dig one out still – from one of the press agencies, or from police headquarters. The official photograph of the International Brotherhood of Radicals, Revolutionaries, Dreamers, Lunatics, Anarchists and Assassins. With one bewildered baronet along for the ride. There I am for all eternity, at the end of the front row of seated grandees, looking damned uncomfortable and trying to spot the nearest exit.

By the nearest exit I ran into Bliss, at last. She'd clearly been enjoying herself immensely; but then she didn't have diverse bands of foreigners trying to kill her. 'I saw your speech!' she bubbled. 'If you're thinking of doing this sort of thing more often, I know someone who could help you with diction. And with writing your–'

'I will not be doing this sort of thing more often. Thank you. I'm leaving now and I'm going to live up a mountain where hopefully I never have to see another human ever again.'

Leaving was easier said than done. For every step we made towards the street, another over-dressed and over-earnest foreign chappie would throw himself at Bliss and offer undying devotion, a visiting card and the chance to write a monthly column in his newspaper. In the end I more or less man-handled her into a horse-cab, kicking away the last scented Belgian pamphleteers as I went.

'See anyone you recognized?'

'No.' She shook her head. 'Do you think I could actually write this book, on the impact of labour relations on the family? I had some rather interesting conv–'

'No. I did see someone I recognized. Well, sort of. Brother of the chap who took the toss into your piano. I'm not onto them so much, but they're certainly onto me.'

We rattled back to Shulstoke Hall, Bliss chattering about the plight of the worker and I musing on the plight of the fugitive baronet.

During the lengthy journey across the front hall at Shulstoke, I passed the vast bald foreigner going the other way. He'd covered the three-piece with a cape now, and looked like one of those marquees they put up in St James's Park for the band. We nodded to each other as we passed. Then he stopped, and said: 'You have been out for some sport?'

'Depends on your definition. I observed the big Trades Unions meeting in Birmingham.'

His face darkened, and he shook the big head. Quite an achievement, for he didn't seem to have any neck to support the movement. 'I do not understand why your Government tolerates these people.' There was probably something patriotic and liberal I was supposed to say at this point, but my sympathies were entirely with him. 'Perhaps because these lands have not seen violence for many generations.' Again the big head shook. His voice was a deep boom, every word hit equally; it emphasized the accent, the treacherous w's and v's and th's. 'In Germany, we know what is civil violence. We know what is war on our frontiers.' Largely because they were invading France on a more or less routine basis, of course, but it wasn't the moment to say so. The big face stared at me – strange pale eyes he had – 'The present society works. We have peace. We have economic success. We have art – music – all that is civilized. Why must you indulge these mischiefs?'

'I said as much to their grand assembly this afternoon.' The most unlikely smile opened across his face. Until then he'd looked bewildered by the world; now he looked utterly in control. Again he shook his head, as if to emphasize how naive I was; I wasn't about to disagree. 'Your pardon, sir,' he said with gravity. 'I am Von Hahn.' I vaguely remembered the name from somewhere. I introduced myself, and we shook hands, and I went up to dress for dinner.

When I was coming down into the hall again, Victoria had just stopped Bliss at the bottom of the staircase.

'You must excuse what might seem an inhospitable question,' she was saying. 'But I'd be obliged if you'd tell me who you really are.'

40.

I stopped dead on the staircase. I wasn't sure Victoria had seen me.

Come on, woman, I was thinking. Bliss and I had rehearsed this in the train. She was the actress, after all.

Victoria was looking pretty formidable. Glorious, of course, but I'd been on the wrong end of that look myself a few times. 'I know Walter Hutchinson, you see. I wasn't quite sure about you, and so I telegraphed him, and he confirms that the company has no book contract with you, and has never heard of you.' Bliss was looking rather startled, and rather defiant. 'The thing is, you see, that while I have no objection to Harry Delamere doing whatever he must to sort out the present predicament, I won't have my father's hospitality abused. Daddy's a funny old stick, but I won't have him made fun of.'

The whole world had stopped. *Come along, woman!* The great Sarah bloody Bernhardt moment. *Come on...*

'You're quite right,' Bliss said. 'It was a silly charade, and I should have told you immediately. My name is Annabella Bliss. I'm a burlesque dancer. Sir Henry dropped through my skylight a few nights ago and I've been helping him.'

I think I covered my face with my hands. When I opened my eyes, Victoria was gazing up at me with disapproval. She turned back to Bliss. 'That's rather sporting of you. And it's a pleasure properly to meet you and welcome you.' Now they were shaking hands again, for God's sake. 'Dropped through your skylight?'

'Yes. Naked.'

'Oh dear. He first appeared to me out of the Thames at Oxford, clambering into my brother's boat like some creature of the deep and claiming he was being chased by the police. I think he was wearing trousers then, but not much else. Bliss, you said?'

'Bliss. We're not famous or anything. My father's a vicar in Suffolk.'

'And you've struck out on your own in London. How splendid. Harry!' This, suddenly, to me as I was trying to slip backwards up the stairs. 'They're expecting you in the study. Big pow-wow. Men only. Behave yourself.' Then she was leading Bliss away across the hall, still holding her hand. 'Is that the Reverend Joshua Bliss? Wrote the pamphlet on *The Pulpit as Schoolroom and Stage*?'

'You must be the only person in England who's even...' – and away they drifted.

There were half a dozen men in the study when I slipped in. Aysgarth's scowl on seeing me would have kept me quiet on its own. The obvious seriousness of the others reinforced the effect.

I helped myself to a glass of water – everything was starting to feel like gambling now – and propped myself discreetly in the corner.

'The French Government has sent a formal note of concern. We've had the German Ambassador himself in to see the Foreign Secretary today.' This from a chap perhaps a little older than me, sleek and smart and dignified. 'They're furious – genuinely, it seems – that their radicals are allowed to wander round Britain preaching the class war. Think we've gone soft.'

'Don't they realize that a bit of subtlety is why we're the only ones who don't suffer revolutions on an annual basis?'

'Precisely their point I think, old chap. Russian Ambassador has named two or three participants on this junket – Latvians, apparently – who'll be strung up as soon as they set a foot in Russia again, but are free here to link up and plot revolutions to their hearts' content.'

'Von Hahn himself is here for dinner tonight.'

There were murmurs of concern. Someone else said 'Von Hahn?'

'The lion of German diplomacy. Otto Immanuel Von Hahn. Actually, a very civilized chap, for a hun. We're talking about getting him onto the Board at Covent Garden, and he's always good for a subscription for an exhibition. Notionally he's the counsellor or the cultural something-or-other at the German Embassy, but everyone knows he's the real power. Been here for ever. The Kaiser's man, they say, and he's a standing invitation to Windsor.'

'What can he do here that's so terrible?'

'I don't think he'll pinch the spoons or pass the port the wrong way, but this shows how seriously the Germans are taking this. For him to be dirtying his hands with commercial affairs…'

'If Berlin decides to think that we are somehow encouraging their workers to make trouble…'

'I thought we were worried about our battleship.' Murmurs of agreement. 'Having these appalling people strutting around freely and prosing about how unfree they are is bad enough. What are they up to in our shipyards? – that's what I want to know.'

'That, I think, is young Delamere's department.' It was the old man again, from Admiralty Arch. Half of them hadn't realized I was there, but the old man had turned to me automatically. 'I think you were sniffing around today, Sir Harry. Any more sign of a connection to the sabotage and the murder?'

'It's there,' I said. 'I thought it before, and I know it now. One of them threatened to finish the job on me. But nothing I can prove.' I shook my head. 'It's not all of them, though. They're not one coherent outfit. Some of them, certainly; perhaps a more extreme element.'

'You'll pardon me, Sir Harry,' – the old man again, sounding like he didn't care whether or not I pardoned him – 'but is there any chance their attitude to you is unrelated to the trouble at the yard? Might there be any other reason for someone to take against you so strongly?'

Magnus Lord Aysgarth made a noise inappropriate in a host.

'What,' I said, 'the workers of Europe have suddenly taken it into their heads to avenge my bookmaker for a couple of unpaid bills? I'm no-one's best friend, sir, but if these philosophers want to strike a blow against the oppressor there are surely a couple of other addresses they'd try first. I'd probably join them.'

That comment went down as well as you'd expect. But they didn't argue. Someone asked: 'where are they off to next after Birmingham, on this damned national tour of theirs?'

'Glasgow.'

'Glasgow?' There was alarm in the question, and everyone turned sharply to the speaker. It was Stackhouse again, my chum from the Thames Ironworks. He'd been silent before this, better than me at knowing his place and keeping his mouth shut in grand company. 'It's just...' He looked at the expectant faces. 'That's where the H.M.S. *Colossus* is being laid down, in Scotts' yard – at Greenock, a couple of miles down the Clyde.'

That got them worried. I confess I've not been following our battleship programme closely, but I assumed the *Colossus* was another Dreadnought. Eventually, someone said: 'I still can't see what they're up to. Some act of mass sabotage?'

'I'll have a regiment around the docks! Like to see them try to get past a couple of Maxim guns.' The speaker looked like a man who would like to see it, too.

'Pardon me,' I said, remembering my exploits in the burning drawings office, and the conversation at Admiralty Arch. 'But I'd gathered there was some particular bit of kit that we're sensitive about.'

'That's rather a good point,' the old man said. 'Mr Stackhouse–'

Stackhouse got the point immediately. 'The fire-control tables are assembled at the Dreyer works, then transported by train to the dockyard – ours, or Scotts', or whoever else is building the particular ship – for installation as part of the fitting-out.'

'Perhaps you could confirm with your opposite number in Scotts the timetable for the *Colossus*'s fire-control table. We want it to get there in one piece.' Stackhouse nodded.

That was that, as far as the great men's fretting went. We decamped towards the dining room, where the rest of the houseguests were gathering. It was the usual elegant scrum: a dozen and a half men sharp in our regulation penguin suits, mingling with the diverse colours of the women's dresses, rustling and gleaming and touched with jewels. After what I'd seen and heard during the day, tonight it seemed even more fragile and foolish than usual.

As promised, a few of the more respectable of the foreign visitors to Birmingham had been invited to dinner: a French philosopher, a senior newspaper man from somewhere, and one or two heads of national associations for something not-too-likely to frighten the horses.

'Ah, Delamere;' the Foreign Office chappie touched my arm as I was making for the double doors and wondering who I'd be stuck next to. 'Let me introduce one of our foreign guests: from the confederated trade association of Switzerland; Mr Hertenstein.'

Again the eyes; again the sleek blond hair. Again the ice smile.

Our handshake was held a moment too long, our hold on each other's eyes broken with difficulty. And then I walked into dinner beside my would-be assassin.

41.

I've been inclined, and sometimes obliged, to spend a lot of my time in the dustier parts of the world, and often to travel on a budget. One gets used to eccentricity, discomfort, and even threat. I've dined in everything from a palace to an upturned rowing boat, eaten most parts of most mammals, and done so in some damned odd company. But I can remember few meals quite as odd as that night at Shulstoke.

I've dined with dangerous men. I've dined with men who might easily have decided to do me mischief. I don't think I've ever dined with a man who had clearly stated his intention to murder me.

(With the exception of Magnus, Lord Aysgarth, now I come to think of it; but on that occasion I'd been fairly hopeful that Victoria would get him to moderate the sentence.)

Tonight I could look down the table and see death. And occasionally death would look back down the table and see me, and catch my eye.

Hertenstein was perfectly turned out, well-mannered, and charming. His careful witticisms were going down a storm with the ladies either side of him. I even saw Aysgarth smiling at one of his remarks. The Swiss was the only one of the relative radicals placed near his host – the table plan must have been quite a challenge, given Aysgarth's feelings about newspapermen, intelligent women, the French, and me – and once or twice I saw him speaking earnestly and Aysgarth nodding thoughtfully.

My assassin wasn't even the odd part. One knows the score with killers, and rubs along civilly until the crisis. Killers I'm used to. Diplomats, not so much. The whole atmosphere was damned eerie: so much tension, and no-one saying a word about it. It's just not the done thing to discuss European revolution, you see; not with the ladies present. The British officials were uncomfortable in the presence of the foreign diplomats, having tolerated the radical visit to the country. And both were uncomfortable in the presence of the token radicals. Everyone talked about anything, except what they were thinking.

The constipated politics of the men left the ladies to dominate the discussion, for once. That was easy enough, because Victoria had more brain and wit than all the men put together and was able to lead discussions on everything from Nietzsche, Matisse and the Curies to a recent epidemic of croup among the local poultry, all while maintaining a hostess's vigilance about the performance of the servants. Aysgarth's legendary capacity to talk about hunting – apparently a full hour uninterrupted and without drawing breath – was a social asset at last. His suggestion that the house party should partake of a mass slaughter of rabbits the next day – pheasants still being out of season – met with great approval, largely because it was something to talk about. He topped it by bragging of Victoria's skill as a shot, which actually rather annoys him but gets deployed when he knows it'll play well.

Only once did the thunderclouds break.

I'd happened to see one of the introductions, when my man Hertenstein had been presented to Von Hahn, the Kaiser's favourite opera-lover. The Swiss had made some witticism, and offered his hand. The big German took it like Hertenstein had just wiped his backside with it, and dropped it immediately. Hertenstein had merely smiled. During the dinner conversation Von Hahn gave the impression of being much more comfortable with the cultural stuff, and as everyone was avoiding politics he was one of the better contributors. He didn't agree with Victoria on Ravel or Mallarmé, but his disagreement was interesting and well-informed. He spent a few minutes prosing about Debussy, and even if most of us couldn't have told Debussy from a chicken sandwich we were happy enough with the distraction.

And then the French philosopher chappie said something along the lines of 'surely the arts are the field that are seeing the most fundamental revolution, because we are re-evaluating not only how men interact, but how they feel'. He mentioned some Russian name which I didn't catch. Von Hahn had stiffened immediately, and was looking rather stuffed and hot. One of the visiting diplomats, I assume French, jumped in and said something obviously critical to his compatriot in rapid French, and the compatriot said something rude back at him and added in English that the arts were also the field where the ruling class had been allowed to become most complacent and decadent. Von Hahn wasn't having this, and said something pompous and rather naive to the effect that the arts should be what elevated men above the chaos of their animal politics.

Hertenstein piped up. 'Perhaps they are grown sceptical, when they are encouraged to look upwards, and then they find that their pocket it has been picked.' It was said pleasantly, but everyone could see he was needling Von Hahn.

'I speak of absolute beauties,' Von Hahn said stiffly. 'Not these mammal appetites and political games.'

'No one here will deny the power of music. But some of us may question if a man who cannot vote or feed his family has so much time for Brahms.'

Von Hahn glared at him, massive and still missing the point. 'There are some foods too rich for a simple stomach. They cannot be digested, and the organism rejects it. Perhaps it is better that this man stays loyally at his work, and does not try to taste cultural beauty.' The big head came forwards, the eyes glaring, and the words heavy. 'Because – it – may – kill – him.'

I happened to be glancing at Bliss at that moment – you can't blame me – and I saw her look rather shocked. It had been a clumsy line from the German, with its tone of threat. It didn't even make sense in the context. Accordingly, no-one could offer a reply, and we all looked at our plates for a bit. At last Aysgarth – who probably feels the same way about Brahms as he does about revolution and hadn't been following any of it – said something hopeful about the autumn weather for the next day's shooting. Von Hahn was silent for a time, a great wounded elephant. Hertenstein was immediately chatting with his neighbours, and looking pretty pleased with himself. At one point he caught my eye again, and smiled, and raised his glass to me.

That's the stuff, I thought. *I do like an arrogant opponent.*

42.

As I trekked across the hall towards the front door and the possibility of fresh air, I saw that Von Hahn had cornered one of the Foreign Office men. I couldn't hear what was being said, but it looked pretty one-sided. The Englishman was just looking uncomfortable and a bit scared, as Von Hahn stood close and spoke at him in an emphatic growl. His glare alone would have killed.

The night was crisp and fresh and I breathed it in gratefully.

'Hoping the stars will elevate your soul,' a quiet voice said beside me, 'or just walking off some of your mammal appetites?'

It was the old man. He looked more ghostly than ever, under the moon.

'My soul and my appetites are just fine, thank you, and I don't need advice on either. How's your diplomacy?'

He smiled faintly. 'The Foreign Office chaps are frantic. Their own mammal appetites are always for civility, whatever else may be going wrong. And the Germans seem very angry, and the French worse.' Still the smile. 'The Foreign Office would tolerate revolutionary outrages in Pall Mall and an outright ban on modern poetry as long as their cordial relations with the other foreign ministries were maintained.'

'Doesn't that prove the radicals' point?' Again his infuriating smile. I wondered what the old man was, if he wasn't Foreign Office. 'I take it you're not frantic.'

He shrugged. 'Us deciding to tolerate this radical conference won't affect whether there will or won't be war with Germany.' Gods, that was one hell of a jump; for a moment I felt rather out of my depth. 'But it might help preserve enough stability in our military and industrial manpower to be able to fight successfully if there is war.'

'And if we've one Dreadnought fewer?'

He looked at me. 'I'm sure you'll look after us on that front, Sir Harry.'

'Are you indeed?' I glanced over my shoulder. We were still alone. 'About that: the very elegant Swiss, Hertenstein – he's the one who's planning to kill me. One of my points of sympathy with Von Hahn.'

The old man seemed almost interested. 'Is he now?'

'I mention it so that if he's successful, you'll have a bit of a head-start in picking up the trail.'

He was gazing out into the darkness. 'Most helpful...' he said distantly.

At last I saw it. 'I'm your decoy,' I said, trying to sound careless. 'Aren't I? And perfect for the job. You've let me loose to run around in the undergrowth, and you aim that I flush them out. And it's no particular concern of yours whether I get mauled in the process.'

He put his hand on my shoulder. 'You seem a resilient sort of chap, Delamere. Reckon you'll stand a bit of mauling.'

It was the sort of stuff that chaps were supposed to say to each other in 1910. I can't say I felt all that inspired.

43.

I enjoyed a smoke in the darkness. I was glad of the solitude.

I'd been brought up to know that the enemy was the chap with the different flag and the funny hat. Nice and clear that had been. And the hats give you something to shoot at. Now I was in a Europe where Englishmen and Frenchmen and Germans and charming murderous Swiss could all think the same way and dangerously. And an old buffer of a German music expert, and a French diplomat and our own Foreign Office were united in worrying about it. I was starting to feel that getting throttled in bath-houses was the easy bit.

I was up in my room and starting to undress, when I heard footsteps, and then a knock at the door.

Quinn usually stops by at this stage in the proceedings to review the plan for the morning and check I've got something improving to read. I was about to speak, but the door opened anyway.

It was Annabella Bliss. She was in and had the door closed before I could say anything.

She was wearing one of her stylish dressing gowns, and looking rather bothered. 'Don't tell me,' I said. 'Someone's been chasing you over the rooftops.'

To be honest, I wasn't really in the mood. But a chap does his duty. I smiled. 'Did you know this was my room, or were you less–?'

'Don't try to be funny. I didn't come to–'

I never heard what she didn't come to do, sadly. Footsteps outside again, and another knock. Bliss jumped at the noise, and then darted across the room and into the wardrobe.

Well, for goodness' sake… That's what you get from a stage career, I suppose. Wardrobes are the worst place to hide: obvious, and a dead-end. It's a lesson I only had to learn once, in Rome in my younger days, but it almost killed me.

Once she had the door properly closed, I called a 'come in'. I was bare-chested but at least still had trousers on, and after recent events I was feeling that dignity and decorum were luxuries I could probably forego.

It was only Quinn, of course. He closed the door behind him, and stepped forwards. 'Evening, sir. Just came to–' He was sniffing. He stopped, and took another, deeper sniff. Then his expression changed. Bliss is a damned stylish woman, and cool with it, but her perfume tends to the melodramatic. Quinn looked at me, just about holding his stone face, and gave a little nod. 'You must excuse me, sir. Hadn't realized.' He started to turn.

'Stand fast,' I said. 'I'll get her out of the wardrobe.'

I did so. Bliss stepped into the room again looking a little pink, but contrived a demure 'Good evening, Mr Quinn', which he reciprocated suavely. Easy for him; he was the only one of us properly dressed. He started to make his apologies again.

'Stay a bit, Quinn. Whatever she's here for, apparently it's not that. If this is the revolution I can't say I like it.' I looked at Bliss. 'Please don't worry. You're quite the pleasantest thing Quinn's ever found in my wardrobe. Happens all the time, don't it Quinn?' He smiled encouragingly at her.

We stood there in a little triangle, Quinn in his formals waiting for the next Boer attack, Bliss looking uncomfortable and charming in her dressing gown, and me between them trying to remember if I still had my fly done up.

'Well, this is nice,' I said.

'No,' Bliss said. 'It's not.' I looked at her. I'd got to know her over the last few days as a steady, unflappable sort of girl. Now she was clearly unhappy. Her lovely face was frozen, as if she was holding herself together with difficulty. 'The man who wants to kill you,' she said; 'he's here.'

'Yes, I know. The Swiss. He's the brother I was telling you about. Elegant sort of—'

'Not him!' Her voice was low, urgent. 'The man in the carriage that night near the theatre. The man I heard ordering your death. It's that enormous German.'

44.

'What?'

She nodded.

'Surely that's nonsense.' She looked cross. 'It can't—'

'When did you get so smart?' She gazed at me, still pink. 'I suppose as you've been so right about everything else...'

Somewhat harsh, but it slowed me down. 'He's the right shape,' she said. 'And I know voices. I notice what's distinctive about them. As soon as he started talking at dinner I thought there was something… Like a memory I couldn't catch. Then I realized he sounded like the man from the carriage.' Her voice clear and strong now. 'And then at the end, when he was saying all the nonsense about primitive men and art, he used the exact same two words he'd used in the carriage, about you.' I didn't need her to repeat them, but she was enjoying her certainty. '"Kill him."'

She shrugged. 'There. That's it. Nighty-night.' She blew me a kiss. 'Sweet dreams.'

We watched her go.

Quinn waited to see if I'd say anything. I was still watching the closed door.

The whole damn' business was upside down.

Eventually, he said 'You fancy it, sir?'

I breathed out heavily. 'It ought to be nonsense. It is non-sense.' I looked at him. 'But she knows what she's talking about. Doesn't spook easily, that one.' I shook my head. 'But Gods, if by some mad chance it's true…'

He waited.

'How on earth does Von Hahn tally with the murderous phi-losophers, anyway?' Another breath. 'All right. Standing orders:' I said. 'If in the next few days I get shot, stabbed, strangled, dynamited, or pitchforked to death by the peasants' revolt, you are to seek out the old man who's lurking around here. You seen him? Looks about ninety and so damned dusty he's not there. Sort of deep fellow we used to see whispering in ears in Bloemfontein.' Quinn nodded. 'He's canny, and he's the only sensible one I've met in this business. If I take the low road to the Cape, you seek him out and you tell him everything, yes?'

'Right ho, sir.' His usual even growl. 'Think we'll try to avoid that contingency, though, eh?' I nodded doubtfully. 'Plan of at-tack for the morning, sir?'

'In the morning, Quinn, I'm going to take out my frustrations on a lot of rabbits.'

'Chancy business, sir. All those guns.'

'I know guns, Quinn. I can do guns. It's all this damned diplomacy and speechifying and running around in the shadows that's getting on my nerves.' He nodded. 'Doubt they'll try anything here. Too obvious. And even if Von Hahn is involved somehow, he's not going to take a pop at me himself. They don't like that sort of thing on the Covent Garden Board of Trustees.' He nodded again, but he wasn't convinced. Nor was I.

He glanced around the room. 'Locked door tonight, sir.' I nodded. 'Chair under the handle.'

'Alright Quinn. If I get rattled, you'll find me in the wardrobe.'

45.

Stepping out the next morning I felt better than I had for several days.

My situation was still ropey. Even assuming Bliss's staggering story was true, it didn't mean that the Swiss – or some of them – weren't trying to kill me. Or had I got that wrong, somehow? Was Hertenstein one hundred percent elegant charm, with just an unfortunately heavy-handed way of expressing familiarity?

He was irrelevant today, anyway: not part of the house party, he'd gone back to Birmingham after dinner and wouldn't be murdering rabbits or anything else for the moment.

At the very least, Bliss's story was a complication. Von Hahn didn't seem a natural revolutionary; but perhaps he'd got caught up by some of that modern music. I thought again about the street outside Jolly's Theatre, and I thought about Annabella Bliss. She wasn't the hysterical sort. She'd been enjoying herself at Shulstoke, not spooking at shadows. I trusted her.

So a senior German diplomat wanted me dead.

Someone wanted me dead, anyway.

But the morning was clear and sharp, and two minutes out of the front door I stepped onto rough ground for the first time in weeks, and ahead the English landscape opened to welcome me.

I'd stuck Bliss with Victoria for the shoot. She'd no intention of staying indoors and sewing, or whatever it is that women do when men are out slaughtering things. I didn't want her with me: partly for her safety, and partly for my flexibility. And there was no safer place for her than Victoria's side. Aysgarth hadn't been exaggerating when he'd bragged about his daughter's skill as a shot. She generally rejected a shotgun as being unladylike, and instead favoured an imported Winchester rifle, the 1894 model – and if being able to kill a man at 200 yards isn't as la-dylike as all hell, I don't know what is. They don't make many ladies like the Honourable Victoria Carteret. For rough shooting and on Aysgarth's land no-one was going to complain. I knew few eyes better, man or woman.

I'd watched them away, Victoria in her tailored outdoor el-egance, Bliss in a similar tweed business she'd pulled together from the Jolly's dressing-up box – too tight for her, but no-one was protesting – and a hat I suspected was left over from a pro-duction of Robin Hood. Golden and dark, willowy and volup-tuous. If I hadn't been trying to forestall European revolution and save my neck, I'd have enjoyed my luck more. Even with all the nonsense, I enjoyed it a bit.

That left me and Quinn. He was supposed to be loading for me, as I ambled through the undergrowth blasting away at the fauna. But I'd given him the Webley, in case he wanted to pot a rodent or two, and because – as I'd learned in southern Africa and repeatedly since – he's a handy sort of chap in the melee. Besides, my host seemed to have given me a weapon that hadn't seen effective use since the Crimea, so I doubted I'd risk it blowing up in my face too frequently.

The bracken and then the trees rose around us. The smell was rich and natural, tree bark and wet earth and plants. I felt as if I was re-entering my element. The restrictions were fewer out here. I was in steady and trusted company. And I was armed; albeit with something I'd be better using as a club.

The familiar sound of gunfire rose around us, first a few scattered shots as the more intrepid disturbed a rabbit at his breakfast; and then a steady popping as everyone settled to the mayhem.

Five minutes after we set off, at a junction in the path, we met Hertenstein.

46.

He doffed his hat and even managed a little bow. Mischievous bastard. 'Why, Sir Harry!' he said. 'How very martial you look.' He peered more closely. 'An 1870 single-barrel Pace, surely. What a splendid museum piece.'

Quinn had stepped away to the side. Hertenstein probably assumed this was deference; I knew my valet was improving his field of fire.

'Hardly suitable for the modern revolutionary, Hertenstein. You know your guns, it seems.'

'Ah, the Swiss have always been weapon-makers of the highest expertise.' He looked the perfect country gentleman, from his Jermyn Street boots to his soft hat. Lucrative business, radical philosophy.

'Mm. And mercenaries.'

It hit him more than I'd expected, and I noted the point.

The charming smile went out like a light. 'This is why you are doomed, Delamere. Because you have no true loyalties, and no true values.'

'Can't afford them, old chap. What brings you here, anyway? Come to spread sedition among the local rabbits, or are you selling arms to the pigeons?'

'Ah,' he began, and then froze. He'd pulled his hands out of his pockets suddenly, and Quinn's reaction had been immediate. The Webley was out and rock-steady.

Hertenstein licked his lips. And then he produced a big smile, and opened his empty hands. Slowly. 'I was invited only to enjoy the walk. I believe in the great power of the multitude, but I am myself a creature of peace.'

'That's what all the rabbits say. Go carefully today, Hertenstein.'

'Likewise, Sir Harry!' And off he strode.

We watched him go, until he was a long way off. 'Charming fellow, eh Quinn? Nice to do business with professionals.'

'Right you are, sir.' The Webley had disappeared as swiftly as it had appeared. 'A killing gentleman.' He sniffed. 'A talker, though.'

'Mm.' I considered the paths, and pointed our way ahead. 'Skirmish order now.'

We set off bush-style, constantly scanning the ground around us, anything from five to ten yards apart: close enough to cover each other; far enough that we couldn't be caught by a single shot and had a dramatically greater field of vision between us.

Blending in with the landscape doesn't have to mean wearing animal skins and sticking leaves in your hat. But it must mean adjusting your rhythm, and your movements, and your awareness, until the terrain around fills you completely and you become part of it. The present moment, the products of your senses, must become your whole existence. Any inclination to think – about anything, about what you had for breakfast or whether revolutionaries would consider it acceptable to murder a night-watchman – destroys your focus. No creeping, no tip-toes; but you find yourself slowing, and swaying, with the ground under your feet and the wind that gusts and the branches that wrap themselves around you like old friends. Ideally, you don't notice you're doing it; but it's the grandest sensation.

We went on for ten minutes or so. The English woodland grew around me. My boots slipped into and emerged from its earth. My arms and legs swung among the tree limbs. My hands gripped bark. The leaves whispered to me. The rich smell of it all filled my body.

When I glanced round, I saw Quinn had stopped, his palm raised. Then he pointed.

Perhaps forty yards off through the leaves, I saw Hertenstein. He had stopped under a tree and lit a cigarette. Bad form on a shoot of course, but that's foreigners for you.

Quinn was beside me. 'As you intended, I think sir,' he murmured. 'Tracked him nicely.'

'Just lucky, Quinn, as always. Sort of chap it's best to keep an eye on, eh?' He nodded.

I wanted to watch Hertenstein. Partly to see whom he spoke to. Partly to stop him sneaking up on me too easily, to use one of the variety of concealed weapons no doubt available to such a determined creature of peace.

After a couple of minutes he finished the cigarette and whatever reflection had occupied his philosophical soul, and set off again through the woods.

We followed. Never on the same path; never closer than twenty or thirty yards. Distantly around us, I could hear the banging of the guns as they went to war on the local rabbits.

Had he been invited, as he said? Probably; easy to wangle the suggestion during the previous evening.

Was he really just walking? Surely not.

Once I saw him pause and chat to someone coming in the other direction, then pass on. It had been a momentary courtesy, surely. No time for a substantial exchange. No point in contriving such a rendezvous for a short one.

Once or twice I saw other figures near me. But I barely registered who they were. A nod of fraternity in our pursuits, and move on, and always the fringe of blond hair moving through the leaves ahead of me.

Time passed. I knew the movement of each twig, but I couldn't have distinguished a minute from an hour.

And then, ahead of me on the faint track I was following in parallel to Hertenstein's, I saw a figure.

At first it was no more than that: a tweedy shape amid the greenery. Then immediately it was clear. That massive form was unmistakeable.

Otto Immanuel Von Hahn. Last bastion of classical music, and the man Bliss thought wanted to kill me. My hand had come up fast, and I knew that Quinn had frozen behind me.

My whole body felt alive and alert. Surely there was significance here. More immediately, how was I to track two men?

Von Hahn didn't seem to be moving. Another who couldn't do without a cigarette? Stopped to get his bearings, or have a piss? Automatically, my eyes were moving to and fro Hertenstein as well. But Hertenstein was walking on now, and even away from this parallel track.

With one finger of my raised hand, I beckoned Quinn forwards. I didn't hear him, not a foot-fall among the leaves, but then I felt his breath over my shoulder.

I turned my head over my shoulder until I was whispering almost directly into his ear. 'Another of the mourners at my funeral. I stick with Hertenstein. Once we're clear, give it a couple of minutes and then approach the big hun. Tell him I urgently want to meet him. Remember that oak we passed, at the fork in the path three hundred yards back? There; send him there. Don't go with him, but track him.'

Silence. Quinn didn't like it. I didn't blame him. But he knew better than to chit-chat in these circumstances. 'Aye sir,' he murmured eventually, the seaman's acknowledgement the Army had never managed to train out of him.

I began to shift to the right, off the path and through bracken, to where Hertenstein had been. Von Hahn I would leave to Quinn. I didn't know if they were linked – it seemed madness. But I had to split them. Quinn would make sure Von Hahn went to that oak. If he wasn't the bad man Bliss thought, my absence could easily be explained as miscommunication. If he was, then I didn't care so much about inconveniencing him.

I reached the path Hertenstein was on, saw his figure through the leaves ahead, and set off after him.

We were heading roughly north through the woodland, the ground rising gently. I knew the slope through my feet, and my leg muscles, and the changing play of light through trees.

Occasionally Hertenstein hesitated, or stopped, or looked around him at the warm beauty of the woods. I know that he never saw me.

Half a mile later, he stopped again. This time he leaned against a tree, his back towards me, and from the movement of his arm I could tell he was smoking again.

I lowered myself to my haunches: even less chance of discovery; ease the pressure on legs and feet. In the pause, consciousness returned, the active part of my brain ticking over while my unconscious took a breather from its dialogue with the terrain.

I've never been to India, but in East Africa I met an Indian chappie who'd hunted at home and come to try his luck against a different menu. He told me that when you're hunting a tiger, the great trick is to see things from the tiger's point of view. The land; the movement of wind and water and smell; the priorities.

I've found it a useful habit on all sorts of occasion.

It still didn't tell me where on earth Hertenstein was going. I refused to believe that he'd got himself invited her for a solitary ramble. He had something to do, or someone to meet. But he was going a damned long roundabout way, if so. If he wanted a discreet conversation with anyone, there were better ways and places, surely. And what could he be doing, so far from anyone else?

I realized I was speculating, and uselessly. I would follow him, and–

The tiger's point of view. *You damned fool, Delamere...* I felt my face clenching in anger, at myself. Was the tiger being followed, or was the tiger *leading*?

47.

So far from anyone else...

I scanned the ground around me. Still ducking low among the bracken, I stuffed the butt of my gun into a rabbit hole, so the barrel stood more or less upright. I perched my hat on the end of the barrel. Then I dropped, and on my belly began to wriggle through the bracken to one side. The ground was falling away in this direction, and a slight channel worn by a trickle of water gave me a path. I went dead slow. I was trying to avoid disturbing the bracken too much. A track of waving undergrowth is the surest sign of the fugitive animal. And if my hypothetical hunter was anything better than an imbecile, my hat-on-a-stick gag wouldn't hold him for long.

I made ten yards this way, the earth rich in my nostrils and smeared all over my kit. With my slow, rhythmic progress, hopefully the ruffling of the bracken would look like the wind. I was at the top of a kind of gully: at the moment I was just a few feet lower than the ground either side, but in front of me the gully widened and dropped away deeper than I could see through the undergrowth.

Now I turned to my right, and scrambled slowly up one side of the gully. When I stretched my head up over its lip, I had a bit of a view through the bracken back the way I'd come earlier. If I turned my head to one side, I could see part of my hat, on its perch just protruding above the leaves. And if I rolled onto my back, even though I couldn't see Hertenstein as he was, I had a chance of spotting him if he moved off.

I stayed there a full quarter hour. Watching the ground ahead, through the bracken stalks and fronds. Periodically rolling my head around to scan as much of the ground to my side and behind as I could, without disturbing the leaves above me.

If you stay in that kind of situation long enough, your mind starts to play tricks.

And if you stay even longer, your mind has time to consider and discard the tricks and know the truth.

In this way, after that quarter hour, I knew that there was a boot twenty yards away from me.

Not a rock, a dead animal, or a trick of light on earth and stalk. A boot, gents' outdoor, usual arrangement of laces and so on.

Thanks to the bracken – a vast jungle from my ant's perspective – I couldn't see the toe or the heel of the boot, and I couldn't see any leg and body above it.

It was possible that it was just a boot – lost, abandoned, or fallen from heaven. But that didn't seem very likely.

As I watched, I thought I saw it wriggle slightly.

Then a gust of wind rose slowly and shivered the bracken, and I stared hard. Now I caught a glimpse of leg, close over the boot. He was crouched on his haunches, whoever he was, facing towards where I'd left my gun and hat. From a glimpse of elbow, cocked low against knee, I deduced that he had a long-barrelled weapon held ready.

My priority had to be survival, now. Escape.

The boot shifted again. In that second he'd moved more than he had in a quarter hour. Something had changed; something had caught his attention.

The question for me was whether my gun was part of my survival and escape.

I turned my head, towards my little decoy. I could see the barrel of my gun clearly, perhaps fifteen yards off.

Which was a shame, because last time I'd looked it had been covered by hat. That last gust of wind had caught the hat. My cover was, rather literally, blown.

I turned back to my hunter, and now the legs were moving. He was rising from the crouch. He'd seen what I'd seen, and he knew what I'd done, and he wasn't hesitating.

A man with the instinct and skill to wait as long as he had waited, utterly still, would easily follow the track of my crawl through the undergrowth. Inside twenty seconds he would know my direction of travel. And he'd have my gun, and he'd know me unarmed.

I launched myself up from the gully, crouching low and running hard. I didn't want to give him an easy shot, but I made no attempt to hide. Somewhere to my side there was movement but I was focused only on my pumping legs and my scrambling hands and then I dived forwards through the bracken and if he'd had the chance of a shot the moment had gone. I wrenched my gun out its rabbit hole, and rolled onto my back and round and the gun came up to my shoulder and I was ready to fire.

For an instant I'd had a glimpse of hat and perhaps head beneath it, but I still wasn't sure I wanted to shoot, and it would have been a risky shot at best. As soon as he'd seen that he wasn't going to win the race to my gun, he'd stopped, and then pulled back and ducked.

So there we waited, each crouched low, knowing that another armed man was just a few yards off and waiting for movement.

The bracken fronds shivered in the breeze. I could see the individual drops of moisture on them. As if they too were sweating. I could hear every roaring detail of the silence of the woods.

My treacherous hat was lying beside me, where it had fallen from the gun. I put it over my right hand, and raised it slowly until it was just over the bracken again.

Smart chap I was up against. He wouldn't fall for this one again. So he wouldn't blow my arm off. That was my plan, anyway.

The hat still poking out of the undergrowth, with my left hand I gripped my gun by the butt end. With the barrel, I jostled a bracken stalk beside me. Then another stalk a foot or so away. And so on, until my arm was straining to hold the gun at its farthest possible reach, and one final spasm of the barrel set the leaves rustling a couple of yards away.

Slowly, slowly, I pulled the gun back in again, avoiding every single bracken stalk as it came. I regathered my muscles under me. Then I counted to ten.

Too soon, and he'd still be looking in this direction. Too late, and he'd be having second thoughts about my apparent crawl and looking in this direction again.

I rose up out of the bracken like a jack-in-the-box, gun up and striding forwards through the undergrowth. He was good, and he was fast. He'd shifted himself a bit and when he sensed my first movement he'd jumped to one side and rolled. 'Don't!' I said. I was faster still. Speed and height meant I saw him and had time to adjust my aim, and he was only half-turned when he knew that I had the killing shot and he had no chance.

He stopped instantly, lifted his hands slowly, gun to the sky. A real professional, this. It only made me more watchful.

Slowly, he turned towards me. 'Drop it,' I said. He rested the butt of his gun on the ground, and let the barrel fall away into the bracken. Minimum chance of earth getting into the breech or barrel. The gun was still in play.

I glanced up to his face. Well-built chap. I'd have recognized him from build alone. One of Hertenstein's two mastiffs, whom he'd introduced the previous day. 'Very impressive, Mein Herr,' he started saying. 'I did not–'

I wasn't listening. Professionals don't talk; so why was this professional talking? My eyes, and above all my ears, were open to the woods around me and ignoring the chatter.

Perhaps I heard something. Or perhaps I only thought I did, confirming what I knew had to be true.

With my gun still pointing ahead, and making no sudden movement, I shifted a couple of paces to the side and looked over my shoulder.

The second mastiff was standing twenty yards behind me, gun up and ready.

Killing shot.

48.

'Well that's hardly fair, is it?' I said. Gun held vertical and in left hand only, I spread my arms slowly. I can act the professional too; sometimes. I glanced at Number One. 'Might as well pick yours up again now.'

He nodded, and did so. No smile, no elegant wit. These men did killing, and nothing more, and they were very good at it. I wondered if one of them had stabbed Sinclair, or Merridew, or the night watchman Tulliver. The second man was only ten yards away now.

As they advanced from either side, I took a step forward and turned slightly, so that I was directly between them and presenting as thin a target as I could. Negligible advantages against two killers with shotguns. But every little helps.

I was standing in that position, glancing side to side between them, when I saw a third figure rising over the crest of the slope twenty yards in front of me.

'Why, Sir Harry,' Hertenstein said. 'Have you perhaps miscalculated the risks of a rabbit shoot?' His voice was oily, breathing triumph.

Life has given me fair opportunity to reflect on how my end might come. Instant fatal heart attack while enjoying the embraces of a dusky lady would obviously be ideal. Anything relatively quick and sporting – preferably far from England, doctors, sick-rooms and hordes of gawpers – would be acceptable. Getting knocked off in my prime by a couple of professional hunters, while I was trying to do some good, would be neither unlikely nor too bad a way to go.

'We see you at last, as I have promised.'

But damned if was going to turn up my toes in front of this leering assassin.

Anger makes you do unpredictable and unwise things, and in this case it might have saved my life. Faced with two armed men and one unarmed, with one shot left to you, whom do you aim for? All I could think of was not giving this bounder an easy triumph, and perhaps throwing a spanner in his works. I pulled my gun in to me and dropped to one knee and the barrel came up and I cheerfully spent what I assumed might be my last breath taking a snap-shot at Hertenstein.

I got him in the arm, and he looked shocked as much as hurt. Turning, dropping, and armed with little better than a drainpipe, I consider it one of my better shots. Hertenstein gasped, and swore, and clutched his wound – shotgun'll make a bit of a mess at twenty yards; the revolutionary band would be short one violinist, at least. Then he turned, and hurried away. His plans surely called for him to be well away from my death, and now he had some running repairs to make too. His final glance at me, as he ran cradling his arm, was pure hate. *See you soon, old chap*, I was thinking; his sort and mine are always on converging paths.

As an unexpected bonus, I'd bought myself an extra second with the two killers. They couldn't believe I'd gone for the un-armed man, they weren't sure what to do about their wounded boss, and I was still standing between them. I launched myself at the nearer, my empty gun held at my waist. I jabbed it towards him, and he flinched, and he was adjusting his aim and mak-ing to pull the trigger when my barrel whirled round his and knocked it aside. Professional killers they might be, but they'd not gone through British Army bayonet drill. The shot roared past my ear.

I followed up with the butt of my gun, swinging it round into his jaw and sending him stumbling away. I took three racing steps to the side and as the other man's shot exploded over the bracken I dived headlong into my gully. I scrambled forwards, and threw myself into a roll. Rolling and scrambling would car-ry me fast down the gully and away before they had a clear shot.

I made all of about three yards before I tumbled into the trunk of a dead tree, hidden under the bracken and blocking the gully. For a moment I lay dazed and tangled in my arms and legs, and when I worked out where up was, I found it occupied by two armed killers. Their guns were up and ready and pointing at me.

Still they didn't speak, and they didn't smile.

'Persistent bastards, aren't you?' I said. 'Right ho. Fun while it lasted.'

I heard the shot and I flinched instinctively. Part of my brain was bracing for pain, and part of it was already making its first shocked steps to the afterlife, when some more useful part worked out that I hadn't actually been hit.

Above me, the nearest gunman went pale, and spun, and toppled into the gully at my feet. He'd been shot in the heart.

The other gunman was as surprised as I was. He still had me at disadvantage, but now he was gaping around the woodland and wondering where the shot had come from. He glanced down at his dead comrade, and I knew he was trying to gauge direction from the wound. He took a couple of steps forwards, swinging his gaze and his barrel side to side.

The second shot tore his chest away and threw him backwards into the bracken. He never saw where that one came from, either.

I stepped out of the gully, and watched as a figure emerged from the undergrowth with shotgun held ready.

This I had not expected.

It was Magnus, Lord Aysgarth.

He stomped towards me, and past me, and stared down at the two bodies. Then he turned and glared. Even by his usual standards, it was ferocious.

People react in strange ways to killing someone. Aysgarth was angry and, I suspect, a little shocked. Either way, his face was purple and clenched.

'Thank you, sir.' And dear God I meant it. 'That – that first – that was one hell of a shot.'

It didn't seem possible, but his face got more purple and more angry. He made to say something, but couldn't even manage that.

Then I saw; then I understood. And I gasped at… at what I had brought to his family.

'Yes, that's right, damn you,' he growled.

That first kill would have been something special even for an excellent shot. Aysgarth was a good shot, but he wasn't excellent, not with the havoc wrought on his eyes and muscles and nerves by umpteen decades of idleness and English dinners. The second shot had been his. But the first, as I saw it again on the dead man's chest, wasn't even from a shotgun.

It was the clean precise wound caused by a rifle, and even for a rifle it had been something special. There was only one person using a rifle today; one person with the skill for such a shot.

I closed my eyes a moment. I should have protected her from this.

'It didn't happen,' I said eventually. 'She was not involved.' Then: 'I can't ask you to like it, sir. And I won't waste breath trying to thank you more. Please believe that this is about more than me.'

He glared at me some more. He didn't like it, but he knew. He was still damned angry – at me, at the whole madness. 'And them?' he managed eventually, a growl. He nodded curtly at the two bodies.

I saw his point. Dead foreigners lying around the place lower the tone; and shooting one's guests is bad form, even for the Aysgarths. I nodded. I was thinking hard. 'Go. Leave them to me. I'll… arrange things.'

He growled some more, and turned to go.

'She's the best of you, Lord Aysgarth.' He turned back. 'I know what you think of me, and you know what I think of you. But through her I know what's good in you. And, for what it's worth, you were right that I'm not good enough for her.'

'Go to hell, Delamere.'

'Very much on my way, I think.'

49.

Half an hour later I stepped out of the undergrowth onto the back lawn of Shulstoke, where the guests were starting to mill around a cold lunch laid on tables. I walked up to my host.

'Rather a bad business, sir,' I said too loudly. 'Looks like a couple of poachers. Some kind of accident – or perhaps an argument between them. They're both dead, I'm afraid.'

Aysgarth looked blankly at me. Either he knew he'd be hopeless trying to act emotion, or his mind was no longer registering the chaos I had raised on his land. He turned away and beckoned to his head gamekeeper.

While the head gamekeeper was digging up a couple of lads to come with us – they'd have been enjoying a pint of ale in the kitchen, far from the spread of pies and wines on the lawn – I found that the old man had drifted up behind me.

He murmured: 'You all right, Delamere?'

'Still alive, anyway.'

'Good show. And, er, the scene of… of whatever has just happened?'

'Will support the story I have told.'

The ground where the two bodies now lay, the presence of some tricky fallen branches at the edge of the gully, was consistent with one or both of my two assassins having stumbled. Some of their fancier clothes and kit had been buried. Both now had shotgun wounds. Grim old business, international diplomacy.

'Good show. Looks like you belong in this game after all.'

'But they don't!' I'd turned on him, and was hissing my irritation. 'These people are the closest I have to family, and they don't belong in it.'

Wisely, he didn't try to say anything. He just rested his hand on my shoulder a moment, and drifted away again.

I was gone another half hour, leading the gamekeeper and his lads to the scene and offering some fatuous upper-class gestures of help as they got on with the clearing up.

When I got back, the last of the guests had gathered from the house and the woods for their lunch. As I came near, Aysgarth was talking to a couple of the foreigners.

'Had rather an unfortunate incident out in the woods this morning. Fatal, I'm afraid.' Von Hahn was one of the foreigners. I saw his expression of polite concern. 'Couple of poachers got tangled up with each other somehow; they're both dead.'

Von Hahn frowned, in confusion. And that was the moment when I came into his vision, somewhere behind Aysgarth's shoulder.

For one instant Von Hahn's eyes went wide. Then as quickly his self-control took over again, and he was nodding bland concern at Aysgarth, and no-one who hadn't happened to be looking at him at that very instant would have noticed a thing.

You knew.

You bastard, you knew what was supposed to happen.

You were expecting one unfortunate accident out in the woods. But you weren't expecting two, and you certainly weren't expecting Harry Delamere to come out of the bushes in one piece.

Bliss had been right. The German government had declared war on the Delameres.

And I still couldn't prove any of it.

The morning's drama had left me damned hungry. I ploughed through more than my share of veal pie. At one point, lurking over the sandwiches, I saw Victoria opposite me.

She was looking a little pale. We watched each other for a moment. We didn't say anything. She knew what I felt, and I knew what she felt, and it was no damn use saying any of it. It never was.

I was reaching for an unwise second glass of wine when I saw the old man again, and saw the faintest nod of his head to beckon me.

He was standing with one of the Foreign Office chaps, and Hugh Stackhouse. Stackhouse was looking hot and bothered. 'Someone's been in my room!' he said, trying to keep his voice down but failing to hide his concern. 'Been through my papers.'

I thought about Hertenstein. He could have drifted into the house, between most of the party leaving and the time he'd bumped into me in the woods.

The old man said: 'Anything taken?'

Stackhouse nodded, looking grim. 'The plans of Glasgow docks, where the *Colossus* is fitting out.'

50.

The Council of War took place the next morning, in Birmingham's New Street Station. It's a grand location to discuss the safety of the Empire: a vast glass canopy soaring over the tracks, all one single span without columns, held together by a jungle of intricate ironwork far above. There was a monstrous bustle of steam and noise and people around us, as the engines coughed and hissed to a stop and belched out smoke, and wheezed into movement again ahead of their trains of ornate carriages going to north and south, and every class of humanity flowed along the platforms under the heavy elegance of the lamps.

We were eight: the old man, one of the Foreign Office chaps, Sir Percy Savary himself up from London, Stackhouse and another man from the Thames Ironworks Company, Inspector Bunce and his Assistant Commissioner, and me. We had the waiting room on Platform 1 to ourselves. A policeman on each door saw to that.

The business with Stackhouse's papers had rattled the Government properly. Hence Savary's presence. They'd been more than uncomfortable that the next stop on the international revolutionary pilgrimage just happened to be the city where the newest Dreadnought was getting ready. Now there was a clear indication that something was planned right in Glasgow docks. The threat was clear and direct.

I'd had a bit of trouble with the Foreign Office man, who'd refused to consider that the German government might be involved. I'd started to say something undiplomatic about wanting to see him running for his life through the undergrowth, but the old man had interrupted and suggested that given various indications during recent days it would be judicious to have the possibility of German involvement in mind until we could clearly rule it out. Everyone had politely accepted, and I'd not had to admit that I'd been involved in the deaths of two more foreigners. Bunce was keeping quiet in the presence of his superior, but from his scowl I could see that he was as sceptical about my German spies as he was about everything else I'd ever said to him.

'It does make sense, I suppose,' the other Thames Ironworks man was saying, 'that Germany should want to delay our Dreadnought schedule.'

There was general nodding at this.

'They don't care about your Dreadnought schedule,' I said.

The nodding stopped. As usual, I was contradicting everyone.

'They want a fire-control table.'

There was mixed grumbling at this: doubt or concern. The old man only nodded, as if he'd known this all along.

'But the chaos at Wapping, around the *Thunderer*, and now they're obviously planning something against the *Colossus* at Greenock.'

'What, exactly?' I said. 'They're going to throw stones at it?

Paint dirty pictures on the side? Steal it? I've never hijacked a battleship myself,' – Bunce looked sceptical – 'but I assume there's more to it than when you jump a chap's horse while he's having a piss or bump-start a motor-carriage.' Bunce was wondering whether he'd just heard a confession. 'Even with a concerted programme of sabotage, how much could they delay a ship?' I glanced at Stackhouse, who shrugged in agreement. 'A week or two? That's hardly going to change the balance of power in Europe, is it?'

They waited. In their defence, I'd had more time to think all this through.

'Unless they sail one of their own battleships up the Thames or shell Glasgow docks – and I assume even the Foreign Office would ask questions at that point' – the Foreign Office chap looked non-committal – 'they can't actually stop the battleship. But from what you've told me, the one thing that might alter the current balance of power is if Germany gets her hands on a fire-control table.'

Stackhouse and the other Thames Ironworks man were nodding gravely.

'I thought you said that this Swiss radical was the man,' Sir Percy chipped in. 'We must not overlook the radical threat. The basis of our nation's—'

He was about to start on the benefits of British democracy, so I jumped in. 'I kept tripping over that point myself, sir. Swiss, German, who knows what he really is? I'm sure that there's low-level sabotage at the yard caused by these hotheads. And I think the Germans have wanted to use the radical activity in the yard as cover for their own interests; they've certainly used the conference as cover, and they've used it to get some of their people here incognito. But I kept asking myself: what would these people have to gain from the trouble of the last week, beyond a general sense of jolly mayhem? And what on earth would a bunch of

Swiss revolutionaries want with a fire control table? What are they going to do: put it on a rowing boat and go round and round Lake Geneva lobbing mortar shells into France?'

I shook my head. 'While we've been fretting at all these revolutionaries with their speeches, and the general threat of radicalism in the shipyards, the Germans have had a very specific objective.'

Stackhouse began, 'I still don't see—'

'I think they started with bribery, or some light blackmail. Perhaps they tried others first, but in any case they came to David Sinclair. I suspect they got their hooks into him right enough – poor chap could never refuse a loan – and eventually suggested he could buy his way out of trouble with the technical drawings for the fire-control table. But at some point he baulked. Poor man was being pulled apart.' I thought of Pamela Sinclair, and her wrecked face and her wrecked life. 'By that point he knew too much about who they were – perhaps he'd seen how they were using the trade union and the international radical visit as cover – and so they killed him.'

I hesitated. 'I'm also worried about an acquaintance of his. A man named Samuel Greenberg, of the Commercial Correspondence Confederation. Sinclair had been spending quite a bit of time with him, and that was somehow bound up with his concern about the yard.'

The Assistant Commissioner leaned towards his man. 'Bunce, have you, er…come across, this, er…?'

With impressive speed, Bunce switched from his expression of scornful dismissal to one of complacent competence. 'All part of the enquiry, sir', he lied. 'We'll track him down.'

He looked at me bleakly. In a moment of weakness, I repeated the names for him to write down. Then I pressed on. 'With Sinclair unco-operative, and then out of the way, the Germans had to try something else.'

'They attacked the shipyard,' Savary said. 'Destroyed vital

drawings.'

'But what would that achieve?' This from the other Thames Ironworks man. 'We can replace them inside a day, and they don't get the details.' He shook his head, and Stackhouse echoed the movement.

'No.' The old man. 'They didn't burn them. Now I call that smart.' He looked at me, and smiled grimly. 'They set a fire to cover the fact that they had removed one set of drawings. The fire-control table, no doubt.'

The Foreign Office man said: 'So why all this–'

Sir Percy Savary was coming up slowly but hard to stop: 'So they *do* have a set of our drawings? Of the fire-control table? But this is disastrous! Our nation's–'

'No,' I said. 'Well, yes and no.'

This had the clarifying effect you'd expect. I looked warily at Inspector Bunce. 'You see, I was in the drawings office that night.'

Bunce's eyes went wide. He didn't quite know what it meant, but he knew things were looking up in his campaign to get me back into his cell.

There was a general harrumphing from the others – all except the old man, who was watching me with his usual style, a faintly amused appraisal. 'I'd, er, discovered that these important drawings had been called forward to the yard, and I was trying to follow them.' Bunce was looking wolfish. 'Anyway, long story, but I'd disturbed the papers so that when these chaps broke in after me, and took what they thought were the technical drawings for the fire-control table, they actually got something else. The fire-control table drawings burned.'

'You're sure? Those very particular papers?' Thames Ironworks man. The intensity was understandable, I suppose, given that we were discussing one of the most precious documents in Britain.

'I'm sure. I… I used them as a torch to set fire to the door.'

They were all gazing at me, a general sense of bewilderment and disapproval. 'I destroyed them, but' – I looked at Bunce – 'it worked out rather for the best, I think.'

'Indeed.' The old man. 'Then we tightened security on the drawings, and the enemy have to find another way.'

'Right,' I said. 'And the only way left to them is to steal the thing itself. And that's why the German agents, pretending to be Swiss or whatever as part of the radical delegation, are heading for Glasgow now.'

'So it's… sort of a race,' Stackhouse said.

'I hope not quite so melodramatic,' I said. I glanced between him and his colleague. 'When does the fire-control table get to Glasgow docks and the ship? Is it there already, or will it come up later when the fitting-out is further advanced?'

The colleague was uncomfortable. He glanced at Stackhouse, and then the rest of us. 'Well, our company is not building the H.M.S. *Colossus*, of course, so I don't–'

'But you were sent here on behalf of the industry, I think.' The old man: quiet and cold. 'And you have that information.'

'Get on with it, man!' Sir Percy. Loud and hot.

The colleague opened his briefcase. Then he searched his pockets until he found a pair of wire-rimmed spectacles. Then he dropped his spectacles, and Stackhouse had to help him find them. After various attempts at stabbing himself in the eye, he got the spectacles installed, and started riffling through the papers in his case, methodically flicking over each page corner with a wet finger.

'It shouldn't be in Glasgow yet,' he said.

Our set of tense glaring faces told him that more was needed.

'It should come up by train when the vessel is ready for the command systems to be installed.'

Sir Percy Savary's face in particular looked close to explosion.

More flicking through pages. 'Ooh. I see. Yes, it should be due around about this time.'

He didn't even bother looking up at us. Another page turned. At last he found it. 'Today,' he said, looking rather hunted. 'It goes up the west coast railway line to Glasgow today.'

I looked at Stackhouse again. 'Now it's a race.'

51.

I'm not the heartiest supporter of our diplomats and police, as I hope you'll understand, but I must give them their due. Once they had a clear problem and a clear plan of action, they moved damned smartly.

Well, the police, anyway. The diplomats continued to faff, but at least they didn't get under people's feet too much.

The Foreign Office didn't believe my theory that the German Embassy was behind it – 'but he and the Permanent Under-Secretary saw *Giselle* together last week; it *can't* be true' – but they did at least acknowledge the theoretical proposition that a German campaign of bribery, industrial espionage, theft and murder would in principle offer an occasion for a re-appraisal of the tone of the diplomatic relationship.

The police, in the shape of Inspector Ernest Bunce, still fancied me guilty of... something. Anything. But while they worked out what it might be, they'd acknowledged that the possibility of foreign agents stealing a piece of vital naval technology would be a crime, and one that they should stop. The Assistant Commissioner and the old man had been very clear, and Bunce to his credit had had policemen and telegrams flying all over the place.

Stackhouse and his colleague had checked the paperwork and confirmed that the fire-control table for the *HMS Colossus* would be in a crate in its own railway wagon, which would be attached to the London-to-Glasgow train at Crewe.

Here at Birmingham we were off the main line, of course. Bunce had hauled in the Station Master and interrogated him about train times. Two minutes later he was hurrying Stackhouse and I out of the waiting room and the station and into two motor-cars, which somehow were ready and running with police drivers goggled and gloved and waiting for us.

Bunce yelled instructions over his shoulder as the cars began to move, and the world disappeared in dust as we started careering through the chaos of Birmingham and out into open country. All I knew was the choking dust, and vague shapes that loomed at us and disappeared as the car veered away, and a constant exchange between the horn and shouting angry passers-by.

It's about twenty miles from Birmingham to Tamworth, and we did them in as many minutes. I'd think that a fair speed on a railway train; in a motor-car it was staggering – literally. The vehicles had good strong springs – perhaps a special police adjustment. They might have been robust protection for the car's mechanism but the passengers got shaken to hell. When the cars skidded to a halt outside Tamworth railway station, on the main line north, we pretty much fell out of them and weaved on bewildered legs that would not answer properly away and onto the platform.

'What the devil do you people think you're playing at?' The train was already there, and obviously had been for some while. Dimly I saw a uniformed railway official stomping towards us. 'Don't you people know what it means to hold this train?' Clouds of steam, and faces watching us from every window. 'Your interference means chaos–' But Bunce had pushed him aside and told him to get on with it, and then we were tumbling into the first door we saw and collapsing into seats and breathing hard. Bunce had no idea what it meant to hold the train, but he'd done it.

We were four: Hugh Stackhouse of the Thames Ironworks Shipbuilding Company, and I, and Bunce and a man who'd been in the second car with him, and who I now saw was another policeman. Uniformed, this one, though you could barely tell under the dust. We all looked like we'd come through an explosion.

Something about the policeman seemed familiar.

Bunce saw me looking at the uniform and the ruddy face above it. 'You probably don't remember Sergeant Bulstrode, Delamere,' he said. 'Sergeant Bulstrode doesn't like you either.'

As introductions go, it wasn't the most suave. I was about to explain exactly how little of a damn I gave on either point. But the Sergeant jumped in quickly. 'That's all right, sir,' he said. The voice was a measured west country trudge. 'These things happen in the course of duty.'

I had no idea what they were talking about, and wasn't all that fussed in any case. Between international espionage, revolution, murder, and the incessant attempts to kill me, the moral judgements of individual policemen about my mis-spent life weren't a large concern. Bunce was determined to elaborate. 'Twice he almost got his hands on you, Delamere. Ready for the arrest. And twice he got knocked out in the confusion. Lot of confusion around you, Delamere. Not to worry, Sergeant: third time lucky, eh? Shouldn't be too long now.'

I looked at Quinn's victim a little more closely. I wondered what he really thought of me, and whether over time he would remember more about his night in Jolly's theatre. It seemed that keeping Sergeant Bulstrode apart from my valet would be prudent.

Mercifully, a conductor slid open the door to our compartment.

The voice was as gloomy as the face. 'Thought it was going to be an elopement,' he said. 'It usually is.' He looked without interest at four dusty men. 'I s'pose not.'

'Police business,' Bunce said. 'Let's be away.' The train was already moving hard. The thump-thump of steam belching from the locomotive came clear, and I could feel the acceleration pressing me against the seat.

The conductor didn't seem impressed. 'About the revolutionaries, is it?'

'What?'

'Lot of young fellows talking about revolution. In Carriage G.'

He shook his head, indifferent. Raikes, I suspected, would be short one proletarian when the great day came.

52.

At Stafford, Bunce leapt from the train while it was still slowing, and ran for the station building. Halfway there he saw the conductor, diverted, and yelled something which clearly caused the conductor no joy. The Glasgow express was going to be a little less express today, and relations between the Railwaymen's Union and the Metropolitan Police considerably less cordial. Bunce raced on into the telegraph office.

The minutes passed, while the Glasgow express built up steam and her conductor did much the same. After five minutes, Bunce emerged from the telegraph office and strode, rather than ran, back to our compartment. Another northbound train was pulling in on the opposite platform.

Our conductor contrived to get the train moving just as Bunce's hand and foot reached for it, bringing the Inspector swaying and stumbling through the door and into his seat. Rather sporting by the lugubrious conductor, I thought. As I closed the door, trying not to shut Bunce's foot in it too hard,

I saw a couple running across the platform towards our train. Too far and too blurred for me to be sure; a man and a woman, certainly. The man got a door open in the very last carriage, and pulled the woman in after him.

When Bunce had come upright and stopped swearing, I said: 'Anything?'

'Questions, not answers,' he said, before he'd remembered that he didn't like sharing information with me. He turned to Stackhouse. 'Need you to tell me exactly what's going to happen with this apparatus of yours, sir, when it joins our train at Crewe.' Sir, you see? Bunce could tell a worthy taxpayer when he saw one. Chaps like Stackhouse – polite, obedient, working for influential ship-building companies – were just the sort of chaps that policemen liked to serve.

'Of course Inspector. Yes, that's rather sensible of you.' Nauseating, it was. 'At the factory, the fire-control table will have been packed in a special crate – to protect the mechanism. The crate is then loaded onto a standard railway goods wagon. The wagon is locked, and the guard has the key. A goods engine pulls the wagon out of the factory on the rail spur to the main line, and I gather it's a short journey to Crewe. At Crewe the whole wagon is treated like any other goods car; it's coupled to the end of whichever regular train is going in the right direction. In this case the Glasgow express. This is all worked out and agreed in advance with the railway dispatchers, of course. I've never been part of it myself, even when it's coming to our yard in London, but it seems to run pretty smoothly.'

Bunce was nodding like a connoisseur of the railway freight business. 'Right you are, sir. Well, we'll try to keep it smooth today. We're expecting the trouble in Glasgow, of course. But one step at a time, eh?'

I stood, and slid open the compartment door.

'Going somewhere, Delamere?'

'Obviously, Inspector. I could piss out of the window, but I'm pretty sure there's a by-law against it, and at sixty miles to the hour the wind makes it a little tricky.'

My destination was the last carriage, but to get to it I had to pass the conductor's revolutionaries in Carriage G. I wasn't particularly worried: whether they were part of Raikes's legion of dreamers or the narrower sub-set of Hertenstein's thugs – or indeed some new outing of local enthusiasts – I doubted they'd want to be diverted from their respective causes of overthrowing the bourgeoisie and stealing British secret technology by starting a fight with me. But either way, I didn't want complications, not at this point. And I was something of a celebrity among the radical movement, of course; got the photograph to prove it.

One complication I particularly wanted to avoid at this point was Hertenstein. If he was to be involved in some attempt on the fire-control table at Glasgow, he might well travel up on this train. His gang would presumably stay among the group of international radical tourists for as long as possible. He seemed a chap who was willing to dirty his hands. Hand, anyway, now I'd blown a hole in one of his arms. If I suddenly hove into view outside his compartment window, I couldn't guarantee that he wouldn't go for me just for the hell of the thing. Nor, indeed, that I wouldn't go for him.

I swayed onwards from Coach E towards the back of the train. I found a newspaper in a luggage rack on the way, and had it part-shielding my face as I stepped through the jolting doorway from F into G.

It was the same arrangement as all the other coaches, the type that's been around for a few years now, with a corridor down one side and half a dozen compartments opening off it. As the conductor had suggested, Coach G was the radical jamboree wagon. Each compartment was full and more with my comrades from Birmingham. The same diversity of clothes and accents, the same holiday atmosphere. If I have one hope for my fellow man, as he contemplates upturning all Europe, it is that he seems fairly easily distracted by a free lunch and a day out. Some of the compartment doors were open, and the corridor was full of cigarette smoke and chatter.

I got the impression they were in different national groups for each compartment. Garlic and weak cigarettes in one, no doubt, then comic opera, then sausage and philosophy, and then whatever it is that distinguishes Belgians. All very jolly.

Until the last compartment in the carriage.

The door to the last compartment was closed, and the curtains were half drawn. No suggestion of boisterousness; no sound. From behind my paper, and between the curtains, I could see half a dozen men sitting orderly and silent. In that brief glance, they seemed solid and intent. The same physical presence, the same certainty, as the two killers who'd come for me in Shulstoke wood. I couldn't see the man himself. But I knew, instinctively, that these men were Hertenstein's.

53.

In the last carriage, I found what I'd expected to find.

'Cheap tickets today, is it?' I said. 'Fancied a trip to the seaside?'

Quinn stood, and grumbled a courtesy. Bliss smiled up brightly. She was still looking a little flushed from her sprint across the platform, and terribly pleased with herself.

I sat, and Quinn followed. 'What in hell do you think you're playing at?' I was deliberately not looking at Bliss, but I could tell her expression had changed.

Quinn's voice dropped from grumble to growl. 'It, er, wasn't appropriate to leave the lady alone sir.' Meaning she'd fluttered her eyes at him and begged to come. 'Thought it best to catch up with you sir. Able to lend a hand.'

'Charming idea, Quinn. But getting yourselves killed ain't lending a hand.' They were a liability – Bliss in particular. I wanted to keep her clear of the official party, and preferably alive. I'd also had the rough idea of staying alive myself and perhaps stopping a war; having to worry about the relative movements of Bliss, and Bunce, and the party of revolutionaries, on one single-corridor train was going to make that harder. I turned to her, and I didn't hide my irritation. 'Annabella, charmed as I am and so forth, please believe that you can't help and you can only complicate, and you're at great risk. Yesterday, three men tried to kill me. I shot one of them. I didn't kill the other two, but I did have to interfere with their dead bodies in order to disguise who did. The game is getting more unpleasant, and more dangerous.'

It was supposed to intimidate her. She just glared at me. 'I run my own risks, Harry Delamere,' she said, very haughty. 'And I do as I see fit without consulting you.'

'My compliments', I said. 'Stay here. Keep the curtains drawn on the compartment, and the door locked. Only open up if you're sure it's me – or I suppose the conductor. Do not, under any circumstances, wander around.'

Bliss looked out of the window.

In the doorway, Quinn murmured 'sorry about this, sir. But she—'

'I know, I know. She's best with you, anyway. With your life, you hear?' He nodded. 'Glad you're around, Quinn.'

He produced what passes for the Quinn smile. 'Looks like it might be another lively day, sir,' he said. And from unknown pockets he produced and handed over the Webley, and a packet of sandwiches.

54.

At Crewe the train stopped for ten minutes. This was part of its regular schedule, and today it gave time for the extra wagon with the fire-control table to be added.

Bunce dashed off to the telegraph office. He'd be expecting answers to questions he'd asked at previous stations, and sending more. Efficient, as pestilences go. Quite a few passengers took the chance to stretch their legs, and I joined them.

Stackhouse walked off towards the back of the train to watch the extra wagon being shunted in. As Bunce had said, the trouble was due in Glasgow. But Stackhouse was incapable of anything less than professional care.

The philosophers of Carriage G were quick off, chattering happily. Crewe railway station's an impressive place, if you're interested in the lot of the working man. Not one of the fine architectural specimens: a sprawl of brick and iron and wood and wire built and run in the service of the industrial age. The group arranged themselves for a portrait photograph against a locomotive on the adjacent platform. This time I wasn't invited to join them.

The photographer was just preparing to make the exposure, when I heard what sounded like a shot. It came from the direction of the front of our train.

There was so much noise: the constant belching of steam, the thumping as it was forced through pistons, and the screaming of whistles, and the shouted instructions.

And then another shot, surely. And a scream.

I still wasn't certain. I made for the front of the train anyway.

At the locomotive I found Bunce, shouting up to the driver. 'You hear that?'

'What?'

'Shots, maybe!'

The driver shrugged. His fireman, comically short beside him, shrugged. 'Maybe,' the driver said. 'Over there maybe.' He pointed.

I followed Bunce between the back of the locomotive and its tender, stepping over the tracks and ducking under the coupling. It's all much bigger when you're close up. On the next platform we found a uniformed railway man, gazing around confused. He also shrugged at us. He also had heard something. There was no sign of the something.

I dislike running around to no purpose. I dislike the impression that I'm getting jumpy.

Back on our platform, another uniform was trying to comfort a shaken woman. She was fighting tears, fighting for breath. This was Bunce's element, and he was quickly engaged. A masked man, she said. Two masked men, perhaps. What exactly? Where exactly? It was difficult to say. What exactly had she seen? It was difficult to say. A mask? Well, she hadn't seen all of his face...

Bunce looked angry; frustrated. He looked at me, presumably wondering if this also was somehow my fault. I said: 'Perhaps she broke into the Thames Ironworks shipyard, too.'

He didn't find it funny. Nor did I. We were both edgy, both confused. Chasing shadows.

The whistle shrieked from our train. The conductor yelled something. Bunce knew he'd get nothing more from the woman, and we hurried back.

We met Stackhouse, at the door to our compartment. 'All right?' I said.

He nodded, stability restored. 'Coupled up now.'

Another whistle, and we boarded.

We'd passed Warrington – wherever on earth that is – when there was a knock on the compartment door.

It was Quinn.

I wasn't all that pleased to see him – I'd hoped to keep him away from the official party, as I'd said – and Inspector Bunce certainly wasn't. 'Where the hell did you spring from, my lad?'

Quinn has a strong and subtle sense of the hierarchy of things, and I don't think it includes policemen talking to him like that. Particularly not policemen who'd spent a day or two messing up his domestic order. 'A scheduled service on the spur line from Birmingham to Stafford,' he said stiffly. 'No doubt you were aware of the possibility.'

'This is Sergeant Bulstrode, Quinn,' I said quickly, pointing to same. 'Quite the warrior for the cause, eh sergeant?' The sergeant grunted complacently, and nodded at Quinn. 'You'll not believe it, Quinn, but the sergeant was knocked out twice in one evening, on the track of these villains.'

Quinn considered the Sergeant. 'Now I call that low,' he said at last. 'Assaulting an officer doing his lawful duty.' It was shameless. The sergeant started to say something sturdy and fake-humble, and Bunce started on who the real villains might be, but Quinn wasn't finished. 'I wonder if I could invite you into the corridor, sir,' he said to me. 'There's a... a particular view hereabouts that my cousin Gerald insists is worth looking out for.'

I followed him out of the compartment. 'Gerald?' I said. 'Always the danger of over-elaboration, Quinn. And you'd better watch yourself around that sergeant.'

Quinn glanced dismissively back towards the compartment. 'Devon accent, sir, I fancy. Nothing to worry about in that head. Next time I'll hit him properly.'

'Well?'

He checked that we couldn't be heard from the compartment. 'Your hefty German acquaintance, sir. Thought you should know: Miss Bliss says he's on the train.'

It wasn't a shock or even a surprise.

'Is he now?' My mental sketch of the mechanisms of European chaos was becoming a little complex. 'Wait – how in hell does she know? Telepathy? Lucky guess?'

'She insisted on going to the lavatory, sir, and–'

'Oh, Christ. Disguised as a…?'

'I convinced her that a veil was enough. She's… wilful, sir.'

'She's a pain in the arse.'

'If we will involve the ladies in our activities, sir…'

'She more or less saved my life, Quinn. And she looks damned fine in a burgundy corset.'

'That's a lot of detail, sir. Perhaps next time just a courteous word of appreciation, or flowers.'

'Alright, alright. Did Von Hahn see Bliss?'

'No, sir. She was definite on that point.'

'I don't doubt it. She was dressed as a station porter by this point, of course, or a rhododendron bush.' I reflected. 'Very well. Back you go and keep an eye on her. I'd like to keep you in tactical reserve, Quinn. Behind the kopje, where the enemy can't see you, yes?'

'Aye, sir. You worried about him?'

'Well, I'm more worried by the revolutionaries on the train. And the revolutionaries not on the train, the Metropolitan Police, and indeed the conductor. But he's on my list, yes.' I considered. 'He's surely not going to be doing any dirty work himself. So why is he on the train?'

55.

As we pulled in to Wigan, where the branch lines come in from Liverpool and Manchester, half a dozen policemen were waiting on the platform. I assumed this was the fruit of one of Bunce's earlier telegrams. He sent one of them forward, just in case there was any trouble at the locomotive. One he kept with him as a runner. Two went to lurk around coach G, to keep an eye on the radicals. What they were supposed to do there wasn't clear, beyond cautioning the tourists for being foreign without due care and attention. And two he sent as far back as they could go – coach H that would be, where Quinn and Bliss were, just before the luggage wagon and the special wagon.

As usual, when Bunce stopped trying to think, he was impressive. There wasn't anything more that could be done to protect the fire-control table, solitary in the last wagon. And trouble if any wasn't expected until Glasgow docks. But Bunce had gathered what forces he could and deployed them as best he could.

One of his policemen had also brought an update on Bunce's preparations. 'All lining up nicely in Glasgow,' he said to Stackhouse. 'It'll all be ready for us, sir.' He waved a telegraph form like his winning ace. 'Special measures, as I requested.' He looked down proudly at the paper. 'Glasgow police and detectives will meet you on arrival Greenock Docks Stop. Known radicals watched Stop. Military standing by Stop.' Each 'Stop' was proof of the brisk efficiency of the British constabulary, and treated accordingly. 'Regular movements at yard suspended Stop.' He looked up. Stackhouse was nodding polite approval. 'Not sure we'll need the Army in this. Not ideal. Upsets the civilians. Anyways, we'll be ready in case anyone does try anything against your apparatus.'

He moved on to the next telegram. 'Hel-lo…' he said hungrily. Clearly a special day for police efficiency. 'And another little breakthrough in the business of your colleague – Mr Sinclair.' Stackhouse was interested. 'Investigations had shown that Mr Sinclair had seen a lot of one Samuel Greenberg.' Delamere's investigations, he might have added; he didn't, though.

'Was that what made you suspicious of poor David?' Stackhouse said. Bunce sucked his teeth. Bunce was suspicious of everyone; hardly fair to particularize.

'We didn't know anything about this Mr Greenberg. But we found out his lodgings, and there were some photographs there, and we copied them and showed to them to his landlady and to Mrs Sinclair. We know what Greenberg looks like now.' He was rummaging in an inside pocket. 'Makes it more likely we can find him, ask him some questions.' He glanced at me, as grim as ever. He was anticipating that the mysterious Greenberg would be able to confirm my involvement.

I confess I was interested myself. Greenberg was perhaps the one man who could explain what had been on David Sinclair's mind before his death. So much so that I'd become increasingly concerned that he'd suffered the same fate as Sinclair. If all those policemen could finally be put to good use and root him out of wherever he was hiding…

Bunce pulled out a sheaf of papers from his pocket, to add to the sheaf of telegrams. 'Here we are,' he said. He was glancing between one of the telegrams, and a photograph he'd brought with him. 'Sources confirm Figure B Greenberg.'

He passed the photograph to Stackhouse. Stackhouse shrugged, and shook his head. I took the photograph from him, before Bunce could stop me. Not a very clear reproduction, but adequate. Three men, relaxed but at some formal event, smiling towards the camera. A, B and C had been pencilled in beneath them on the reproduction.

Like Stackhouse, I shrugged and shook my head, and I passed the picture back to Bunce.

Inwardly, I felt that familiar cold stab.

Once again, Inspector Bunce was going to be disappointed. He wouldn't be getting any useful information from Figure B, the man who called himself Samuel Greenberg. Figure B was dead. I was certain of this, but it didn't seem prudent to mention it to Bunce.

I recognized Greenberg.

The last I'd seen of him, he'd been smouldering on my carpet.

Bunce and Co. hadn't recognized him because, by the time I'd finished with it, his head hadn't been of the recognizable sort.

For Bunce and for me, Samuel Greenberg had been the key to understanding the original mystery, and I'd shot him.

Once again, it felt like the moment to stretch my legs.

56.

In the dining car I found Otto Immanuel Von Hahn.

It was the wrong hour for anyone to be eating. He had the carriage to himself, and his isolation increased his grandeur. Amid the best of the finery that the London and North Western could offer, and behind the pure white tablecloth, he was vast and serene.

He saw me, and the big face spread in a smile. He unrolled his hand and offered me the seat opposite him. Von Hahn would always behave as if he owned wherever he was.

He probably did. No doubt he was a major shareholder of the London and North Western Railway. And a regular whist companion of the Chairman of the Board.

I sat.

He lifted a wine bottle. 'A surprisingly adequate white,' he said. Again the deep boom of the words, the heavy manipulation of foreign letter sounds. He made to pour me some of the surprisingly adequate white, but I shook my head. He frowned. 'I thought that this abstinence was only when you gamble.' I said nothing. 'Ah, you see this meeting as a gamble!' I smiled. Suddenly he looked grave. 'It was your choice, Sir Henry, to enter my casino.'

'I'm a lucky fellow.'

He shook his head. Still the grave expression, the wise uncle trying to share important wisdom. 'You must know this, Sir Henry: the house – always – wins.'

'I'm rather a bad sport, if I think the game is rigged. Liable to tear the house down.'

He considered this seriously. He nodded. 'Tell me', he said. He tapped a book that lay beside him on the tablecloth. 'What sites of interest should I visit during my excursion to Glasgow?'

'I'm English. I could tell you more about Cairo and Constantinople than I could about any British city.'

He beamed and nodded.

'I thought it was the docks you're interested in,' I said.

He shrugged. For him, shrugging was an enormous movement, like a buffalo coming out of a swamp. 'I leave these things to the mechanics.'

'Yes, you do, don't you? Bloody mayhem across the country, and it's all your doing, and we'll never be able to prove any of it.'

He watched me silently, satisfied.

'Men like Greenberg, who was your front man for bribery and blackmail and running secret agents: they must come out of the shadows to do your bidding; they must speak, they must leave their fingerprints on everything, they must run the risks and sometimes they must die. Men like Hertenstein the first, the brother: he had to show himself, and fight me to the death.' Von Hahn took a sip of the wine. 'But not you. You stay in the shadows, and you leave no marks, and you run no risks.'

'You were a junior officer, Delamere, I think. But you understand how armies work.' The words growled out, unfamiliar in his accent. 'A general who forgets the battlefield and focuses on the capture of one strongpoint, a general who picks up a sword and runs to the front of the attack, this is an imbecile.'

'And now your agents are going to try to steal a fire-control table.'

He was silent for a time, just watching me. There was a faint superior smile lurking in the eyes and mouth. I resisted the urge to punch him in the face.

At last he said: 'I have not heard of such a thing.' He was more serious suddenly. 'Is it yet another machine by which England exercises her aggressive dominance over the world, while other nations must struggle for crumbs, for enough air to breathe?'

I considered him. 'You're doing alright for crumbs and air, Von Hahn. Come on, admit it. I still can't prove anything, but satisfy my curiosity. You set your agents to all of it: to the attempts to buy or steal a copy of the technical drawings, and now to steal the machine itself; you're behind all those deaths. And you've tried to kill me... what, three times?'

He considered the wine, swirled it gently in his big paw.

'I decline,' he said at last, 'to satisfy your curiosity. Bragging is a bad habit, anyway. So no, you do not get no confessions out of me, Sir Henry.' He smiled. 'It might be amusing to put us against each other in the witness box, and see whom your establishment believes. The honoured foreigner over the disreputable Englander, I fear.'

He pulled a watch on a chain out of his waistcoat pocket. 'But you must allow me my discretion.' The watch was sized like the man, a great gold onion. He looked up at me. 'four-twenty-eight,' he said.

'You have an appointment?'

'No, Sir Henry.' Still the all-powerful gaze. 'You do.'

I took a breath. 'Oh really? And what is this appointment?'

For a moment he looked as though he might tell me. Then he smiled and shook his head. 'Sir Henry, I have been observing you for many days now. You are a man of action. Not so stupid, I mean, but you are best in the moment of crisis. I think I leave you to respond according to your instincts.' Another big smile. 'That is the sporting approach, I think!' He'd enjoyed that one very much. His big body shuddered.

He wasn't fat, I realized now. Just vast. A great ox, arrogant and utterly sure of his greatness and his power.

'You're running a risk, Von Hahn. A man like me – reckless, disreputable – perhaps I might do something desperate just to stop you.'

He gazed at me for a few moments, eyes narrow. Then he shook his head. 'No risk, no. The man who is in control, this is the man who may calculate. In the calculation of an intelligent man, there is no risk.' He leaned forwards again. 'It is the man who finds himself hunted in the theatre or the forest, and must fight for his life, the man who is trapped in an office and must run through the fire, this man runs risks.'

It was rather a good point.

'You must decide if you wish to play this game, Delamere. You have now... one minute to decide.'

'I decided a while back. I'm taking you on.'

He looked as if I'd made a dirty joke. 'My fight is not with you personally, Sir Henry Delamere. You are... incidental. If you are destroyed by interfering in my affairs, this was your choice. But – how would you put it? – outside the boxing arena, there shall be no underhand tactics.'

'And you trust me to be so sporting?'

Suddenly he looked ominous. 'Yes, Sir Henry, I do.' He leaned forwards. 'You act the lone wolf, but even you have your points of weakness; points of... affection. You were seen with a woman in London. And of course the most wonderous Lady Victoria.' He pulled back, which meant he'd seen the immediate hardening of my face. He watched me carefully for a moment. Then he relaxed, and smiled again. 'This, you see?' He waved his hand towards me. 'This emotion. Emotion is weakness, Delamere. Affection is vulnerability.' He sat back.

I did the same. I considered him. At last I smiled at him. 'Very well, Von Hahn. I think you'll dislike defeat more than you'd dislike danger. So you sit back and watch, and see what happens.' I leaned forwards. 'I think you've miscalculated.'

Again he gave the great shrug. And again he pulled the watch from his pocket, and this time he placed it carefully on the table between us.

The ticking of the second hand was loud.

'I was saying to someone a short while ago,' I said, 'that I couldn't work out why you're on the train.'

Cold, cold eyes. Tick, tick, tick.

'Why Sir Henry: a pleasant day out, and a little sport – surely this is the most English of diversions, no?'

Together we watched the second hand tick round, and then reach the half-hour.

From somewhere back along the train, there was an explosion.

57.

I ran back through Carriage D, and through Carriage E, pushing past concerned citizens. Our compartment was empty, the door wide; hasty departure.

At the near end of Carriage F I found Bunce, and Stackhouse, and the Sergeant and another policeman crowded round the door of the lavatory.

'Caught short, Inspector?' I said. 'Must be tiresome in your business.'

Stackhouse said: 'Some kind of explosion.'

I peered between their bobbing heads. Inside the lavatory, a policeman was beating out a few last flames, on the scorched and pocked cubicle wall. There had indeed been a small explosion.

'Clever way to start the revolution,' I said. 'With the privies out of commission, we'll all explode naturally.' But I doubt they heard: I was already striding down the carriage towards the back of the train.

In Carriage G, the revolutionaries were milling around like everyone else. But not the last compartment. The six solid silent men I'd glimpsed through the curtains had gone. I hurried on into Carriage H.

'Stand fast sir!' The compartment door beside me was half-open and Quinn's arm had shot out to block my way. I glanced at him, stepped into the gap. He nodded towards the back of the train. 'Gunshot, while everyone was fretting about the explosion.'

I drew the Webley from its inside pocket. Another gunshot rang clear from the rear of the train, and then a scream from somewhere. 'Bunce!' I yelled. 'Come out of the privy. You're missing the party.' From the next carriage, I heard the bellowing of an Inspector barging his way through a couple of dozen radical tourists. 'Sit tight,' I said to Quinn, and set off towards the back of the carriage.

Bunce was less cautious than me, and we reached the end of Carriage H at the same moment. In the last compartment a policeman was lying on the floor, unconscious, with a nasty-looking knock on his head. Round the corner, at the very end of the carriage, another was lying on his side, groaning and clutching at where he'd been shot. Beyond him was the door that led through the end of the carriage into the regular luggage wagon. The door was half open, and the luggage wagon was in darkness.

Bunce lunged forwards to his wounded man and I grabbed him back and another shot cracked. 'Idiot', I hissed. 'I want you alive to see me proved right, remember?' I raised the Webley. 'Ready?' He nodded.

I fired twice through the gap into the darkness of the luggage wagon, and Bunce swooped to his man and dragged him back into the main corridor. Two more shots echoed back.

More of Bunce's policemen had come up now, and were looking in concern at their wounded comrades. 'Quinn!' I called down over the heads. 'Medical detail!'

'What in hell are they up to in there?' Bunce hissed at me.

'Hacking their way out of the other end of the luggage wagon, I guess. Then through into the wagon beyond, where the fire-control table is.'

I heard a smash from the luggage wagon. Bunce said: 'Cover me again. I'm getting in there.'

Cautiously, I stuck my head around the corner at the end of the corridor, until I could see the doorway again. 'Tempting,' I said. 'But I think the game has changed.' Through the doorway I could see flames spreading rapidly in the darkness of the luggage wagon. Smoke began to drift out towards us. 'I guess they're through and away.'

We both took deep breaths, ducked low, and stepped through the door and the short concertina passageway that joined the carriage to the luggage wagon. The doors would normally have been locked, and I could see where the locks had been hacked open.

The luggage wagon was a little inferno, a box of darkness with a fire blazing at its heart and spreading. Everything in the luggage would burn nicely, and I guessed the smash had been an oil lamp. 'Sergeant Bulstrode!' Bunce yelled, and the sergeant acknowledged. 'Three men! In here now!' Through the flames and smoke, in the back wall of the wagon I could see a rough rectangle of daylight where the attackers had hacked through. I sensed the policemen behind me. 'Jump to it!' Bunce hissed between coughs. 'Drag away anything that's not burned. Find heavy clothes in the trunks and beat out the flames.' It was smart thinking, and immediately the policemen were at work.

Dimly, in the rectangle of daylight, I saw figures moving.

'Give me two yards' run-up first,' I said. The fire dominated the centre of the wagon, but it wasn't climbing at the walls yet.

It didn't seem so deep. I'd probably make it.

Someone said 'What?' and grabbed at my arm and I pushed them away. I stepped back to the doorway, handed the revolver to Quinn, and took in a breath of goodish air. Then I turned. It didn't bear too much thinking about. I put one arm up over my face, and took a three step run towards the flames and leapt. Something snagged at my boot but didn't stop me and I landed and stumbled and dragged myself forwards. Another couple of yards and I was at the back wall.

I raised my head above the sill of the rough doorway they'd hacked in it. Immediately they were in front of me. They'd hacked a matching doorway in the rearmost wagon. One was standing in that, holding another by the belt as he bent and fiddled with the coupling between the wagons. For a moment they didn't see me, then I must have moved again in surprise at their proximity. Two faces gaped, and the one hanging over the coupling swayed dangerously over the gap and swore at his mate. The other yelled something. I could see more movement in the wagon beyond.

The man working at the coupling and the man holding him both had their hands full. It was a moment's chance. I braced myself between the two sides of the doorway, put one boot on the sill, and swung a kick at the crouching man. He went stumbling back, pushing his comrade. The coupling held; they were still attached to the train. I was swaying wildly, clinging to the shattered planks of the wagon and trying to hold my balance on one leg on the narrow sill. The sky and the countryside reeled around me, and then below me the rushing stones and sleepers of the railway track.

I got myself up and steady in the doorway, and was immediately confronted by a pistol projecting from the rear wagon just a foot from my face. I flung myself backwards into the luggage wagon as the shot roared over my head. Angry, stupid, I was back in the gap in an instant. Chummy was bent over the coupling again. I pulled myself into the doorway. As I got there, he was rising with something metal in his hand and I jumped for him.

We both toppled towards the other wagon. And now the movement changed sickeningly. Whatever I was standing on seemed to change direction, and then one of the bandits got an arm free and landed a punch on my shoulder and I swayed backwards again. The wind and the world roared around me and I was tottering on God knows what bit of the coupling, and the enemy were accelerating away from me and I was alone and swaying in the sky and then I fell.

58.

The world was a wild blur of light and wind. Now I pretend I remember fragments of what I saw as I fell: the smouldering luggage wagon, or perhaps the other wagon with the fire-control table and the faces of the bandits dropping away behind, the sky, the Cumbrian landscape, the horrendous rushing of the track beneath me.

I saw none of it. I fell and it was sickening and I knew it was the end. My whole body jerked and twisted and my head jarred on something and I was stunned. I felt my boots dragging on the rushing ground and I flailed desperately. My arms, somehow, were flapping at the coupling. My feet were being flung around by contact with the ground and I was horribly aware of the metal wheels of the train whirling and screaming near, and still I hung over death.

I doubt I've mentioned my tailor before.

Why would I? Cockayne is nothing out of the ordinary: ordinarily hysterical about occasional delays in the settling of my account; ordinarily susceptible to little fads of cut or embellishment from the continent; ordinarily expensive.

I mention him now, because at that moment of imminent death he was suddenly very much in my mind. By some fluke, as I'd dropped towards the railway track a prong of some kind on the coupling mechanism had contrived to get hooked up under my waistcoat towards my armpit. As the Glasgow express raced on, and I tried to lift my battered swinging feet away from the track and my arms waved uselessly, I was held up solely by this prong and swinging wildly around it. My life hung, very really, by a thread: specifically, the thread that Cockayne had sewn across the shoulder of my waistcoat. So, as I say, he was suddenly in my mind. Always banging on about traditional craftsmanship, Cockayne, and now I had to wonder how committed he really was.

I knew I had to stop writhing or I'd tear it. I managed to get my legs tucked up under me, though God only knew how long I could hold that, and I managed to hold my waving arms still. For one frozen moment, I contemplated the metal prong and the wrenched bit of waistcoat that hung from it, close against my face.

Say what you like about tweed, but there are times when a gentleman has to rely on a good strong-woven bit of British cloth.

I felt my legs tiring, felt my arms instinctively scrabbling for purchase. I saw the twisted material straining in front of my eye.

Then something jerked one of my arms up, and then the other, and I was looking up into the face of Inspector Ernest Bunce. With my wrists gripped in his hands, he adjusted himself, and then heaved me up until I was perched on the coupling with my hands clutching the rough door frame.

We stared at each other through the doorway.

'Bunce,' I gasped; 'is there any chance you're starting to believe I'm innocent?'

'No,' he said cheerfully over the rattle of wheels. 'But you're about the most incompetent guilty man I've ever met, and that's got to be good news.'

59.

Bunce raced off down what was left of the train, yelling for the conductor.

I staggered wearily after him, through the smouldering residue of the luggage. Then Quinn was there, of course, and somehow he had a flask of brandy, and soon enough I was starting to feel chipper again.

He plonked me in his compartment with Bliss, and went off at my request to find out what Bunce was doing. Bliss gazed at me, rather appalled. 'Where did you get to?' she said.

'Under the train.'

One of the side-effects of a reputation for smart-aleck remarks is that no one believes you when you say something surprising. Mercifully, she didn't comment. She took one of my hands, and started to examine it with apparent fondness.

Suddenly there was the smell of perfume. 'Why on earth are you putting – Damnit!' My hand stung fiercely.

She tutted. 'Alcohol base in the perfume,' she said. 'You're badly scratched.' I looked at my hands. I was badly scratched. I sat back and let her finish dousing them in floral scent and tried not to cry out again.

Quinn appeared in the compartment doorway. 'We'll be in Carlisle in a moment,' he said. 'The Inspector'll alert the local police from there, and we'll reverse up the line to chase that wagon.'

Bliss said: 'Would either of you care to tell me what on earth's going on?'

The train was slowing now, and the first buildings of Carlisle appeared through the window.

I told her: the explosion, distracting most of the police while Hertenstein's ruffians overpowered the two guarding the door to the luggage wagon; the gunfire and the burning luggage to hold the police back; hacking their way into the special wagon and uncoupling it so that it dropped away from the speeding train, leaving them free to make off with Britain's secret naval apparatus. 'Worked out handily for them,' I said, looking to Quinn. 'We were going up a gradient at the time, so as soon as they uncoupled their wagon they were moving away from us back down the slope. That'll give them a few more minutes to play with.'

We hadn't quite stopped in Carlisle station, but I saw a policeman racing away from the train towards the station building. As soon as we had stopped, there were two or three voices shouting 'Stay on the train! Stay on the train!' It was hard to believe that among the policemen and revolutionaries there were still a fair number of regular humans. Regular humans presumably increasingly bewildered at what was happening to their day out. And they hadn't yet seen what the bandits had done to their luggage, either. Already the train was heaving and belching and starting backwards. Again, Inspector Bunce had had his plan and worked it quickly. I wondered what the conductor was making of it all.

A minute later Bunce himself was with us, a face suddenly in the compartment doorway, wild-eyed and determined. His pistol was already out – if he'd ever put it away. 'We'll get them now! They've only minutes! There's no way they can unload it in that time!' Immediately he was away to what was now the front of the train, the ruined luggage wagon.

'We should, too,' I said. 'They can't have brought another locomotive up in time: even if they could steal one, they'd have to capture umpteen signal boxes to keep it on this track after us. Their wagon will have rolled gently to a stop, and now they're trying to manhandle a damned great crate off it and onto a cart or a motor car while the police close in.'

'Take a while for the police to get there,' Quinn said. He nodded at the dramatic landscape outside the window, the hills all around us. 'Bad country.'

'I guess they knew whereabouts they were stopping. But fewer roads for the police is fewer roads for them, too.'

'Pretty desperate business.'

He was right. It was a pretty desperate business.

And where was Hertenstein, anyway, while his gang were up to their desperate games? Lord knows I didn't admire the fellow all that much, but he struck me as the kind of villain who'd be on the spot for the main event. As when he'd popped up in the woods to enjoy my execution.

By natural progression of thought, Von Hahn came into my mind. He was presumably still sitting in the dining car, enjoying his white wine. Was that glacial calm, that arrogant certainty, affected by the noises of the battle he had started, or by the police toing and froing?

It didn't seem likely, as I thought of his face.

None of it seemed likely. Not for a man who calculated likelihoods so finely.

Bliss said: 'It must have been a clever plan.'

I kept starting to stand, to go and join Bunce in the luggage wagon for the imminent battle. And I kept hesitating. 'It was a clever plan', I said. 'Back and forth and always looking in the wrong direction.' I shook my head. 'And... so what?'

Annabella Bliss nodded thoughtfully, and said: 'The duck's mask.'

I gazed at her. 'I don't really have time, but: what?'

'One of the essential ideas of magic; one of the very oldest principles of the stage. Actually, it's French: *les deux masques*; but we're a bit behind on our French reading skills in the London theatre. The audience knows they're being tricked; they're looking and they're looking, and they're determined the magician won't catch them out. And then they spot it, they see the trick, look behind the mask. And they're so pleased with themselves they don't realize there's a second mask. The real trick is somewhere else completely.'

Quinn said: 'like when you're playing Spot The Lady on the street corner and someone's picking your pocket?'

'That's it.'

'It's a charming bit of cultural history,' I said, 'and I'll know when to pop out for a gasper when I'm next at Jolly's, but I can't see how it's relevant.'

And yet; and yet... It reinforced my discomfort.

Von Hahn was more than explosions. Armed battles with the police were far too chancy for him, surely.

I looked at Bliss. I waited for the flip comment, the petulance at my scepticism.

But it wasn't there. She was just watching me, patiently; gazing with those big brown eyes. Then she said, quietly: 'What is it, Harry? What have you seen but not seen?'

And then I was racing down the corridor, shoving people aside left and right and yelling 'Bunce! Stop this damned train!'

60.

Bunce wouldn't stop the train, even when I'd tried to explain. I didn't have anything certain that I could explain. He'd been the policeman in charge when foreign agents had stolen Britain's most important bit of naval technology, and now he was going to be the policeman in charge when it was recovered. I didn't entirely blame him.

That didn't stop me cursing him pretty comprehensively for his stubbornness and stupidity. It made me feel a bit better, at least, and then I went looking for the conductor.

A few minutes later I felt the train slowing, and before it had stopped I had dropped down to the trackside and was running beside it. I knew what I was going to find, and speed wouldn't change it. But I was losing time nonetheless. Near the back of the train I caught up with Bunce and Sergeant Bulstrode and Stackhouse, all running.

Fifty yards ahead of us, beyond the back of the train, sitting alone and proud on the track, was the lost wagon. There wasn't a village or even a house in any direction. Just the emptiness of Cumbria, and in the middle of it that wooden wagon.

No one seemed to be nearby. Bunce covered the last twenty yards with his pistol up and ready, and I let him go ahead. He needed to see this himself, and first.

There were boxes and cases strewn around the side of the wagon. The sliding door was still open. Bunce stood in front of it, looking up into the wagon.

I was destined never to make Inspector Ernest Bunce happy.

'It's not there, is it?' I said. 'It's never been there.'

61.

Bunce was staring at me, at the world, in bafflement. Never a man to baffle sedately, he was looking damned angry about it. Strangely, it reinforced my respect for him. He would never give up, this policeman.

I walked up to him, stood right in front of him, clasped him by the back of the neck, and stared into him. It was strange enough that for a moment he didn't resist. Nearby, Stackhouse was staring into the wagon, still half full of baggage, and Sergeant Bulstrode was saying something about fresh wheel-ruts in the track that ran alongside the railway line.

'Inspector,' I said, 'your success – your career – and my inno-cence are the same thing now. Now more than ever, we need to think clear and we need to think fast.' He stared. Angry, but not entirely stupid. 'Unless you plan to chase a cart or a motor-car across rough ground on foot, you have no time to waste here. There is no use fooling around the wagon. If we have any chance of success, it's back on that train, moving forwards. That's where the next station is, the next telegraph office. That's where rein-forcements are. That's where the battle is.'

He stared a bit longer. Then he nodded. Just once, but it was a beautiful sight. Then he was bawling at Sergeant Bulstrode and dragging Stackhouse with him back to the train.

I don't think he was brandishing his pistol in the face of the conductor with intent to threaten – he just hadn't got round to re-pocketing it – but that was certainly the impression the conductor got. Within moments the train was accelerating northwards again. God knows what the regular passengers were thinking.

Bunce all but pushed me into a seat and sat down opposite. 'Talk', he said.

'At the next station telegraph office, you will get the local police to that wagon, and you'll get them following the wheel marks of the vehicle that came along that track to pick up the men. That's good. Maybe you even catch them. Either way, you won't get the fire-control table.' Bunce was doing his not blink-ing trick again. 'It was never on this train.'

His eyes went wide. I was losing him again.

'These are clever resourceful men, Inspector. Hijacking the fire-control table en route, and transferring it on to a cart, and trying to get away across country, that's a hellish long shot. A dozen ways it can go wrong, they've nothing to gain from a scrap, and they end up in a race which they're not guaranteed to win. Could they have got the thing out of the wagon and onto a vehicle, with no heavy lifting apparatus, and be out of sight, in the few minutes it took us to get back there?' I shook my head. 'Same with our original idea, that they were somehow going to snatch the thing from under your nose in the docks.'

The train was slowing again, as we approached Carlisle. Bunce felt it too, and I could see him bracing for action. I had to hurry.

'It's all just to distract us, and above all to delay us. D'you remember back in Crewe, when the wagon was being coupled? And right at that moment, our attention was distracted to the opposite end of the train, with shots and screams that didn't mean anything?' He frowned. 'They probably improvised that bit when they found that we were on their train. Anyway, that was when they switched it.'

'Switched it?'

'Put the wrong wagon on our train. They've got a few friends among the working men, haven't they? Stackhouse here saw *a* wagon being hitched up. But he couldn't tell it wasn't *the* wagon.' Stackhouse looked uncomfortable. He shook his head at Bunce.

'So where the hell's the right one then?'

Again the buildings of Carlisle and then the station rose outside the window. The train was coming to a stop.

'Somewhere in Britain. When you send your telegrams organizing the local police, get the conductor to send one asking for details of any special chartered trains travelling north on this line this afternoon. Then we'll find out where the hell it is.'

62.

Another policeman was thrown off at Carlisle with a set of messages to send. We continued northwards, as fast as the Glasgow Express would go.

We continued because Bunce would have exploded if he'd tried stopping. And northwards, partly because it still felt like forwards, partly because there was an empty wagon blocking our way southwards, and partly because of my instinct that this was still the logical direction for the Germans to bring their prize.

They'd have chartered a locomotive to pull the wagon, but they couldn't disrupt the regular timetables of the railways. And they still needed to get the fire-control table onto a boat and away quickly, and that meant a port. There weren't so many ports with railway links to the water's edge. And if they still hoped to be inconspicuous as they loaded, they'd be better in a large port.

'Anyone know how big Glasgow docks actually are?' I said. There was a general shaking of heads.

Stackhouse said: 'The *Colossus* is at Greenock, and I think that's several miles down the Clyde from the city. Never been there – not our yard, not our battleship – but I get the impression it's quite a sprawl. Different bits of docks on both sides of the Clyde for miles.' He saw where I was going, and looked doubtful. 'You don't think they're still going there?'

'Where better? One of our biggest ports, ain't it? Lovely place to lose a railway wagon and a boat.' My brain was working better now. I think the brandy helped. 'And when they first planned this, they'd reckon that even if we had detectives or soldiers waiting at Glasgow, we'd stand them down once the wagon had failed to arrive.'

At Lockerbie there was a telegram waiting for Bunce. Someone going by the name of Engineering Projects Limited had chartered a special train, to run from Crewe to Glasgow this afternoon. Locomotive and tender, one passenger carriage plus one goods wagon. Just sometimes, very very occasionally, I get a thing exactly right. I think it's worth celebrating when it happens.

Bunce got his pal the conductor in, and starting quizzing him about journey times. The conductor was unhappy about the whole business: a heated Bunce, combined with the implied abuse of his beloved railway network, got his back up properly. Eventually, we convinced him that it was the German agents who were disrupting his timetable, not us, and he started to co-operate.

'But they must be running about the same as us!' he said after a moment's thought. 'Those times you said are close enough to ours.'

'Behind us or in front?' Bunce asked.

'Can't be sure. Even if they'd started behind us, there's enough stretches of double track on this route they could have overtaken us any time; it's mostly double track from here on in to Glasgow. That is, if they could manage the points.'

I thought of Hertenstein, and his smart ruthless gang, up against an isolated signal man. 'They can manage the points,' I said. 'What's the next station?'

'Lesmahagow.'

'I beg your pardon?'

'The junction. They call it Motherwell now. Plenty track there. They'll have to slow with the big bend, but they won't need to stop.'

I glanced at Bunce. 'When are they due there, according to the timetable for that special?'

'6.30.'

'That's 40 minutes.' To the conductor: 'How long until we make whatever you call it?'

'Approximately 40 minutes.'
'Here's your race then, Stackhouse.'

63.

A couple of miles short of Motherwell station the railway line makes a sharp curve left, and we saw them.

A goods wagon, a carriage in front of it, and a locomotive smoking steadily. Hertenstein's band of German professional assassins and their prize, Britain's most precious piece of naval technology, chased by Inspector Ernest Bunce and Sir Harry Delamere and a couple of hundred holidaymakers who'd made the mistake of travelling on the Glasgow Express.

For a moment, I thought it was a trick of light or distance. 'They've stopped!' Bunce into the wind.

'Signal,' the conductor said.

No sooner had he said it, than they started to move again. But it took time for their locomotive to gather momentum, and we were still going at speed, and in a moment we had gained dramatically. 'Faster!' Bunce was shouting.

The conductor was unimpressed. 'We have to stop at Motherwell anyway.'

'No we damn well don't!'

'Listen mate, you ever seen a train wreck?' Even this stark warning was delivered dully. 'Even if you 'ad the authority to make us miss the stop, which you 'asn't, you can't straighten out the Lesmahagow loop. If we don't slow right down on that bend, we goes over.'

Bunce was livid. Fortunately he had an idea before he could take it out on the conductor. 'But they'll have to slow as well, right? Fair's fair.'

I was still gazing out the window, willing us closer to the goods wagon ahead. They only had a hundred yards on us, and we were still gaining.

'Course they'll 'ave to slow as well.'

'Right then! We'll have them on the bend then!'

'Doubt it.'

Bunce swung round into the conductor's face, and now his pistol was definitely threatening. 'Old'un, you are properly trying my patience now.'

A hundred yards only. In the distance there was a town, coming nearer.

To his credit, the conductor wasn't backing down. With a finger, he pushed aside the pistol barrel. 'Just after Motherwell there's a signal. Up ahead the east-west lines and the local traffic start merging with the London and North Western. Most likely we'll be 'eld there a few minutes.'

'No!' As if to torment poor Bunce, we all felt the train starting to slow as we neared the station and the bend that was making itself so notorious. 'This is supposed to be an express!'

'You're the one who keeps buggering about with it. Backwards and forwards, backwards and forwards. Take a day for the timetable to recover.'

Our locomotive came level with the back of their train, and began to pass it. The wagon – the secret apparatus in it – felt so close.

'Don't stop! Ignore the signal!'

If I was nearer the front of our train I could actually touch them…

'You gone stupid, mate? You ever seen a train wreck?'

Bunce actually roared his frustration.

The buildings of Motherwell were around us. We were going ever slower, and the bend was becoming more apparent. Still we were gaining on the train. Still that goods wagon grew larger in front of me.

'If we stop at the signal we'll lose them for good!'

Already I was walking forwards along the train.

Beside me, just yards away, we came level with their goods wagon. For a moment we seemed to match them for pace, and then we even gained a few yards. I was running down the corridor now, yelling and shoving my way through.

If the conductor was right about the signal, our advantage would last moments only. Our momentum and my run had carried me ahead of them now, but suddenly the two trains started to separate. I saw their locomotive moving away, saw them slipping away from me.

We were coming into the station, and the two trains were diverging either side of a platform. Suddenly we started to slow dramatically, and for the first time I saw them pull ahead a fraction.

Already I had the door open, was ignoring the cries of concern from the passengers around me. The details of the platform were drifting past me, benches and lamp-posts and advertisement hoardings. Beyond them I saw the other locomotive, and then the tender behind it.

I jumped for the platform and hit it and stumbled and kept moving, fighting to stay upright. I cannoned into something, someone, pushed it away and turned and raced across the platform. Their passenger wagon was moving ahead of me now, and then it disappeared behind a hoarding. Now their goods wagon filled my vision and still I ran. Five yards away and starting to accelerate past me. A final desperate burst of sprinting. Just yards away from me, and on a stupid instinct I lifted my arm towards it, and the corner of the wagon passed in front of my eyes and I could almost touch it and there was the back of the wagon and the empty track behind and I leapt forwards into the void.

Death and the Dreadnought

64.

Recent experience had made me a bit of an expert on the architecture of goods wagon ends. They have a set of iron rungs leading up one side of them. I got a hand on one of these and was jerked madly forward and my shoulder screamed, and then a desperate scrabbling foot found another rung and I got my other wild arm in and grabbed and I was on.

For a moment I was triumphant. I'd made it. I'd caught them. I'd finally come to grips with the elusive wagon, which the Germans had worked so hard to steal and hide from me. There was a good chance they didn't even know I was there: my run across the platform had been hidden from their passenger carriage; and what I'd just done was too ridiculous for them to contemplate.

That's the trouble with these logical planning fellows. Bit of lunacy throws them completely.

On the downside, I was now clinging to the back of an accelerating train. I had little idea where it was going, and no idea when it was going to slow down.

But – partly out of stubbornness at my achievement, and partly because the alternative was letting myself fall to serious injury or death – there I stayed.

My predicament wasn't so uncomfortable. Bit of a surprise at first, of course, but once I had hands and feet all comfortably on rungs, I was stable enough. Sheltered behind the back of the wagon, I found the wind was bearable.

And thus it was that I journeyed from Motherwell to Glasgow on that September afternoon: clinging to the back of a speeding railway wagon, while the scenery of southern Scotland flickered past me. I'd almost recommend it as the economic option, should you find yourself hard up and needing to get north.

It's a journey of some twenty miles. For a locomotive only pulling one tender, one carriage, one goods wagon and one well-dressed stowaway, it took around half an hour. Towards the end I was feeling the strain. I could be steady enough, but for that I had to keep myself pulled close in to the wagon, and my arms started to feel it. In the end I squeezed one whole forearm behind the rung and more or less jammed myself in place. Now and then a freak of wind would rush a gust of smoke and soot into my face.

I can't pretend I'd been very aware of what was happening around me, not in the first moments of the escapade. I'd not heard or seen any other train nearby, or passing. I had to assume that the conductor had been right: the other train, with Bunce and his policemen, had been held near the station and was now well behind. I was on my own.

Once I'd got used to the somewhat unconventional accommodation, I wasn't worrying about the journey. I was worrying about the end of the journey. I took it for granted that Hertenstein and his First XI were in the passenger coach ahead. Sometime in the near future the train would arrive at some isolated bit of dockside, and they'd be all over the goods wagon unloading the fire-control table. They would find it hard to miss a man in a tweed suit stuck to the outside. At this climax of their operation, they wouldn't be fooling around.

The infinite stone dourness of the outskirts of Glasgow passed around me. I tried adjusting my grip on the rung. It didn't help.

Glasgow, by extension, was another problem. Back in the open country, I'd had the world to myself and there was no chance of anyone seeing me. In a built-up area, when the train would probably be slower, any number of signalmen or navvies might be lurking around the track; pedestrians would be stopping at level-crossings, and bored domestics would be staring out of back windows. And they would see a gentlemen in correct country wear hanging off the back of the train, and surely one of them would shout or scream, and Hertenstein would learn he had an unexpected passenger.

Through the suburbs we rolled. Occasionally, for a bit of variety, I would twist my head around and watch the backs of the houses, the little fragments of domesticity and squalor. Otherwise I rested my chin on my straining forearm and concentrated on gently flexing and easing the muscles in my legs and arms.

In particular, if we passed through one of the Glasgow stations en route the docks, I would certainly be spotted. I'd at least have the chance of jumping off the wagon and getting lost in the crowd, but I didn't want that. I wanted to stay with my prize. I had to wait for the moment when… when what, exactly?

We rolled on. The stink of smoke and soot hung heavy around the wagon. I had to wait for the moment when I had worked out what I would do when the moment came.

We didn't pass through any of the Glasgow stations. The special had been booked onto lines that went through the southern districts of the city without the risk of getting stopped at a signal in a station. Understandably, from the German point of view. Once, at some significant junction of the tracks, I saw a signal box passing beside us, and I pressed closer to my wagon and hoped the signalman in the box was particularly busy, or blind.

Then we stopped. The sudden jolt of the wagon was matched by a great thump in my chest, as I wondered if the crisis had come. I stared around me. We weren't at the docks. We were still in the outskirts of the city, surely: houses and factory buildings around us. From ahead I heard a shout, and remembered that I was clinging to a vehicle full of very efficient murderers. I wrenched my forearm out its rung, and shifted round until I was held by one hand and one foot only, ready to jump at whoever appeared round the back of the wagon.

Then we started rolling forwards again. I lurched and swung from the rungs, and pulled myself back in. Below me I saw the tracks, different sets merging and diverging. Points. Hertenstein's gang had had to switch lines manually.

Of course they had. When they'd chartered the special, they'd had to give ninety percent of their true course so that the train would be routed properly at the many junctions between Crewe and Glasgow. But for the last stretch they'd no doubt given a false destination.

Again, I had to admire the planning. They would have hoped that the authorities wouldn't have known about the switch, wouldn't even know that the fire-control table had been snatched, certainly wouldn't be tracking the train. But just in case, Hertenstein had given a false destination: in no circumstances would there be any policemen lurking when he got there. I was even more isolated. As far as the London and North Western Railway was concerned, the Germans and their booty, and I, had just ceased to exist.

The houses were gone now. First we passed factory buildings, and then fragments of open country to the south, and then the buildings were growing up around me again, more factories, and then warehouses. At last, over my left shoulder, I glimpsed water: the River Clyde, and the route to the sea.

65.

A grey brown world of wharves and warehouses, rough ground and rough buildings, as we weaved through the docks that crowd the banks of the River Clyde, as it opens out westwards from Glasgow. A bustling shouting world, as I watched gangs of workers scurrying over the waterfront and the ships tied alongside it and pressed myself tight into my wagon. An industrial jungle, into which I was disappearing.

Then things seemed quieter, as our train coughed its way into a new section of the docks. The Clyde was clear to the left. No one to see us here. No way Bunce could track us through the maze of junctions and docks.

I was on my own with Hertenstein and his gang, going wherever they were going. Germany, presumably; if they didn't find and murder me first.

I reached into my jacket for the Webley.

And then I remembered that I'd given it to Quinn to cover me, back on the Glasgow Express.

I was obliged, it turned out, to confront a gang of ruthless foreign bandits armed only with a packet of sandwiches.

The train was going at walking pace. We were nearly there, wherever there was.

I could have dropped off the back of it, and they probably wouldn't have seen me. But they might; and what would I achieve? I had to watch them, I had to stay with them, to the very end.

I wondered if I should have been dropping a trail of breadcrumbs, from my sandwich. But the rats would have got them long before the police bloodhounds did.

The locomotive was coughing hard now. Warehouses to the right. The river to the left. No signs of life. We were definitely slowing.

I poked one eye round the edge of the wagon. A couple of hundred yards ahead, a steam yacht was moored to the dockside. Journey's end.

Slowly, clumsily, feeling the strain in muscles frozen by the half-hour clutching at the rungs, I climbed up onto the roof of the wagon. I squirmed forwards, keeping flat.

We were a hundred yards from the yacht now, coming in

parallel to it along the waterfront. Elegant thing: two masts for when they wanted to pretend to be sailors; funnel in the middle for steaming back to Germany without any fuss. Already there were men bustling around on the deck. Hertenstein wasn't one to dawdle.

And not another soul. Glasgow's supposed to be one of the great cities of the Empire, a heaving metropolis of humans. And I couldn't see a single solitary one of them, not for a mile in any direction. Typical of the Scots to be so damned contrary.

Then, in the distance, my eye caught movement. At first I thought I'd imagined it, and then I couldn't interpret it. And then the odd shifting in the distance resolved itself into a man on a bicycle. A man on a bicycle, heading towards us.

And so what? Shouting would only ensure my death sooner. I had no other way of–

Then I was wrenching into my jacket pocket and pulling out the packet of sandwiches. I opened it, removed half the sandwich and scribbled on the paper 'HELP. SMUGGLERS. URGENT ALERT POLICE.' The cyclist was fifty yards away. In my haste, and my attempts to cling to the roof, and the last jolting of the train over the dockside the letters were mostly illegible, but hopefully he'd get the gist. I repackaged it around the half-sandwich.

Just in time. The cyclist – some kind of dockworker – was coming level with the train, and paying it no attention. He didn't see me half rise, didn't see the arc of my arm; and nor, I think, did anyone on the yacht.

It's probably typical of my odd life that one of the finest feats of marksmanship I will ever have pulled off was executed with half a sandwich against a Glasgow watchman on a bicycle. Two moving vessels, just as Hugh Stackhouse had described the challenges of naval gunnery. The sandwich packet took a long trajectory across the dockside and caught the cyclist smack in the face.

I didn't even need a fire control table.

He wobbled, and fell, and then I lay down flat again. I had to hope he'd instinctively look at what had hit him, that it would be half open, that he'd investigate, that he'd have the sense to hurry to the police. A lot of hoping.

Stretched flat on the wagon roof, as the train juddered to a halt, I ate the other half of the sandwich.

Duck pâté.

Now I could only wait. Before the train had completely stopped, I heard doors opening. Then below me, between the wagon and the yacht, there was movement. Hertenstein's gang were quick about their business.

I daren't raise my head. I couldn't be seen from immediately below me, but anyone who walked towards the yacht could turn and see me, and I was in plain view of the deck. Any movement might attract fatal attention. I fancied I heard Hertenstein's voice. Otherwise, the men were quiet. Orders given, orders followed, no fuss.

There was a shot, and I felt my heart kick. Then the wagon door slid open. Not a man to trifle with a lock, your hun. Immediately there were boots up and echoing around in the wagon. I could only wait, and hope reinforcements arrived before the fire-control table was loaded aboard the yacht and the yacht was away to Germany, and hope fervently that none of the Germans bothered to look up at all.

'Hoi! Wha' the 'ell d'ye think yeer playin' a'?'

For a moment I assumed it was directed at me. In another moment, I realized that this squawk had been in the most unGerman accent imaginable.

It was the cyclist.

I almost swore aloud. I couldn't resist twisting my head around to look. Perhaps he hadn't even read the message. Perhaps he had, but his pride was too wounded at being struck down by an unexpected sandwich. However it was, rather than doing the logical, sensible thing and going for the police, the stupid sod had come over to investigate.

I could see him now. He was wheeling his bike towards the wagon. He looked unhappy, and he was ready to expand on the point. 'Wha' en God's name d'ye–'

He stopped. He didn't sound a man who'd shut up easily, so he'd obviously seen something pretty striking. From what happened next, it must have been Hertenstein appearing round the end of the wagon with his pistol out.

There was silence for a moment. Then Hertenstein's voice came quiet and clear: 'Go away.'

One last time, the watchman's pride overcame prudence. 'No I w–' and the gun fired and there was a yell of pain.

Surprisingly, he wasn't dead. At this stage I doubt Hertenstein would scruple to murder another innocent, but perhaps the watchman had been too far off. Or perhaps Hertenstein was using his wrong arm because someone had shot him in the other. That was one the watchman owed me.

That was the end of that episode. My great hope had manifested itself as one angry Scotsman, who'd jumped into something beyond his imagination and got shot for it. Had he not still been alive, swerving and swearing on his bicycle, it would have been tragedy. Instead it was merely farce.

There was one benefit only from the whole nonsense: the distraction gave me the opportunity to drop down from the landward side of the goods wagon, out of sight of all the Germans gathered on the other side and watching the fleeing cyclist. It was twenty yards to the nearest buildings, and I did them at a sprint and ducked into an alleyway.

66.

Instinct, and the familiar sense of an impending bullet between my shoulder blades, told me to keep running. About as far as Edinburgh would have done nicely.

Unfortunately, I had spent the last hours desperately trying to catch up with the damn crate and not to get separated from it. Now, a minute or two before it was hauled up the gangplank onto a yacht for Germany, was not the time to set off in the other direction. The alley ran perhaps thirty yards between two warehouses, and by the end of it I had slowed to a walk.

Good thing I had, too. Otherwise I'd have knocked down the man who suddenly appeared at the other end, instead of just surprising him. He didn't look the kind of chap who liked surprises. I was starting to take in just what an imposing shape he was, and noticing the similarly hard-looking men around him, when a voice nearby said: 'Delamere?'

The voice – the nasal sneer – was unmistakeable.

It was Raikes.

Had this hero of the mob not been normal-sized and normalish-looking I'd have spotted him sooner. For a moment, I was as surprised as he was. 'Raikes? What the hell are–... But of course.' The information from the police; the radicals coming up by train for their next big meeting. 'You're here with the revolutionary pilgrimage, aren't you? Next stop on the touring holiday. But there's not much to sabotage in this part of the docks, surely.'

He was still staring at me, and at last I rubbed a hand across my cheek and saw how black the soot had left me. He was about to answer my remark with something similarly childish, but stopped himself, glancing at the man beside him. There was something like deference in his manner; I'd have been less surprised if he'd broken into *God Save the King*.

'Mr Scoular here is Secretary of the United Society of Boilermakers and Shipbuilders hereabouts', he said formally. 'His territory now, Delamere.' Scoular might have puffed up at this flattery, but there wasn't room for any more puffing. He couldn't have been more than five foot six, but he wasn't much less broad. A very solid man indeed, and he looked damn' tough. I supposed one didn't get to rule the Glasgow docks without overcoming a challenge or two on the way. Scoular appeared to have done so with his head: it was a battered, mottled, shaven head, and it didn't seem to like the look of me.

Raikes pointed a distasteful finger at me. 'Mr Delamere is the last gasp of the British aristocracy, brother Walter. The final glass of champagne, eh Delamere? Bona fide war hero, and a proper gent, aren't you? Probably a murderer as well, but really no more than the rest of his class.'

Brother Walter was considering me with distaste. 'What's he doing here, then?' I think that's what he said, anyway. His accent was broad, angular Glaswegian; for all I could make out, he might have been inviting me home to meet his sister or just clearing his sinuses.

'Mr Delamere has a deep interest in the affairs of the working man, don't you Delamere?' The quiet level voice as ever, the sarcasm soft and thunderous. 'Quite the connoisseur of dockyards.'

I got a word in at last. 'Out on that dockside is a steam-yacht. The men around it are German spies. They're stealing a top-secret piece of naval apparatus.'

The Scottish lump looked confused. I couldn't blame him; he'd not been following the narrative from the beginning. Raikes just watched me, cold.

Then he shrugged.

'While you're having your committee meeting, they're getting away. You don't care?'

'If it's any help, I loathe the German government fully as much as I loathe the British.' The Scottish chap made a noise of agreement; or perhaps he was suffering from bronchitis. 'Should they annihilate each other, I would find it efficient as well as satisfactory.'

'That apparatus in German hands means the deaths of British sailors.'

'They're doomed the moment they take their shilling from this war-mongering regime.'

'Your fantastical revolution is being picked off, man by man, while you debate the right typeface to print the pamphlets. They killed Merridew, once the Secretary of your Union. They killed John Tulliver, the night-watchman at the Thames Ironworks yard.' I glanced towards the Scottish chap. 'They've just shot one of yours, too.'

I saw the Scottish chap's eyes harden. I saw Raikes, very slowly, as if tasting uncertainty for the first time, licking his lips.

67.

The Battle of Bethlehem Quay has, over the years, gained rather a grand reputation in the annals of British radicalism.

As one of the very few people who witnessed it – indeed, as the chap who started it – I may say that it wasn't exactly Waterloo. Not much more than a dozen or two fellows on each side, and what you'd call an inconclusive result. But that only increases my respect for the English and Scottish Trades Union men who fought it. And the philosophers who have since used it to show that radicalism isn't incompatible with patriotism, well, they've got a point.

Painful though it is to admit it, I had to admire Raikes in that moment. Insidious weasel he might be, but when it came to the crisis he had more than his share of cold courage, and that's the rarest kind.

I thought they weren't going to make it in time. I watched from behind an enormous metal mooring bollard fifty yards away, as Hertenstein and co. went about their business with their usual efficiency. There wasn't a crane at this isolated bit of the docks, but the gang had had a couple of carrying poles all ready, and these were rapidly lashed to the crate, and it was manoeuvred down from the wagon onto the dockside. There Hertenstein insisted on having a look inside. He'd not wanted to slow the train before, I suppose, but now he wanted to be sure what he'd got. Didn't fancy saving up the great unveiling of his prize for when he was standing in front of the Kaiser, and then finding that he'd smuggled out a crate of novelty knit-wear from Lancashire.

And still I was alone on the dockside. I confess some pretty ungenerous thoughts about the British Trades Union movement in that moment. It would, no doubt, be impossible for them to order a bowl of soup without having a two-day conference first and translating the proceedings for the benefit of the Bulgarian delegation, so God only knew how much deliberation they'd need for this job.

And now one of Hertenstein's men had taken a chisel to the side of the crate, and it was lying on the dockside, and Hertenstein was looking pretty pleased with himself, and he was turning to some little chap who'd just hurried down the gangplank from the yacht, and the little chap was peeking into the crate and then nodding.

Then I heard boots, and I turned.

No more than a dozen or two of them, and pretty rough, but the relief column coming into Mafeking can't have looked any sweeter.

Raikes was out in front. I can't say I'd ever found his cold-eyed insolence very charming when directed at me, but his capacity to maintain it when walking silently towards a gang of armed assassins was damned impressive. His Glaswegian colleague was beside him. Scoular didn't look the sort to shirk a scrap, and in his own dockyard he couldn't be anywhere but the front rank. Their men were in a loose squad behind.

For a moment I wished I'd given them a couple of pointers on close order infantry tactics, but immediately I saw it hadn't been needed. They'd spent years in running battles with the police, and they knew what they were doing.

They were past me before any of the Germans saw them, the steady tramp of boots relentless over the dockside. Then one of the Germans was calling to Hertenstein, and even at distance I could see his concern.

And still Raikes's band tramped on. It was madness; they'd be shot down in rows, I could see it, I knew the ruthlessness of these Germans.

'Ho there!' It was the first noise they'd made, and it was the Scottish leader. 'I demand to know yer business in ma yard!' And still they tramped forwards.

Now I saw Hertenstein's predicament, as he gazed at this scruffy band bearing down on him. He surely didn't want a massacre: he didn't want the attention, he didn't want the delay, he didn't want his own men left here wounded. He could slaughter Raikes and comrades, but it would only be a distraction from his desperate need to get his prize onto the yacht and away. He took a step or two towards the approaching Trades Union men, as if to offer parley, hoping at least to stop them.

They didn't stop. They were thirty yards away from the wagon and the yacht now, and Hertenstein's dilemma was clear.

He solved it with his usual instinct. He pulled out his pistol, and held it high. Behind him, at least half of his men did the same. There were shouts from the deck of the yacht, and now the crew was mustering. Quick onto the firing-step, the Germans.

Raikes and his squad stopped still. But each man had reached into a pocket and found a knife, or a cosh, or a marlin-spike; a few had dropped to the ground. Fair enough, I thought, until I saw they weren't ducking but prising up stones.

The two bands faced each other across the dock-side: Raikes and the Scottish street-fighters, versus Hertenstein and his assassins.

I saw Raikes and his Scottish mate looking at each other.

'I'm obliged to carry on, Mr Raikes.'

'Your docks, Mr Scoular. Quite proper.'

And they nodded to each other, and they carried on towards the killers, and their squad followed.

Hertenstein yelled something, and fired a shot in the air. The Scottish flinched, but pressed on. A volley of shots into the air from the Germans, and still they came, and Hertenstein yelled another order and now the shots were aimed at the oncoming men. I heard the cries of pain, saw two stagger or stumble – three – four. The Germans were deliberately aiming at arms and legs – God, but Hertenstein knew discipline – and it worked. The Trade Union men broke and ran – staggered – round to the left of the locomotive and relative safety.

So much for the preliminary skirmishing. It put Raikes and Scoular and their men along the landward side of the train, wounded but damned angry. On the other side, between the train and the yacht, Hertenstein and his band were rather wondering what to do with themselves. With typical speed, he had his men detailed. Some were firing through the gaps between the train's coaches – and under the coaches, at the feet, which was rather unsporting – while he had a squad wrestling with the crate and its precious contents.

All very handy, but now they came under a hail of stones, thrown over the roof of the train. It ain't so easy to prise up a cobble, but the street-fighters were experts, and strong too: they had the things arcing over the coach in numbers enough to do damage. Before the Germans had worked out what was happening, a couple of them had been hit on the head and gone down – get hit on the head by plunging fire from a cobblestone and you surely feel it. Then I saw some of the Trade Union men climbing up into the passenger carriage, and while the barrage of stones continued over the roof, they opened a second line of attack with things thrown from the carriage windows down onto the bewildered Germans on the dockside. You wouldn't think there was much loose and throwable in the average railway carriage, but you've not reckoned with an inventive Scottish street-fighter with a knife in his pocket and revenge on his mind. Wood panels, glass, light fittings: a storm of miscellaneous debris showered over the Germans, and they replied with increasingly random and angry gunfire. And all the time Hertenstein was urging his squad up the gang plank onto the yacht with their booty, the crate still minus its side-panel. It was about now that some bright chap in the train re-invented Greek fire from the resources available to him, and burning cushions began spinning out of the carriage windows towards the retreating Germans.

The London and North Western Railway were going to be more than unhappy when they got their train back. I hoped they'd touched Hertenstein for a hefty deposit up front.

The Battle of Bethlehem Quay was rather brief, and rather chaotic. But well before it was done, I was in the water and paddling unseen down the shadow of the dockside and then round the stern of the yacht.

68.

I had my pick of a couple of portholes within stretching distance of the waterline. The fracas on the dockside gave me time enough to choose carefully, and confidence that everyone would be on the deck and looking the other way.

I found myself in a bunk room: crew quarters, presumably. Unfortunate, because it seemed the sort of place where my wet footprints would be more out of place. Fortunate, because I had my choice of four kit-bags. Inside a minute I was out of my wet gear and in some other chap's trousers and wool pullover. My wet boots I had to live with, and I was disappointed that no one had thought to keep a spare hat; not being easily recognized was likely to prove important.

My suit I had to stuff under a bunk; couldn't risk someone on deck seeing it popping out of the porthole. I was sorry to see it go: good quality tweed, as I say, and I'd come through a lot in it.

I had to move fast. I had a few minutes, surely, while the kerfuffle continued top side and the Germans concentrated on getting the crate onboard and secure, and getting away from the shore. After that…

I stuck my head out into the corridor as boldly as I could. I'd taken advantage of the swim to wash the soot off. At distance, I looked like someone who belonged on the boat. There was a fair chance that the crew and the men who'd come up on the train didn't know each other much. I should be well, as long as I kept my distance and met no one who knew my face.

Which of course Hertenstein and possibly quite a few of his gang did.

I had to move fast.

I was more alert to noise now. From up on deck there were gunshots, as the Germans completed their fighting retreat onto the yacht. To my right, the corridor ran forwards twenty yards or more, doors on both sides all the way; to my left it was only a few paces to a right-angle turn in the corridor, presumably where it met the stern.

Reconnaissance. I had to use my minutes of relative freedom to know my way around.

I took the few paces towards the stern. There the corridor turned and ran across the yacht for a dozen feet or so, and then turned again into what was presumably another corridor, running forwards along the port side in parallel to the first.

In the middle of the cross passage, a set of wooden stairs led up onto the deck, through an open hatch. The noise from the outside was much louder here. Immediately above me was a great heaving and thumping. Still no raised voices: just the quiet command of Hertenstein.

The crate was onboard, and presumably being secured on the deck.

One, two gunshots, but this was just keeping the Scots at bay. Soon they would – and then I heard a shout from Hertenstein and almost immediately I felt a shuddering through my feet as the engine engaged the propeller. I was committed now, no question. And at any minute all those boots up on deck would he thundering down the steps in front of me for a well-deserved cup of cocoa. Instinctively I opened the door nearest me – and then caught myself. Hiding, or more likely getting trapped in a dead end, was not Plan A.

I started to close the door again, but in doing so I saw that it was a storeroom. And that might be handy. I nipped inside. As I did, the yacht shifted under me, sideward. We were away from the dockside and moving.

The store was handier than I'd hoped. I'd imagined tearing up a bit of sheet or something, but my efficient hosts had medical supplies in here too, including some hefty rolls of bandage. It didn't take thirty seconds to wrap a generous length of it around my head and over one eye. Now I was one of the wounded heroes from the battle with the Scots, and even harder to recognize.

Then I was hurrying forwards along the starboard corridor, opening and closing every door. There would be a time for stealth, but while Hertenstein and most of his crew were up top it was the time for reckless haste and see what happens.

What happens was that I found various cabins, the galley with a cook who clearly didn't want to be disturbed, and the latrine with an inhabitant likewise. I felt he'd no right to be shirking on the thunderbox when the battle and the heavy lifting were on deck. He'd probably risked a first taste of Scottish cuisine and was now regretting it. I retreated quickly. By the time I did there were footsteps in the corridor behind me. I stopped fooling around with doors, and continued forwards. Now I had to blend in: to look purposeful, and to avoid conversation. And I still hadn't found what I was looking for.

Almost immediately I was at the forward end of the corridor, and again it turned across towards the other side of the yacht and there was a set of steps going up. As I reached them, a pair of legs descended beside me. My hand came up to adjust my bandage, so in effect my whole face was covered, and I politely stepped back and beckoned the chap past.

He stopped. He looked at me. He said something in German. I grunted.

He gestured to the bandage, then clapped me on the shoulder. Wounded hero; jolly good. He strode off. I wondered what the German for 'damned Scottish cobblestones' was.

Looking up the stairs, I could see the backs of two and then three men. They were standing still and looking ahead. Unlike the stern stair which led up on deck, this one led up into an enclosed space. It looked very like the bridge.

I looked more closely. One of the backs reached its summit in a fringe of blond hair.

I was standing under Hertenstein. As I watched, I heard his voice. Orders to the man next to him, quiet and short and immediately the chap was agreeing. One did not, I suspect, do much chit-chat with Admiral Hertenstein.

I needed to be near here, but I needed not to be idling and waiting for Hertenstein to take it into his head to look around the scenery or pop down to see if the gents' had come free. I continued my tour of the corridor, sternwards along the parallel, port side stretch of it.

Some of the doors had signs on them, but these were in ornamental gothic script and at waist height, and I couldn't risk being caught bending and peering and looking lost. At the far end of the corridor, by the stern, there was a sudden crowd of men. They'd just come down from the deck by the aft stair. I ducked my head slightly, took a breath, and continued steadily towards them. They bustled into cabins. I had to pray my unknown and unknowing benefactor wouldn't take it into his head to need his second sweater.

I'd gone half a dozen paces, when I heard steps on the forward stairs. I turned, and began to walk towards the bow again. I timed it nicely, so I was just at the corner when the man got to the bottom. If he came my way I'd repeat the bandage performance and continue to the starboard side corridor. I could, I suppose, have continued this back and fro indefinitely, until someone recognized me, or my heart gave out, or we got to Germany.

He didn't come my way. He turned away at the bottom of the stair and I stuck my head round after him. A great kick of luck: he had two flimsy papers in his hand. I was a step or two behind him as he knocked at the first door on the starboard corridor. By the time he was fully inside I was passing the doorway, and a glance confirmed my calculation and my hope: this was the wireless telegraph room. Chummy was bringing a couple of messages from the bridge, to be sent off. Bit of business with the harbour-master, perhaps, or more likely Hertenstein's first crow of triumph back to HQ.

I'd not covered a dozen paces down the starboard corridor before I heard him coming out and the door closing. He was immediately away back up to his station on the bridge, and again I turned and retraced my steps. A deep breath. I copied his knock on the telegraph room door, and stepped inside.

The telegraph operator was sitting in front of his apparatus, his back to me. He did no more than glance round as I entered. He was used to it. The paper was more important than the face.

Unfortunately for me, I didn't have any paper and my face was worth looking at. His glance found my bandage and my hand again adjusting it, and he turned to look at me more fully. He said something in German.

I said 'Verdammte Skotish' and added a sort of scornful grunt in lieu of the German for 'burning railway company cushion'. He said something back to me, and I grunted loudly in agreement with whatever it was. And then I started humming the first thing in my head – it was 'The Boy I Love Is Up In The Gallery', apparently popular this season at Jolly's Theatre – and looking at his desk.

I saw a block of blank telegraph forms at the back of the desk. Still humming, I tore off a couple, clapped him on the shoulder and left.

69.

As I was taking the stern stairs up to the deck I saw that underneath them there was a line of portable oil lamps hung on hooks.

For night use, presumably. It made me remember that evening must be coming on. Sure enough, the sun was low in the sky when I got up on deck.

It was a bit of a shock. At first glance, I couldn't see any sign of land at all. We might have been in the middle of the Irish Sea already. My toing and froing below deck had surely only been a few minutes. But we'd boarded well out along the Clyde, and Hertenstein wasn't dawdling, and now the river had become an estuary and the estuary was widening as we raced westward towards the sea and the long route round to Germany.

I came up on deck cautiously. They might have restrictions on who came and went up here. They might have a guard on the crate. And Hertenstein was the sort of chap to keep his eye on a prize like this himself.

As I came fully upright, the crate filled my vision. It had been lashed to the deck just in front of the steps.

I saw no one. I checked around me again. I peered forwards past the crate to see if anyone was watching from the bridge.

There was still a bit of traffic around us in the Clyde estuary, yachts coming in towards Glasgow before the sun went, and cargo ships finding their anchorage. To the south, far off the port bow, I saw the great bulk of a battleship.

It wouldn't be the *Colossus*: we were well west of her now. This ship seemed to be anchored near the shore, but it was afloat. This should be the H.M.S. *St Vincent*, and the *St Vincent* was a fully operational Dreadnought.

She seemed a long way away. I checked around me again, and then ducked into the open side of the crate.

This was what it had all been about; the whole madness.

It was my first encounter with a fire-control table. The real thing had the same effect as the drawings had had: the same intricacy; the same incomprehensibility; the same mystery.

I reached out my hand, and ran it over the iron base, and the tiers of wheels and levers and devices above. The summit was a large flat dial marking the full 360 degrees, and a confusion of other signs and symbols.

The light was weakening in the sky. I had so little time.

My hands touched this apparatus of the most modern science, more or less witchcraft to me. My feet felt the constant throb of the yacht as it hurried towards the sunset, and its escape.

In less than a minute I was below again, and hurrying forwards along the starboard corridor. And then back again as quickly, and up on deck. I felt the freshness of the wind around me now, felt it whipping at my hair, felt it like freedom.

The shattering of the glass of one of the oil lamps against the crate seemed strangely muffled, in the vastness of the estuary. But it was loud enough to be heard along the deck.

70.

They were alert, and fast. Within moments there were two of them, advancing on me with pistols drawn. And then there was Hertenstein, appearing between them. Just like old times.

I pulled the bandage off my head, and let it fall. Hertenstein considered me, interest and amusement.

'You do not give up, Delamere, do you?'

'You ain't dead yet', I said. 'After you.'

The smile faded. 'And here on my yacht you hope to achieve... what exactly?'

'Well,' I said, 'I had been planning to stop you.'

He looked around into the dusk, the Clyde estuary falling behind us. The amusement was back. 'And yet we still seem to be moving. Good steady course. This craft indistinguishable from any other: the battleship *St Vincent* is just over there, but even if the word is out, we will not be noticed; we will not be stopped.' He shook his head. 'Bad show, Delamere.'

'I know. It's damn' frustrating.'

The swine had the cheek to look really regretful. 'And now Delamere, I fear that you have run out of river. On this voyage I am bringing no passengers.'

'Ah yes, of course. You'll want to make me walk the plank, like all good pirates.' He didn't quite get it, but he knew he'd won and the smile stayed. I looked around me, into the half-light; the sea either side, the stern half a dozen yards behind me.

It wasn't a bad spot for an ending: the last of the sun on the sea, the emptiness and the air around us. 'Look old chap, I know it's a cliché, but would you grant me a last cigarette? As one hunter to another?'

He chuckled. An elaborate wave of the hand, magnanimous acquiescence and smug superiority. But he was wise enough to throw me the cigarette instead of passing it, and his henchmen were watching me intently.

'Everything got soaked in my swim', I said. 'Could I trouble you for a match?'

No trouble at all, for Hertenstein the triumphant. He threw me a box. 'How marvellously British you are, Delamere. All the style. All the running around. And it means nothing.'

'In my defence,' I said, 'the idea was fair enough. As you said, there's no way for the police or the navy to know that this is the yacht to stop. Dozens like it on the estuary. No time to summon reinforcements, or organize a blockade. H.M.S. *St Vincent* there ain't going to start taking pot-shots at random.' He was frowning slightly now, wondering where I was going.

I patted the crate beside me. 'The good old fire-control table. I don't have the first idea how this thing works, but I can take a bearing all right from the dial on top of it. A few bearings, indeed.'

Now the frown was clear. He still couldn't see the threat, but he didn't like the way things were headed. 'Once I'd done that, I added a message to the pile that your telegraph man was sending out. He'd no reason to suspect that the data I sent weren't a progress report from you. The navy and the police will have picked up my message – they'll be listening desperately for any clue as to where you are and where you're going – and it had my initials. It pinpointed this yacht's location by time and by bearing from three landmarks, and gave its course.' Real concern on his face. He glanced across the water, to the outline of the *St Vincent* half a mile away. 'The Navy are going to be pretty unhappy that a washed-up soldier is the first man to use their top-secret apparatus in action. But I'm afraid you're a lot easier to find than you hoped, Hertenstein.'

We gazed at each other. He was breathing heavily, eyes angry. 'Yet still we escape, Delamere. You got your message away, but it achieved nothing. Nothing from the battleship. Only us, and night falling, and the open sea.'

'Quite right. Frustrating, as I say. That was where the plan rather broke down. I told the navy whereabouts to look, but they still need to be able to see you clearly, make sure they know what they're shooting at. I had it all worked out, Hertenstein, and at the very last step I found I was missing one vital element.'

'What?'

I held it up. 'A match, Hertenstein. Cheerio.' The match flared, and dropped, and the deck around us was a carpet of flame as the oil I'd poured ignited. I was already free and running, half a dozen desperate steps. I managed a racing dive off the stern just as the first shells from the guns of H.M.S. *St Vincent* were coming in.

71.

As every soldier knows, the Navy are rotten shots; and this lot hadn't fired a gun under fighting conditions for decades. But I think that made them more enthusiastic. I didn't seem to have taken more than a few strokes through the water when the world exploded behind me, and the air was thick with bits of yacht and German. I hoped the Navy wouldn't mind that I'd persuaded them to blow up the most precious bit of technology in the British Empire.

The explosion, so close behind, was staggering. The waves of sound and shock battered me, and I was left half-conscious and drifting and unable to communicate to my arms and legs. I was aware of them waving vaguely around me, and everything was misty, and I was reaching and falling and I think I saw Victoria, and Bliss, tasted the moistness of their lips, felt the embrace around me, and to be honest that'll do for paradise.

'All right now, sir; let's be having you.'

I'm not much of a theologian, but I'd be pretty sure that God isn't Cornish.

'Easy now. Here we are.'

He certainly sounded Cornish. I continued to drift and drown.

'If you'll just stay still sir, I'll have you safe in a moment.'

'Quinn? What the hell are you doing here?'

'Just passing, sir.'

'In the middle of the ocean?'

'Hardly that, sir.' He was pulling me backwards with easy rhythm. 'More like a pond, this. Not a proper ocean like the Atlantic. Now…' Our progress slowed for a moment, and I trod water. 'There's a launch about here somewhere.'

'A launch?'

'Miss Bliss commandeered it. She somewhat exaggerated your

status and her own, I suspect.'

'Ah, marvellous. Playing the duchess at last.'

We drifted off into the evening, and I managed an intermittent back-stroke and watched the stars coming out.

72.

The Thames Ironworks Company shipyard was silent. As silent as the grave which it had become, for two men at least.

As I trod carefully through its darkness, remembering its weird night-time shapes like old friends, the ghosts came at me. Poor Sinclair, and Tulliver the night-watchman, and Merridew the old union lion. And those on the other side of the ledger too: Greenberg, with his macabre death in my arms; the two killers in the forest; Hertenstein the first, staring up at me as he fell to his death on the Jolly's stage; his brother, and his brother's crew, now just flotsam in the Irish Sea. One doesn't exactly regret them, but you'd rather it wasn't necessary.

I splashed through something that felt thicker than water, and cursed. Once his adrenalin had subsided, I'd have a pretty grumpy Cornishman in my retinue. My best country suit had been lost at sea. There's only so many times you can have a fight to the death in gentleman's correct evening wear before it starts to look rather shabby. My dress shoes hadn't been in great shape to start with, Quinn had had two heroic efforts at cleaning them after my previous visits to the shipyard at night, and here I was again.

The great void loomed up out of the gloom. H.M.S. *Thunderer*. The start of it all. No place more fitting for the conclusion.

As its darkness rose over me, I reached out my hand and pressed it against the chill hull. Such an impassive monster, to have caused so much chaos.

Among the web of scaffolding that covered one section of the hull, I found the steps to the entrance doorway halfway up one side. There, I was swallowed by the battleship. Now I used my torch. I hadn't wanted to outside. In here, I'd get lost forever or fall to my death inside a minute.

Jonah inside the whale.

That was about right. Wrong place, wrong time, and taking the blame for everyone else's mischief.

Up on the main deck and enjoying the night air again, I made my way towards the bow. The battleship was an extraordinary vantage point. To the west, I could see the lights of London, a twinkling horizon. Around me the dark jungle of the shipyard. Behind me, the river. Sometime, not too far off, the *Thunderer* would slip back into the river, and point her bow towards the sea and Germany.

From the bow, I could look down and see the yard offices, scene of my skirmishes with fire and with mob. Far below me, against the keel, was where Sinclair had died.

I switched off the torch, and waited.

Life was getting back to normal. Whatever that meant. Quinn had kicked me out of my rooms for a few days, while he oversaw the redecoration of the sitting room and told heroic lies to the tradesmen to get a bit of extra credit. So I was still dossing chez Bliss, which was fine. No more congenial place to lie low and recuperate.

Sir Henry Irving, to whom Bliss kept referring, turned out to be her bloody cat. So that was one bit of mystery cleared up without too much melodrama.

I was pretty sure there was no one chasing me now. Even Bunce, though he wasn't convinced that I didn't deserve to be banged up for something, had accepted or been told that he should lay off.

The whole business had been hushed up, of course. I don't know whether anything was ever said, but in effect the Foreign Office politely overlooked the fact that the German Embassy was running a wholesale programme of sabotage and murder out of Carlton House Terrace, and the Germans didn't make any fuss about the Royal Navy declaring war on a German pleasure yacht. Funny business, diplomacy.

Hertenstein, and his yacht, and the German scheme, were debris in the current of the Irish Sea now. So was the navy's fire-control table. The Germans never got their hands on one, but the programme was delayed nonetheless. I gather the government got more cagey about how the thing was being managed and looked after, and it was another year or two before they were being installed in Dreadnoughts.

I was in reflective mood, melancholy if you like, as I stood on the deck of H.M.S. *Thunderer* and waited for my guest.

It seemed colder now, high above the docks, far from the lights of the city. I fancied I felt the first spots of drizzle.

'Delamere? That you?'

The figure rose out of the darkness of the deck. It became a shadow, and the shadow took on contours, and at last the lights gave it features.

It was Hugh Stackhouse, of course.

'What the hell do you mean, dragging me out here like this?'

'What the hell do you mean, Stackhouse, by accepting?'

He was silent.

'What on earth would tempt you to traipse out here, after such a bland message from me?' Nothing. 'Something on your mind?'

'Something's on yours, clearly.'

'Mm. Yes indeed.' Against the distant lights of London, and the few lights below us in the yard, Stackhouse seemed as he'd always seemed: an indistinct presence; an outline. 'You got a middle name, Stackhouse?'

'You're joking.'

'Humour me.'

He grunted scorn. 'Marston.'

I heard it with a sigh and a smile. 'Thank you. A private bet with myself. I won.'

'It's cold out here, Delamere. When you've finished fooling around…'

'I'll be more than glad to be shot of this business. But the story's not done yet. I told Victoria Carteret that I'd find out who killed David Sinclair. Tonight, I fulfil that promise.'

'Your German friends, surely. You proved that.'

'No.'

His face was becoming more distinct to me now, as my eyes adjusted. Steady; watchful.

'No. That would have been the last thing they wanted. They were aiming at some discreet espionage. They wouldn't want blood. They wouldn't want to draw attention to themselves. No one had known that anything was happening at all. Then, in the instant of Sinclair's death, all London was paying attention. Same with the trades union men. Last thing they'd want would be that kind of attention; that kind of suspicion. No, Stackhouse. Someone else. There's always been someone else.'

Still the shadow was silent.

'The Germans wanted a fire-control table. They had a few preliminary attempts at it. They found that the secrets were too closely guarded at the Dreyer company where it's produced. So they shifted their attention to the Thames Ironworks Company, to see if there might be opportunities there. I suspect they were instrumental in stirring up some of the union trouble, but that was just for distraction. What they really wanted was someone on the inside; someone they could persuade to work for them.'

Stackhouse shook his head. 'Poor David.'

'He was ideal, wasn't he? Congenial chap; addicted to gambling; constantly in debt. The Embassy had a front man for this sort of business: Samuel Greenberg, and his sham Commercial Codswallop and Chaos outfit. He got friendly with Sinclair, and worked it so Sinclair was heavily in his debt – for favours; for money. Soon he was in a position to offer to wipe the slate clean, and more, in return for just a tiny favour of his own. Perhaps he presented it as engineering curiosity, nothing sinister.'

Again Stackhouse shook his head. 'And so Sinclair betrayed us.'

'Looks that way, doesn't it?' I watched him in the gloom. Another piece of Thames Ironworks Company equipment, in the haunted yard at night. 'But he didn't, of course, did he?'

Silence.

'Everything about Sinclair's behaviour says the opposite. This wasn't a man solving his problems; this wasn't a man with his slate wiped clean. This was a man suddenly realizing what he was caught in, and panicking, and wanting help. There was no way he'd have summoned me if he'd given in and betrayed the secrets and was regretting it; what could I have done to help? But if he hadn't given in, and instead had realized that there was something big going on and wanted advice from someone he knew wandered in and out of the shadows, I was just the chap.'

I waited. My hands were loose at my sides. I didn't want Stackhouse thinking I was a threat.

'The Germans wanted to get their hands on the technical drawings for the fire-control table. And then, by staggering co-incidence, a set is called forward from the special safety of the offices to the shipyard. If nothing else, that showed treachery at the heart of the company.'

'Sinclair requested the drawings.'

The words were flat.

'But he didn't, did he? There was something fishy about the

procedure. Sinclair was worried about the fire-control table, and I guess he asked to check the drawings in the office, and was told they'd been called to the yard. That would have worried him properly, and he'd have checked the ledger to see who had requested them. And he'd have found his own name there. With the drawings still at the yard, the receipt for their return should have been in the ledger. And there should have been nothing for anyone to be particularly surprised at. But Sinclair was very surprised. He took the stub himself – we found it in his pocket. That was panic, not plan. He was frightened – about what was happening, about himself – and who can blame him? He knew now that after he had rejected the approach from Greenberg, someone else in the company had accepted.'

He was silent and still.

'Eh, Stackhouse?' Nothing. He wasn't used to this sort of thing. 'Did you suspect something, and follow him here that night? Or did he summon you for a confrontation, with me as witness? And I was too late to save him.' I'd been thinking about the second scenario a lot in recent days. I knew I would go on thinking about it.

I said: 'Got a knife this time?' I couldn't see his hands in the gloom. 'Perhaps it was your own. Common enough that it wouldn't be traced. Or perhaps one you found here, when the conversation started going wrong. Perhaps you didn't want to risk being stopped with it. Perhaps you calculated. Perhaps you panicked. That how it was, Stackhouse?'

'You're guessing, Delamere. You can't prove anything.' Steady Stackhouse.

'Sinclair learned enough to believe it was you. If he could, others can.'

'Plenty of people work for the company.'

'Very few in your head office. You started to worry. You got the Germans to stage a phoney break-in at the office. You needed them to cover the disappearance of Sinclair's diary, and your own, which you smuggled out the next day and presumably burned. You were worried that his diary showed details of his meetings with Greenberg; and you knew that your own did the same – perhaps more.'

'This is the wildest speculation. It was a break-in. The police know it. Try and convince them it wasn't real and they'll think you're crazy.'

'They'll think I'm even crazier when they find out that I broke in myself.' I saw something alter in his posture. That had been a surprise. 'Yes, Stackhouse. I was there that night. I broke in before the Germans, and properly. I know that the business on the roof was sham. I know there's no way that that diary was stolen that night, because I was there the whole time from when it was last in Sinclair's desk until the police arrived. And I know what was in it.'

He waited.

'Perhaps there was more than I saw. But I saw enough to get me thinking. Greenberg's initials. The number of the receipt for the drawing you'd contrived to borrow in his name. And a set of initials, with a double question mark of speculation: "H.M.S.??" – Hugh Marston Stackhouse, I fancy.'

He had nothing now.

'Second. You told us that someone had stolen the plans of Glasgow docks from your room at Shulstoke. Perhaps they did sneak in and mess things around, to give weight to your story. But there's no way they'd have needed or wanted to take such a long shot to get plans of the docks; and I don't know why you would have had them anyway, given that your company isn't building in Glasgow. But your story distracted police attention to Glasgow, far away from Crewe and the train where the real attack was going to happen. Odd that.'

Silence.

'And there's something else. The police found a Thames Ironworks Company cufflink in my rooms.'

'The police said that was Sinclair's.'

'I'm pretty sure he was wearing others that evening. Anyway, how on earth would one of his have ended up with his murderer?'

'This implicates you rather than me.'

'What, I somehow got it in the struggle and decided to keep it? Souvenir? I ain't that doolally.'

'The Germans took one of his to implicate you.'

'But at the moment of his murder they had no idea about me. Took it just in case, and risk getting found with it? Not very likely. No, after you killed Sinclair, you scared badly, and you rushed to Greenberg to tell all. By this time my head was in the noose, and Greenberg saw a chance to reinforce my guilt by planting some evidence. Those cufflinks and tie-pins are a limited edition. Expensive. Can't have been many made. I know that if the police check, they'll be able to account for the set of every Thames Ironworks Director and Manager. Including David Sinclair's. Except one set: yours. When Inspector Bunce asks you tomorrow, Stackhouse, will you be able to produce your Thames Ironworks Company special cufflinks?'

'Why on earth should one of my cufflinks matter a damn?'

'Because you left the other clutched in Sinclair's hand, when he tried to stop you murdering him. It's the one thing that ties you absolutely to the crime.' I pulled it out of my pocket. 'Seems fitting to bring it back here, don't it? Here!'

I threw it high and slow towards him, and instinctively his hands came out into the night, and one held a knife and one reached to catch the cufflink. I took one fast step forwards and put a straight punch into the centre of his face.

I don't know what I expected. Not in that instant. Not in the whole conversation. I was tired and I didn't care and I wanted out of the whole business.

Stackhouse staggered backwards, arms flailing with knife and cufflink, and he stumbled against the lip on the edge of the deck and fell backwards into the night.

A Dreadnought battleship dwarfs a man, especially if he has the misfortune to fall from it. Hugh Stackhouse fell in silence, gazing up at me, and took a damn long time about it, and it was so far that I didn't even hear him hit the dockyard stones.

Slowly, wearily, I retraced my way back through the hulk of the battleship, and down to solid ground again. I sat down by the body, and waited for the police to arrive.

The End

Author's Note

Sir Henry Delamere's memoirs are naturally a limited and partial picture of the events of Autumn 1910. Although he seems never to have really fitted in anywhere (and certainly not in Eaton Square with the wonderful Lady Victoria, alas), his words reflect the attitudes of his time and place. While he had the junior officer's sympathy for the other ranks, and the outsider's empathy with the oppressed, he was not a natural class warrior.

The practical context of his account – his Boer War service; the Anglo-German naval race, the calendar of the Dreadnought-building programme and its technological details, within the wider tension which would be sparked into war; the topography of the London and North-Western Railway – seems consistent with the historical record. I'm grateful to Messrs Richard Campbell and Ray Wilton, in spirit a pair of Edwardian gentlemen, for their advice on the motor-cars and firearms of the time.

H.M.S. Thunderer was launched from the Thames Ironworks and Shipbuilding Company yard at Poplar in February 1911, a few months after Harry Delamere last spent an evening in her company; commissioned in 1912, and active throughout the First World War, she was finally scrapped in 1927. *H.M.S. Colossus* had been launched earlier in 1910, and was completed and commissioned during 1911. Launched in 1908, by 1910 *H.M.S. St Vincent* was part of the 1st Division of the Royal Navy's Home Fleet.

The Royal Navy pursued two development programmes for fire-control, with Captain Dreyer's becoming dominant for the Dreadnought series of battleships. (There's much fascinating material via www.dreadnoughtproject.org.) Delamere's account of the dramas of espionage and sabotage behind the development programmes could explain the delay in bringing the fire-control table into active service, and why the public record tends to give rather later dates for their installation on seagoing battleships. Though advanced and effective, in the one major naval engagement of the First World War, off Jutland in 1916, the Royal Navy's superior fire-control technology was more than balanced by relative weaknesses in communications and armour-piercing shells. The German High Seas Fleet sank more ships, and escaped to port; but it left the Royal Navy in command of the seas for the rest of the war. So perhaps, in some small way, Harry Delamere had done his bit.

POISON IN PARIS

1.

The train whistle shrieked. It startled the young man standing in front of me, and he looked hastily over his shoulder and out the carriage window. Then he was staring at me again.

'You must guard it with your life, Delamere!'

I slipped the folded paper into the inside pocket of my coat.

'Your life, you hear?'

The paper, whatever it was, was already as close to my body as I could manage without doing something unseemly in a public place. Short of swallowing it, there wasn't a lot more I could do to demonstrate my commitment. I patted my chest pocket, in a reassuring guarding-it-with-my-life sort of manner.

He gazed at my chest long enough that I started to feel uncomfortable. At last he looked up again. 'It's simply the most important thing in Europe.'

Personally, I attached more importance to the heart against which the letter was resting. But apparently that wasn't the official opinion of His Majesty's Government.

Two shrieks from the train whistle, and again he was startled. He was fidgeting to get out of the train compartment, back to whatever passed for routine in the British Embassy in Constantinople. I was starting to feel that the power of the mysterious paper was less that everyone wanted it, and more that no sane man wanted to be anywhere near it.

'You'll hide it, yes?'

I was on the verge of suggesting the one remaining place where it could more intimately be hidden, but you're not supposed to be coarse in government work. Gentleman's business, espionage. The greater the secret, the greater the number of non-gentlemen who are being done over. But they're usually foreign.

I just nodded.

'My Foreign Office colleagues will be waiting as soon as you arrive in Paris,' he said. Again. 'All you have to do is guard it until then.'

'You have my word,' I said.

That, now, is just the sort of nonsense you're supposed to say in government work. He smiled, rather desperately. 'You're a good fellow, Delamere.'

That's pretty debatable, but I didn't argue. I was more bothered by the tone in which he said it: he sounded surprised, as if he'd just learned something new or been proved wrong.

I didn't like it. I wondered idly who'd been saying what about me. Less idly, I wondered why, if I was such a doubtful prospect, the British Government were giving me their damn' secrets to carry.

Again the train shrieked, three blasts that blended into one. This time he looked relieved.

'God speed you.' He nodded for one last time, and turned and opened the carriage door.

Being the sort of chap I am, I was putting more faith in the locomotive of the Orient Express to speed me to Paris. But again, that's not the sort of thing one's supposed to say. And I wouldn't turn down a bit of help from the Almighty or anyone else. I restricted myself to a manly, dependable sort of smile as he glanced back at me over his shoulder.

'Go well,' I said, and he was gone.

He glanced left and right along the platform, as if expecting the four horsemen of the apocalypse to be thundering down it at any moment. A pair of uniforms appeared instead, Turkish policemen, and he watched them pass in front of him.

Still glancing warily from side to side, he walked a few paces away from the train and turned and sat on a bench.

I'm not one of these espionage chappies. If someone's going to stab me I'd rather it's in the front, and reading other people's letters is undignified as well as dull. But I've done enough shady things in my time to know he was even less of an espionage chappy than I. He couldn't have made a worse job of it if he'd tooted a trumpet and yelled out 'Gather round, fellows, Harry Delamere's got a secret in his coat!'

I closed the door - he hadn't even bothered with that - and stepped away from the window.

He on his bench, I back against the internal door to the train corridor, we gazed at each other. I resisted the urge to check that his damn' paper was still in my pocket.

Now he was at the furtive glances again, back and forth. I could see the strain in his face: the clamped jaw, the wide eyes. He was trying to urge the train into movement by sheer force of desperation.

I was starting to feel much the same way. Regardless of what the opposition were up to, any more of his performance and we'd have groups of passers-by stopping and peering in the window and lads flogging them refreshments. I had the uncomfortable sensation of being something in a zoo; something caged.

The point about the opposition had got me wondering, too. Instead of all the desperate urgency and patriotic encouragement he'd have been more use telling me whom, exactly, I was supposed to guard the paper from. But no such thing as straightforward in government work.

People passed to and fro between us. One of the pleasures of Constantinople is the sheer mixture of humanity. Every kind of Arab, most of them selling something, all the diverse peoples of the Balkans, usually plotting against each other or with each other or both at the same time, and a good cross-section of western Europeans with our pallid skins and silly games. All of these - all the colours, all the shades of skin, all the extraordinary hats - ebbed and flowed around the platform. Thus the most exotic, the most diverse city in Europe, perhaps in the world, at the end of the first decade of the twentieth century.

The whistle shrieked again, and now I felt something straining in the train chassis, the beast getting ready to move. My man looked to and fro again. Now the crowd was much thinner: they'd closed the gate to the platform, no doubt. A pair of priests, a handsome woman with a box of some kind slung over her shoulder, a couple of Indians, a distinguished-looking old chap, one or two more. Each was showing their own form of rush: checking and rechecking tickets, juggling hand-luggage, staring back to where they hoped their trunks were being stowed on the train rather than ransacked, failing to decide which carriage to make for. As I watched, one of the Indians bent and asked something of my man on his bench. Then the attempt by one of the priests to control a ticket and a book and a small satchel led inevitably to his dropping all three, and he and his mate were scrabbling around on the platform trying to retrieve the ticket before it got blown under the train and pointing and shouting at each other to keep an eye on the satchel.

Another whistle, and they all hurried for the nearest door, trying to maintain the courtesies as they jostled with each other and glanced towards the sound of urgent official shouts from the guard and back towards the unknown fate of their heavy luggage. At last I heard their door slam, and my man was left alone on his bench, his wide eyes staring back at me.

The train strained, and heaved, and at last we started to move clumsily out of Constantinople's Sirkedji station, the first few yards of a million, an epic journey westward across the whole continent, to Paris.

As I watched, the man on the bench slid to his side, and then toppled forwards. The last thing I saw, as we gathered speed and the compartment window took my view away, was the knife protruding from his back.

To be continued.

For advance notice of Poison in Paris, *and other bits of historical chat, pop by www.robertwilton.com.*

Sherlock Holmes and the Adventure of the Distracted Thane

'So we rode again into Scotland, Sherlock Holmes and I; only this time we came at the head of an army.'

A beautiful woman comes out of a storm to tell her macabre tale. And thus the legendary detective is confronted with his strangest case: the murder of King Duncan of Scotland, and the ascent to the throne of the haunted Macbeth.

Dr Watson's narrative reveals the untold story behind Shakespeare's play: a kingdom in chaos, a man possessed, and bloody murder. At last, literature's greatest detective gives his explanation for its most infamous crime.

from the secret archives of
the Comptrollerate-General for Scrutiny and Survey

Traitor's Field

1648: Britain is at war with itself. The Royalists are defeated but Parliament is in turmoil, its power weakened by internal discord.

Royalism's last hope is Sir Mortimer Shay, a ruthless veteran of decades of intrigue who must rebuild a credible threat to Cromwell's rule, whatever the cost.

John Thurloe is a young official in Cromwell's service. Confronted by the extent of Royalist secret intelligence and conspiracy, he will have to fight the true power reaching into every corner of society: the Comptrollerate-General for Scrutiny and Survey.

'a new benchmark for the literary historical thriller'
– Manda Scott, President of the Historical Writers' Association

Treason's Spring

1792: the blood begins to drip from the guillotine. The French Revolution is entering its most violent phase, and Europe confronts chaos. The spies of England, France and Prussia are fighting their own war, for a trove of secrets that will reveal the treacheries of a whole continent.

At the height of the madness a stranger arrives in Paris, seeking a man who has disappeared. Unknown and untrusted, he finds himself the centre of all conspiracy.

When the world is changing forever, what must one man become to survive?

'A rare clever treat of a novel.'
– The Times

from the secret archives of
the Comptrollerate-General for Scrutiny and Survey

Treason's Tide

1805: Britain is militarily weak, politically divided, unsettled by her rioting poor. A change in the weather will bring Napoleon's forces across the Channel and destroy the British Empire for ever.

Only a dead man stands in the way – Tom Roscarrock, unwitting agent to an obscure government bureau of murky origin and shadowy purpose. Behind the clash of fleets and armies, there is a secret world of intrigue, treachery and violence. His life in danger and his motives increasingly suspect, Roscarrock must pursue the complex conspiracy across England and then into the heart of Napoleon's France, there to confront the greatest mystery of all.

'Beautifully written, wonderfully clever, this is a triumph.'
– *Daily Telegraph*

The Spider of Sarajevo

1914: Europe is on the brink. As Britain's enemies grow stronger, the Comptroller-General must confront the man with whom he has struggled for a generation – a man he knows only as the Spider. In a desperate gamble, he sends four agents out across the continent, on a mission they do not understand…

The future of British intelligence – of the British Empire – is in their hands. Not all of them will return. Unique and resourceful, hunted and deceived, they have embarked on a journey that will climax in the town of Sarajevo on the 28th of June 1914.

'A learned, beautifully-written, elegant spy thriller.'
– *The Times*

About the Author

Robert Wilton was Private Secretary to the UK Secretary of State for Defence, advisor to the Prime Minister of Kosovo in the years before the country's independence, and acting head of an international human rights mission in Albania. He's co-founder of The Ideas Partnership charity, supporting the education and empowerment of marginalized children in the Balkans. Author of the prize-winning Comptrollerate-General series of historical novels, he also writes on history, culture and the failures of international intervention in south-eastern Europe, and translates Albanian poetry. A practising life and writing coach, and occasional voice artist, he divides his time between the Balkans and Cornwall. He is neither an adventurer nor a gentleman.

Visit www.robertwilton.com for free stuff, information, and a conversation about the curiosities of history.